THE CURSE OF ENGSTROM HOUSE

Nasser Rabadi

Also by Nasser Rabadi

THE RAVEN HILL BUTCHER slasher novel series

Book one: The Christmas Morning Massacre

Book two: Return to Camp Solgohachia

Book three: Noel Hell

Book four: The Curse of Raven Hill

Book five: The Final Chapter

Book six (reboot of Return to Camp Solgohachia): A New Beginning

Book seven (reboot of The Christmas Morning Massacre and Noel Hell): Winter Graves

Book eight: Santa's Space Station of Slaughter

Book nine: Santa Goes to Hell

Book ten: Into the Santa-Verse

The ENGSTROM HOUSE series

Book one: The Haunting of Engstrom House

Book two: Return to Engstrom House

Book three: The Curse of Engstrom House

NASSER RABADI

The LOVE KILLS series of dark romance thrillers
Book one: Scarlet
Book two: Lust
Book three: Desire

Contents

1

LAST NIGHT ABIGAIL DREAMT she went to the Engstrom House again.

She passed through the darkened doorway and was met by the cold touch of familiar hands. She held them tight and followed their lead through the archaic walls of the dreaded house. The chilled grip numbed her skin until their hold on each other became one, and Abigail could not let go.

A descent down darkened steps. The wicked creaking sent her back in time; old memories swarmed her mind and choked her. A scream was caught in the back of her throat and threatened to pass her lips. She wanted to turn around but her old friend was plunging her deeper into darkness; perhaps their journey down the steps would never end.

"Where are we going?" Abigail asked.

No response from her guide.

The freezing touch of death crept through her veins and spread through her body. Abigail had lost all control of her hand. As much as she commanded it to open, it would not respond.

After all this time, the house's grip on Abigail still had not been released. She was its prisoner.

"Almost there," her guide, her old friend, said. "Do you dream of me often?"

Tears filled Abigail's eyes so that, although the figure had been covered in the house's phantom shadows, the guide became a blur. Even in outline alone Abigail could tell who it was and she shuddered.

A tall slender body. Dark hair. Pale skin. The marks on her throat from where Abigail's fingers had penetrated. Catherine Blackwell.

"I'm sorry," Abigail whispered.

Cat said nothing.

The stairs turned. The girls spiraled together. Spiraled down the rabbit hole of madness that was the Engstrom House; the phantom reality that existed within it, and all the impossibilities that formed its structure.

Abigail's cries turned from whispers to screams. *"I don't want to go with you."*

"You belong here."

The eternally coiling stairway turned sharply and continued to do so, causing the girls to frequently spiral with every couple steps. Cold air rose from the unseen depths and sent long chills creeping under Abigail's skin.

"How many times do I have to tell you I'm sorry?" Abigail's cries lessened back to whispers.

"Until you rot."

"Cat..."

Silence.

The descent continued until suddenly they were on level ground and no longer the seemingly endless stairs. Cat led her through everlasting darkness, moving Abigail past unseen objects and around hidden corners. Cat knew every inch of the place that she now called home for eternity.

Abigail heard dripping water. Her heart was beating at a hundred and fifty miles an hour as she realized where they were going.

"Please let go of me."

"When you rot."

"Cat please. I'm sorry."

"This is where you belong."

Maybe Cat was right, Abigail thought. Maybe it was the punishment she deserved. The punishment she never received for killing Cat in the living room.

Suddenly it was ten years ago, and Abigail was back in the Engstrom House, and the voices in her head were fighting. A spirit had taken over her body; possessed her left hand and wrapped it around Cat's throat. Abigail saw Cat's terrified eyes again; saw the shock and terror that Cat felt in the final seconds of her life.

Abigail wondered what the last thing Cat thought about was.

Then she was snapped out of it when Cat's hand let go of Abigail's, and Abigail was back in the present, back to cavernous darkness that surrounded her. Suddenly Cat held a candle between her and Abigail, and her cold hand brushed against Abigail's cheek.

Cat was disturbingly sickly and frail and dripping wet. Most of her hair had fallen out in clumps. There was no soul that Abigail could find behind Cat's eyes. She was an imitation of the beautiful girl that she had once been. A monster.

"After you," Cat said.

Abigail looked down. The cistern entrance. Abigail climbed through.

Water up to her thigh. Abigail wobbled, taking deep breaths, until she found the wall and braced herself against it. In the cistern she was completely blind, but had a strange sense that there was something alive below the surface.

"Cat please..." Abigail didn't know what else to say. *"Please... please..."*

Cat climbed down a moment later. The candle was left above ground, and was about the only vision Abigail had. Her eyes adjusted to the darkness just slightly so that she could tell that Cat was approaching her.

"I'm sorry." A begging whisper.

Cat grabbed Abigail's face with both of her hands. Abigail didn't fight back; she wasn't going to win even if she tried.

"Why did you kill me?" Cat asked, somewhat calm at first, sounding like her old self—her living self—instead of the grotesque twin that she now was. Then after a pause she cried. *"Why did you kill me? Why did you have to kill me?"*

Abigail screamed.

"I want you to rot."

Cat dunked Abigail's head under the water. She held her there for ten seconds then pulled her up. Abigail strained to breathe again.

"Why did you want to kill me?"

"I didn't want—"

Abigail was plunged beneath the surface again. She counted to ten again but Cat did not bring her up again. Abigail's arms swung around to hit Cat's body but could not find her; an impossible target and an impossible goal—Cat was already dead. She couldn't hurt somebody who was already dead.

She must have been under water for an entire minute before Cat pulled her up again. Abigail was up long enough this time to regain her breath.

"Please stop."

"I want you to rot. I want you to rot down here with me."

"I didn't want to hurt you."

"My life was supposed to change. I wasn't supposed to die."

"Cat—"

Under water again.

Ten seconds went by.

A minute.

Abigail lost count of time.

Her lungs burned. Her jaw opened against her will. Mouthfuls of gross water filled Abigail's mouth and sprawled through her body.

Her eyes shut and she drifted down...

And down...

And down...

Below the surface of the water arms wrapped around her. Abigail jolted and gasped and woke in bed in her fiancé's arms. Henry was asleep.

Moonlight filled their bedroom from between the red curtains that she had forgotten to shut. Abigail squinted and read the clock on the wall; it was three in the morning. She sat up, inched closer to her nightstand, stretched her arm over the edge of the bed to pull the drawer open, and grabbed her bottle of pills from inside. She popped one into her mouth then washed it down with the glass of water that was on her nightstand.

After that Abigail rested back in her fiancé's arms, pulling the covers closer over her body. She couldn't shake the feeling of drowning; the awful feeling of desperately needing air, the feeling of cold, cold water that lingered over her skin...

And Cat's familiar touch.

2

THE DAY THAT CHANGED everything was a rainy day, and Hazel and Ivy were sitting around Ivy's brother's house looking for things to do.

Hazel kicked off her shoes, laid back on the couch, and watched reruns of *Bewitched.*

"I want to show you something," Ivy said.

"Yeah? What is it?"

"Let me go get it. I'll be right back," Ivy said then left the room for a second. She came back a shoebox under her arm and a little book in her hands. A diary. "Look what I found in the closet yesterday. Abigail's not any good at hiding things, is she?"

"Oh, Ivy, do *not* read her diary. That's so rude."

"I already read some of it. I only had a couple minutes alone with it, and I thought there must be something juicy in here. I don't think she likes me staying here much so I was curious if she wrote something about me. She's got this whole box of diaries, one for each of the past like eleven years."

"Really? What newly engaged woman *wouldn't* want her troubled runaway, soon to be sister-in-law to live with her?"

"Stop it."

"When's the wedding again?"

"I don't know."

"What, they haven't picked a date yet?"

"Oh, they have. Henry mentions it a couple times a day but I don't pay attention."

"Come on, put it down, quit it. Abigail's nice enough to let you crash here in her spare room, the least you could do is respect her privacy."

"I'm too curious. There was something strange in here I started to read but when I heard Abigail come home last night I had to put it back…"

"You know what they say about curiosity."

"No I don't." Ivy turned the page, walking toward Hazel without lifting her eyes from the book. Hazel moved over on the couch and Ivy sat next to her.

"I really think you're making a mistake reading that. If Abigail or Henry find out, they might send you back to your mom's house. And I know that's the last thing you want. You and your mother couldn't get along for like five seconds without yelling. But I don't know why you ran away in the first place, all your mom did was find some weed in your bedroom. Was it that big of a deal?"

"Look at what she's saying here… 'Last night I dreamt I went to the Engstrom House again. I passed through the dark doorway and was met by Cat's cold touch. She led me down a spiraling stairway. I didn't want to go with her but I was her prisoner.'"

"What are you even reading?"

"You know the place she's talking about, right? It's down by the farm. You know the one?"

"Isn't that the place they told us was haunted when we were kids? I think when I was younger some of the kids who used to live next door to me told me that people went missing there."

Ivy read again: "'Why did you kill me? Cat screamed. *Why did you have to kill me?'* Holy shit, Hazel."

"I told you not to read this. Put it away."

"Is this a confession?"

"What? Of course not. It's a dream journal, you nerd. It's more likely that your sister-in-law just ate bad pizza that night than she is a cold-blooded murderer."

"You don't believe in dreams?"

"They exist. Yes. But it's imagination."

"But she said she dreamed she was back there again. What's that mean? What happened to her up there?"

"This is wrong. Put it away. You never read her diary, you never even saw it, and you totally don't know it exists."

"Relax Hazel, it's no big deal." Ivy put down the diary into the box and grabbed another one. This one was old and worn—the ugliest one in the bunch. It was out of place compared to the newness of all the other ones. Even the next oldest journal was nowhere near as disgusting and tarnished as this one was.

Ivy flipped through the pages. There were two handwritings in it. Before she read any of the exchanges a folded piece of yellowed paper with flimsy tape on one of the edges fell out of the back. A missing person poster.

She read it out loud: "Have you seen Catherine Blackwell? Age nineteen, hair color black, eye color blue… last seen at the Neon Theater…. Cash reward a thousand bucks."

"That must be who she was writing about."

"What if this girl was never found…." Ivy flipped back to the section on Abigail's dream that she just read. "And Abigail knows what happened to her. Look at the date on the diary entry, this was a few days ago. Holy shit holy shit."

Hazel took it from Ivy's hands. "I don't like reading people's diaries. Can we drop it? This is an invasion of privacy and I wouldn't want somebody doing this to me."

"No way. I wouldn't want somebody doing it to me neither, but we've got to do something about this."

"I'm not convinced we have to do something about Abigail having bad dreams."

"You never know. Seriously. We should investigate."

Hazel laughed. "Do you hear yourself? 'Investigate?' Yeah, just another case for Spade and Archer."

"Spade and who?"

"Never mind. Seriously, put all this stuff away."

"Okay, I'll put it away." Ivy shut the book. "But only if you come with me. Let's go see that old house."

"You're going to get us arrested for breaking and entering, or for trespassing, all based on a bad night's sleep Abigail had."

"Jung said that dreams are an 'encounter with the subconsciousness.'"

"Who?"

"Carl Jung. Read a book sometime. Maybe Abigail's guilt is manifesting in her dreams. What else am I gonna find in those diaries? Maybe my brother is living with a serial killer. This Cat girl's body could still be there. What if we find her?"

"I do *not* wanna find a dead body, that's so disgusting. Seriously let's leave this all alone."

Ivy left the room and came back a minute or two later. "Okay, I put it away," she said, walking to the front door.

"Where are you going?"

"To that old house. Did you want to come with or something?"

"Ugh. You've got to be kidding me. You're so stubborn, you know that?"

It had stopped raining when they left Henry and Abigail's home, but Ivy brought an umbrella with her anyways.

"I think it's this way."

The girls arrived at the old Engstrom place. It was as filthy and ugly as Hazel had thought it would be. The girls went up the hill. The gate opened under Ivy's touch. The girls went through and stood in front of the door.

"You first," Ivy said.

"No way," Hazel stepped back, "you first. You're the one that wanted to come here so bad."

Ivy opened the door a little then kicked it fully open. The door swung back to close but she put her hand on it and kept it open. A step inside. Hazel followed her and sneezed from the clumps of dust in the air.

"We shouldn't be here." Hazel sneezed two more times. "Think we can turn back now? Since this is gonna be your first semester at my school I could introduce you to some of my friends. I think you'd really like Warren. Maybe we could go see if he's home or something."

"Won't you quit it? Here we are with this huge old place that nobody's ever been in in years and you want to turn back before we even spend three seconds looking around. Think of what we might find in here. And besides, you've tried to introduce me to him before but Warren can't seem to take one day off from his summer job."

"Yeah, dead rats and a lot of dust. That's what we'd find in here. Lots and lots of dust. I doubt anybody left anything of interest behind."

"I wonder where Abigail hid the body."

"Stop talking about dead bodies, all right? It's freaking me the hell out Ivy."

"Fine, then you can turn around and go back to my brother's place. I'll look around this abandoned house all by myself and make all the comments about dead bodies that I want."

"I really hate you sometimes." Hazel put her hands on her hips. "I really do."

"Whatever."

"Ah-ha, that's it. I remember where I've heard that name before. Blackwell. The nurse at the doctor's office is named Blackwell. But I don't think she looked much like that girl in the poster."

"Take another look." Ivy brought the folded paper out of her purse.

"You stole that thing?"

"Well yeah we don't have a xerox machine at my house." Ivy held it up into a ray of light. "Well? Recognize her?"

"I dunno." Hazel grabbed the paper and inspected the picture. "There's a resemblance though. I can't really tell for sure."

"What if we stopped by and asked her?"

"What? No, that could be her sister or something. That would be mean to bring it up."

"You're right but I'm too curious about Abigail. Did she do something to this girl?"

"Why are you so insistent that Abigail hurt somebody?"

Ivy was silent.

"So can we go now?"

"You said you'd stay with me so I don't walk around in this place in the dark all alone."

"That's right." Hazel gave the poster back to Ivy.

Ivy put it away then brought out a flashlight. "You really thought I'd come that unprepared?"

"I dunno. I didn't think you had given this spur of the moment trip much thought."

"You know," Ivy took a few steps away from the windows where they were standing and passed through the living room, "Abigail doesn't know this… but I was up late one night a few weeks ago, after I snuck back in the house from our little bonfire at Michelle's place. And I heard Abigail crying. So I went down the steps to check on her, and I found her drinking. She didn't notice me, I don't think. I was just standing there on the stairs and she was crying. This book was on the table with an empty bottle of wine. I know you don't want to think that Abigail did something, and I'm not even saying I *want* her to be guilty of anything, but she has some connection to this place and I'm too interested not to know it."

Hazel followed her across the room. "So you think she was guilty because she was up late drinking and crying? Ivy, that's just called adulthood."

"No, no, she wasn't just crying. I heard her… apologizing. She kept saying she was sorry. And if that journal was on the table with her, with that missing poster too, it's just... I think something happened to Abigail a long time ago."

"Did you take her diary with you too?"

"No, I put that back. Didn't think we needed it. Hey, there's a spider on your arm."

Hazel hit the small bug off her arm; it was no bigger than a cent. *"Kill it kill it."*

Ivy laughed at her. "I'm not gonna kill it."

"Why not?"

"They scare me too."

They laughed together and went through the entryway into the foreign darkness of the strange archaic house. It felt to Hazel like stepping into another dimension; passing into a place that only existed in somebody's mind or in a drawing hidden away in a rotting old book fallen behind a shelf. The old dark house did not seem like any place that anybody could find; it was a world that was uniquely its own.

Darkness had a way of collapsing in on Ivy's light no matter where she shined it.

Hazel did not want to believe anything bad had happened here, but she could not help but wonder about it—she couldn't help but wonder if Ivy was right. It was a huge house with many floors, and if somebody wanted to make another person vanish... if they wanted to hide them in a place they'd never be found... if you had to get rid of somebody... what better place than here?

And then, Hazel thought, if she and Ivy were to die here, nobody would know. Nobody would know where to find their bodies.

She was brought out of that thought by a noise; by footsteps behind them. She and Ivy turned at the same time to face whoever was also in the old house with them but nobody was there; only shadows. Shadows that must have hidden secrets that wanted to stay buried.

"What do you think that was?" Hazel asked.

"I dunno. A rat?"

"That sounded like footsteps. You don't think there's someone else here, do you?"

"Maybe you were right, let's get out of here. This place gives me the creeps bigtime, Hazel."

"Thank God you're finally making sense."

"Shhh not so loud I don't want him to hear you."

"Who? Who's him?"

"Whoever's footsteps that was that we just heard."

The girls tiptoed quietly.

"Hazel help me he's got me! Help me!"

Hazel jolted backwards a step in shock and banged her head into the wall; Ivy couldn't hold in her laugh. She dropped the flashlight and it rolled a few feet away. She braced herself on the wall with one hand and kept laughing, laughing so hard no sound came out. She fell to her knees then rolled on the dusty floor laughing.

"I—I don't know what was funnier, your face, you—you hitting your head—you—I didn't—I didn't even—didn't even do anything, I just said he got me—you jumped so hard oh my God—are—are—you okay? Oh my God that was hilarious. Oh my God."

"You... ass."

Ivy rolled on the floor laughing still. Hazel couldn't help it and rolled on the floor laughing with her too. Then Ivy grabbed the flashlight and they each stood up.

"I don't think there's really anybody in here," Ivy said. "Or they'd have just heard all of that. Especially how loud you knocked your head into the wall."

Hazel rubbed the back of her head. "It's pounding bad."

After wandering around they came upon the back door and stepped outside. Behind the yard was an endless forest. There was a wellhouse on their right, a shed on their left, and near the shed was a table with benches. The doors on the shed on the wellhouse were shut with padlocks. Ivy went up to the wellhouse and turned over some nearby rocks.

"Thought maybe they'd be hiding a key under these."

"It's like the things to discover in this place never end, huh?"

"You could say that again."

Hazel looked up at the gigantic house; even filthier and more decrepit in the back. "Have you done enough 'investigating' yet?"

"Hey, little girl."

Hazel turned. "What?" But Ivy was running into the forest and didn't acknowledge her. Hazel ran after her friend, but did not see any little girl.

"Come back. Are you lost?"

When they came to a stream of water at a clearing in the forest, Ivy stopped to catch her breath. Hazel jogged the last few steps to Ivy's side; she put a hand on Ivy's shoulder causing Ivy to jump at Hazel's touch. She hadn't noticed Hazel had been running behind her.

"God you scared me. Where did the little girl go?"

"I didn't see any little girl. Are you just trying to scare me again?"

"What do you mean you didn't see her? She was right there."

"There's nobody that I can see."

"Her clothes were covered in gunk. When she saw me she ran away... she must have gone up ahead."

"Look, I don't want to go any further into these woods. I don't like how you've been acting today."

"We can talk about that later, there's a little girl in this forest who looks scared and lost. I'm not kidding with you. There really was a little girl and we should find her."

Hazel and Ivy walked straight ahead. The land rose and fell and they passed over a fallen tree. The last thing they had thought they'd find was a cemetery. If they kept going, who knew what else they'd find, Hazel thought. The discoveries in and around the Engstrom place and its forest must have been truly endless.

Curiously they entered. The gate's door was missing. Nearby a metal sign was on the ground that read: ENGSTROM FAMILY CEME-TERY.

Hazel had a creeping suspicion that somebody was watching them.

As she was walking one way, and Ivy was going the other way, she read the names carved into tombstones. Some were easier to read than others—like the ones that belonged to Agatha Engstrom and Joyce Engstrom and Thaddeus Engstrom. Most stones were covered in moss and dirt and were withered indecipherable over the strain of time.

A wink of sunlight caught Hazel's eye. Something pretty near a grave whose tombstone was cracked in half; laying over it was a dead bird whose wings were spread. Weeds had grown over the grave's yellow grass. The grave was below a tree whose twisted and jumbled roots had uprisen from the ground here and there around the area. One particular root stretched up through the ground at the center of the grave, and on it was a golden ring.

Hazel kneeled. The root had protruded from the ground a length of about six inches and was formed into a reversed arch like a curled finger, and the ring was at its center. She tried to pull the ring from the root but the ring did not move.

"What are you doing?" Ivy joined her. "Oh look at that it's so pretty."

"I think the root dug it out of the grave."

"I want it."

"Hey, I saw it first."

"Can you even get it loose? You look like you're gonna pull your arm out of its socket. Let me try."

"Okay but I did see it first."

"Whatever, I won't steal it. It doesn't look my size anyways, you know?" Ivy pulled on the ring and it came free right away. She slipped it on her left ring finger. "What do you know. A perfect match."

"Oh come on, you said you wouldn't steal it."

"Hey finders keepers."

"Whatever. Come on. You know I totally saw it first."

"Okay." Ivy tried to take the ring off, but it wouldn't come loose. "I can't seem to get it off."

"Look if you didn't want to give it to me you could have just said so."

"I put it on just to tease you, but it really won't come off." Ivy extended her hand to Hazel. "You try."

Hazel attempted to pull it from Ivy's finger but Ivy was right; it was a tight fit. A perfect match. It was as if the ring clung to her skin or was part of her.

"You owe me for this."

"Fine. I owe you."

"Let's just get out of here. It's all muddy and these shoes are practically ruined now. All because we had to come out here and 'investigate.' Did you even find what you were looking for?"

3

DARK CLOUDS BROODED ABOVE the convent…

Everybody was asleep except for Sister White, who was headed for her bedroom when she heard the scream. She froze with her hand hovering above the doorknob, too afraid to turn her head and look toward the source of the sound. But then once silence fell over her again, she nervously darted her eyes in the direction of the staircase that ended the hall. That seemed to be where it had come from.

Slowly her hand drifted away from the knob. She stared deeply into the dreary, dusty hallway. Darkness was chained all around her. Terror was still fresh in her heart as she moved that way. If there was somebody who was hurt then she needed to help them.

But no subsequent screams came, and Sister White was doubting if she had even heard anything at all. Was somebody even down those steps this late at night, she wondered. At the top of the steps she furtively looked around the corner. An empty stairway was waiting for her. It led directly down to the cellar.

She anticipated another scream.

Silence—only silence.

And yet she didn't feel alone.

A descent down the stone steps. The nighttime air chilled her lungs. Sister White clasped her hand around the railing so strongly that it hurt. A distant glow of faded orange light smeared the sea of darkness that awaited her and rose steadily, cutting through the murkiness and giving her what little vision she had in order to know where she was going.

In the cellar the light was more pronounced, and Sister White saw that it was coming from the boiler room. The door was shut but from the glass window she saw the figure of one of her fellow nuns pass by.

Was that who screamed? What is she doing down here?

Sister White approached the door. Before she reached it, it opened and Sister Tillman stepped out.

Sister Colleen Tillman.

"Oh hi, Sister White, I was just on my way to bed. Is something wrong?"

"No, I was just…"

"Yes?"

"I thought I heard somebody down here. I thought…"

"You look like you're worried. Is everything all right?"

"I thought I heard somebody screaming."

"That's funny. I didn't hear anything."

"That's—that's good. Well, goodnight Sister."

"Goodnight."

The two nuns went back to the ground floor. Sister White found her bedroom again, and as she opened the door she looked over her shoulder quickly. Sister Tillman was gone, and she didn't know which way she went.

Sister White locked her bedroom door. She changed into her pajamas then crawled under the covers. She was still so nervous from the scream she had heard—or maybe only *thought* she had heard—that she couldn't get comfortable or fall asleep. The sharp scream played again in her mind: so loud, so full of terror, then it died away almost as quickly as it came, as if it hardly had any time to form at all before being silenced.

She tried to forget about it, but the sleepless minutes dragged on.

There was something about Colleen Tillman that she did not like, and she couldn't exactly place her finger on it. Maybe it was the woman's cold eyes that she didn't like—no, it wasn't her eyes, but it was something… something *behind* them.

She just couldn't shake the feeling. It clung to her like death's embrace.

Then a whisper entered her room. If Sister White had been on the verge of sleep then it would have gone unnoticed, but since she was wide awake it caught her attention right away. She sat up in bed, listening carefully past the squeal of her bedsprings for the whisper to make itself known again. It was a few more seconds of silence before the whisper could be heard once more—it was rather a groan than a whisper. A painful cry.

And it was coming from the vent.

Sister White followed that awful sound and pressed her ear to the vent's cover.

A sickly cry: *"Help me."*

She lingered at the vent in disbelief.

"Help…"

Where are you? Sister White wondered, but she knew.

In her closet she had supplies in case of power outages. In one of her boxes she found her flashlight. It cast an uneven shine with a shadow somehow in the middle of the glowing circle it produced. Still, the dismal light was enough for her to see where she was going when she entered once again the chilling and dark hallways of the convent. And for some reason, under the choking blindness of night, it seemed to change from a convent into a realm of horrors. It ceased being a holy place and became something *other.*

Down the steps again…

And back to the boiler room door…

She crept closely to the glass window and peeked in. The furnace was overflowing with fire, and Sister Tillman was on her knees in front of it bowing. At her side was the decapitated corpse of Mother Superior. Her face was directly in front of the furnace, and the corpse was sprawled off to Sister Tillman's right side.

Sister White put her hands over her mouth to stop herself from screaming. In the process her flashlight slipped from her hands and shattered on the stone floor. Sister Tillman immediately ceased bowing and turned her attention to Sister White. Against the shine of the flames, her eyes had become completely black, and Sister White realized what she had not liked about the new woman.

But it was too late to do anything about it…

At the Ashfall Public Library, Ivy asked the lady at the desk if she could help her find any newspaper articles about the old Engstrom place.

"Haven't heard that name in quite a while, young lady."

The lady helped Ivy in the basement archive. Ivy went through the yellowed newspapers scanning their contents for anything useful.

Two very old headlines:

WIFE CLAIMS HUSBAND VANISHED IN 'HAUNTED HOUSE.'

THE DEVIL MADE HER DO IT! NEW INFORMATION ON THE VICIOUS 'ENGSTROM HOUSE' MURDERS!

After going through more newspapers she found another one that interested her:

ACCUSED MURDERER FOUND <u>NOT GUILTY</u>

She made xerox copies of those articles, as well as a few copies of Catherine Blackwell's missing poster, then put them all into a manila envelope she had brought along with her to the library.

The next time Ivy saw Hazel, she gave Hazel her own copy of Catherine's poster.

"This way Abigail can't get rid of the evidence."

"So what did you find out, 'detective?' Think you've got enough to put Abby away for life?"

"A whole bunch. Take a look at these." Ivy gave Hazel copies of the articles she had found at the library's archive. "Can you believe it?"

Hazel read them, or at least read the headlines and partially read the articles themselves. "This is before Abigail's time. What, you think she murdered this doctor when she was like fresh out the womb or something?"

"You're missing the point. This isn't just about Catherine anymore. That house's history is stranger than I thought. I did some digging and I read some newer articles and I put in a few phone calls. This man from the history museum helped me a ton, he actually met this doctor guy. And guess what?"

"God if he actually met this doctor then he must have been a hundred years old."

"Yeah, no shit, Hazel. But guess what."

"What?"

"This wasn't the only time this lady was in the news. She actually moved here. To Ashfall."

"What are you stalking her? You're taking this 'haunted house' business a little too far, Ivy."

"No, no. Look. I'm on to something. I can feel it."

"So what are you gonna do?"

"I'm gonna go talk to this lady. Colleen Tillman. I'm gonna ask her what she could tell me about the house. Maybe she knew Cat."

"Oh come on, I doubt she knew Cat. I mean why would she? Look how old these articles are, and look how recent Cat's disappearance was. There's no connection. And what if she doesn't want to talk to you? I don't think you should go looking for any trouble."

"Well who else am I gonna ask? I can't ask Abigail because she'll know I stole it, and I can't tell my brother because he's gonna tell Abigail. I'm all out of options. Oh, and Colleen would have to see me. She lives at the convent."

"What? Her husband was murdered so she became a nun?"

"Yeah. She became a nun like fifteen years ago. That puts her back in this town at the time of Cat's disappearance."

"You're totally gonna drag me into this, aren't you?"

Ivy pouted her lip. "Pretty please?"

"Oh, all right."

As the girls approached the convent a strong wind blew a sheet of wrinkled paper their way. Along the torn edges were thick pieces of tape that had collected dirt along the sticky sides. Ivy picked it up and looked at it with Hazel.

Another missing poster. This one for two nuns. One of them was Sister White, the other was Mother Superior. The date on the poster was from fifteen years ago. Knots formed in Ivy's stomach as she put together a little connection in her head…. As soon as Colleen arrived, these two nuns went missing. And what about Cat?

Were they making a mistake being here?

Of course it isn't a mistake, Ivy thought, *she's a nun. What's she gonna do, stab us here in the middle of the day, in the middle of this convent, with her fellow nuns all around her?*

Colleen Tillman was now Mother Superior. She had a big desk on the top floor of the convent. Ivy discretely swept her eyes across the office, taking in each detail she could find, but coming away with nothing important. The curtains were open, and there was a pitcher of ice water on the corner of the desk—everything in the room was normal. She studied the woman behind the desk. Colleen was middle aged, pushing about sixty years old. Ivy wondered what was going on in that woman's mind, and if she had really changed or not.

Could somebody go from killing their husband to being a nun?

"So," Colleen said, "my sisters tell me you two are interested in joining our faith."

"Totally," Hazel said.

Ivy twisted the gold ring she had found at the family cemetery behind the Engstrom place. *Here it goes,* she thought, then she said, "Well, not quite, ma'am. We came here with questions."

"Of course. It's a normal thing for young ladies to be uncertain about their life-changing decisions. Ask away."

"No, you don't get it, Colleen—or do I have to call you 'mother' or 'sister' or something?" Ivy continued to twist the ring around and around. It was getting hotter against her skin.

Colleen stared at Ivy as if Ivy had just spit in her face.

"Well, my question isn't about 'the faith.' We don't really want to join. I wanted to ask you about this girl that went missing."

"Ah, of course. We do occasionally have troubled youth that come through our convent. What is your friend's name?"

"Catherine Blackwell." Ivy grabbed a copy of the poster from her folder and passed it across the table to Colleen. "But she isn't my friend and she didn't go missing recently. She went missing years and years ago. And I think it's because she went into the—"

"Oh no." Colleen shook her head left and right. "No, no, no. Poor girl. Well I can tell you I've never seen this girl before. What a shame. Beautiful girl. Catherine…. No, doesn't ring a bell."

"I think she went into the Engstrom place. That's why we wanted to talk to you, because your husband, uh, 'disappeared' there we were wondering what you could tell us about it," Ivy said, catching Hazel's glance. Hazel looked like she could strangle her.

"I apologize with how straightforward my friend here is being, ma'am."

"It's no trouble at all, girls. Yes, my husband Ambrose… had an unfortunate… accident in that house. But I don't see what one thing has to do with the other. I don't know this girl and she certainly hasn't come through our convent."

Ivy frowned. "This girl went missing and nobody ever found her. I don't know what to do about it."

"Maybe she ran away to start a new life. You know sometimes people aren't missing, they just don't want to be found. We've had a couple of my sisters run away before. In fact, the Mother Superior before me left here abruptly in the middle of the night fifteen years ago."

"Is that so?" Ivy said. Another turn of her ring.

Colleen nodded. "I like your ring, dear. Did a boy give that to you?"

"No." Ivy wiped billows of sweat from her forehead, then she covered up the ring with her opposite hand, glancing to the pitcher of ice water she had forgotten about on Colleen's desk, then lifting her eyes back to Colleen.

"What's the matter? You look like you're burning up. Would you girls like some water?"

"No thank you," Ivy said.

"Thank you, but I'm not thirsty," Hazel said.

"Suit yourselves."

The convent's halls were long and dark, and Ivy felt somebody was watching her and Hazel as they left Colleen's office.

"See? I told you it was nothing. What did you think she was gonna say? 'I know where Catherine is, she's been here the whole time?'"

"I don't like how dismissive you're being. If you went missing, wouldn't you want somebody to find you?"

"Not if it's like that lady said—some people leave to start new lives. Maybe Catherine doesn't even know she's missing."

"That doesn't explain the things Abigail wrote about. That she was sorry for what she did to Catherine. That she dreamed she was back at the Engstrom place again."

"Because it was all a dream. Dreams don't make sense. I think you're reading too much into things. Can we give this up now?"

"Maybe. I dunno."

Once they were on the ground floor, Hazel went up to the washroom door. "I'll be right back."

Colleen was alone in her office after her two visitors left, but that only lasted for a minute or two because the door opened and her master joined her. She eagerly met him at the center of the room and ran her hands through his fur, then she gave him a kiss. His long sticky tongue licked her.

He was a black goat with sharp horns and dark eyes.

"Master," she said, "there are two girls who just visited me. They would make great additions to our coven. One of those girls is already corrupted."

TAP! TAP! TAP!

While Ivy waited for Hazel in the strange halls of the convent, obscure footfalls echoed through the silent halls.

Around the corner came a black goat. Its black eyes studied her, and Ivy carefully watched it, and she was uncertain to move. She wanted to run to Hazel but didn't want to startle the loose animal. She wanted to scream for her friend but she didn't want to do anything that might upset the goat and cause it to charge at her with its jagged horns directly aimed at her torso...

The goat bowed its head, then turned around its corner back where it had originally come from.

Somehow, Ivy found herself moving in its direction. For some reason she felt bound to the goat, as if she could do nothing else but follow it. When she passed the corner herself, the black goat was waiting for her, anticipating her touch. She petted him. His tongue rolled out of his lips and he licked her.

She followed the goat as it brought her to a stairway, and upon her descent she vaguely heard Hazel's isolated voice calling after her. But she couldn't break away now—she couldn't stop following the black goat. She was spellbound. She was determined to know where it was leading her.

There seemed to be whispers all around; voices that were hidden in the walls and leaking out of the brick structures that composed them. Something lurked just of reach. Something was just out of her touch. The essence of this convent was not right.

In the basement she was guided through stretches of darkness to a door with a glass window. Within was the boiler room. At that moment Ivy realized that the black goat was no longer with her. She scanned the basement looking for him, but the surrounding details were so indistinct she couldn't tell what more was in here with her.

A hum. A sort of music. Many voices in unison. Behind the door.

The door squeaked on rusted hinges under Ivy's push.

The room blindingly black save for the faint glow of flames that feebly cut into darkness and gave Ivy a little bit of vision. She followed it as deep as it would guide her, the hums becoming more pronounced the further she went, and she passed through the unknown regions of the boiler room on strange faith alone.

Gleaming light abruptly appeared across the ground, still too weak to fully reveal everything around her but enough to illustrate that there was a door up ahead. The light was flickering, and it was coming from a source that was on the other side.

Ivy pulled the door open and the hums stopped all at once. The light source was fully revealed as that of bonfire in the center of a room whose details, still, were hidden by darkness that did not want to remove itself, as if the darkness were enchanted to cover up the hideous details that light was too afraid to reveal.

Human skulls burned on the other side of the fire. Pentagrams were drawn on the floor. An inverted cross rested against the wall on her right, and on her left was a big leather book with jagged edges.

Ivy shut the door and hurried to the stairway and ran back up to the ground floor, and as soon as she came off the final step she bumped into Mother Superior and they were both knocked over. Colleen stood up first, bracing herself on the wall, and Ivy was too scared to move.

Then she lent a hand to Ivy. Ivy took it. It was unusually cold.

"I was looking for the bathroom."

"I'm afraid you won't find a bathroom down there, dear. If you went through any of those doors all you'll find… is your destiny."

Ivy pushed past her and ran out of the building, not stopping until she found Hazel smoking a cigarette on the bottommost step.

"There you are," Hazel said.

"Let's get out of here," Ivy pretended to be calm. "This place gives me the creeps."

"Where did you go? Were you doing some 'investigating?'"

Ivy didn't answer her.

Hazel had borrowed her sister's car, and was driving her and Ivy back home when they saw a nun running down the street, a girl only a little older than Ivy and Hazel were. Ivy watched the nun take off her veil and throw it into the street. She was dragging a suitcase behind her. She seemed so distraught...

"Pull over."

Hazel did so, and Ivy rolled down her window.

"Do you need a lift?"

The nun looked the girls up and down. "Which way are you going?"

"The same way you just were."

The nun opened the back door and jumped in with her suitcase. "Step on it."

Hazel pulled back onto the road. "Are you okay?"

The girl was crying, and wiping away her tears with her sleeves. "No I'm not. I need you to get me as far away from here as possible."

"All right well we're only going like fifteen minutes away from here so I don't know where you—"

"As far as you can take me, it doesn't matter. I'll catch the bus, if you'd be so kind as to drop me off near one of the stops."

"Uh, sure, okay."

"Why did you run away?" Ivy asked. "Did the nuns do something to you?"

33

"The sisters… I walked in on them." The girl took a deep breath. "Oh you won't believe me. Just take me to the bus stop. I'm so sorry I bothered you two, you're so kind for doing this. I don't have a lot of money, but I—"

"No, it's okay, I don't want your money."

"For the gas."

"We were going this way. It's no big deal."

"Hold on," Ivy said. "You walked in on them doing what though? What were they up to in that convent?"

"Worshiping the devil."

4

Ivy and Hazel brought the runaway girl to a little diner. They sat around a table eating lunch, or rather picking at their food during their conversation.

"Really I can't thank you two enough for this. I… I don't have a penny to my name. When I find my way home I'll mail you some money."

Hazel put her hand over the runaway's. "Things will be okay. And don't you dare worry about paying me back."

"I don't think I could have run into two nicer people. And you're doing this for me and you don't even know my name. I'm Tess." She wiped away a sudden tear from her eye. "Oh God I can't wait to be back home. I never should have run away."

"Well, Tess, it's good to meet you, even if it's just for a day. My name is Hazel and my friend here is Ivana, but I just call her Ivy."

"I wish I met you two when I first came to Ashfall."

"I understand what you're going through," Ivy said. "I have problems at home too. It's why I went to go stay with my brother."

"Do you talk to your parents?"

"Not really."

"Me neither. I haven't called them once. I hope they forgive me."

"They will," Hazel said, then sipped her milkshake for the first time. "They're your parents, they kinda have to."

"Yeah. I hope that's the case."

"So Tess, where are you from?" Ivy asked.

"Just a couple towns over. It won't be a far trip."

"Oh, okay. Maybe we can come visit you sometime."

"That would be great. If you have a pen I can write you down my address and number."

"Yeah I've got one somewhere." Ivy reached into her purse and found a blue pen, then gave it to Tess along with one of the xerox copies of a news article from her manila envelope. "Here, you can write it on the back of this."

Tess wrote it down then curiously turned it over and read the headline. "What's this about a haunted house?"

"Oh, that place is right here in town. You haven't heard about it?"

"No I haven't."

"Oh boy, here we go," Hazel said.

Ivy put the paper back in the envelope. "It's sort of the reason we ran into you. Here," Ivy gave her one copy of her practically endless supply of Catherine's missing poster, "I found this, and I think I know what might have happened to her. Or rather who killed her. I think her body's inside of there, and these old articles tie Mother Superior to this same house."

"You think Mother Superior killed her?"

"No, I think my sister-in-law did. But Mother Superior, according to everything I could find, was passing through here one night with her husband when their car crashed in a storm. They went into that house together for the night but only she walked out. The court

36

found her 'not guilty' but I don't believe that either. Then she moved back to the area, and was here around the time of Cat's disappearance."

"Sorry, uh, Ivy, but you're losing me. If it's your… sister-in-law that could have hurt this girl, what does Mother Superior have to do with her?"

"I couldn't leave any stone unturned. I had to follow up. What if Mother Superior had known this girl? What if she could fill me in on something?"

"You'll have to excuse Ivy." Hazel put her hand on Tess's hand again. "She sort of sees herself as Philip Marlowe's little sister or something."

"Who's Philip Marlowe?"

"Oh God," Hazel said. "Humphrey Bogart. *The Big Sleep.* How come neither of you have seen it?"

"I don't even know who that is."

"You two are hopeless. Tess if you stuck around you'd probably replace me as Ivy's bestie."

"Oh that's not true," Ivy said. Then she jokingly whispered to Tess: "Okay it's kinda true."

5

A WEEK LATER...

"What time did you tell Michelle?" Ivy asked. "Why didn't she come with you? You live next door to her."

"She was busy, she had a thing. I told her to meet us there around three."

"It's almost two-thirty. Warren should be here any minute now. God you were right Hazel I'm head over heels for him. How do I look?"

"You look like you always look."

"Come on, there can't be one hair out of place or Warren might lose interest."

"You think any of that matters to a guy? It might matter to *us,* but not to them. Guys only care that you exist and that you don't smell bad or whatever."

"Are you sure?"

"Totally."

"You better be right about this, Hazel."

"Aren't I always right?"

"Ha, sure."

"Did you ask Warren to bring the thing?"

Ivy nodded. "Yeah, he said he got it from the pawn shop or something."

"It's not gonna work. This was really the goofiest idea you've ever had. At least it's got Warren eating out of the palm of your hand, I'll give you that.

"There he is. Are you sure I look okay?"

"I dunno, I'm sure we'll drive past a few totally prettier girls on our way there."

"Really?"

"No, you big doofus."

Ivy sat in the front seat and Hazel in the back. Warren was wearing a black t-shirt and jeans and Ivy got butterflies from sitting next to him. She had a feeling right away that this was a special day. It was a day she would never forget.

"It's good to see you two."

"Yeah," Ivy said, "I'm shocked you were able to get a day off work. They're working you pretty hard at the ice cream parlor for just a summer job."

Warren smiled. "Yeah they are but I don't mind so much. I'm saving up all the money I can. Between this and cutting lawns I'm a rich man."

"So this is it," Hazel said from behind them, cutting off Ivy unknowingly as Ivy was about to speak. Hazel had the Ouija board in her hands turning it over and over. "God, Warren, I didn't know you still liked playing with toys."

"Hey, those things work. Seriously. My cousin told me she used one once and picture frames started flying off the walls in her house and she'd hear footsteps. They had to bless the house to get it to stop."

"Great."

"They do really work," Ivy said. "I've seen them on TV. But I've never used one myself. Is this the one your cousin used?"

"Actually it is. This is the very one."

"Ivy what are you getting so red for? Are you scared of this thing?"

"Nuh-no."

"Awe, Ivy's scared. Look at her blush."

"I'm not blushing."

Warren parked his car. Ivy hadn't even noticed that they had arrived here at the Engstrom place.

"So are you gonna clue me in yet on what's going on?" Warren stepped out of the car.

Ivy opened her door. "Let's get inside and I'll tell you everything."

The house was dusty and dark and empty, and Ivy opened the box of matches she had brought with her and lit two candles that had been sitting around the living room in stainless steel candleholders that were chillingly cold to the touch. Thin feeble strands of light cut through the darkness.

Warren put his hands on Ivy's. "You're freezing. Maybe we should light a fire."

"That would be great."

"I'll go grab some branches from out front. Don't have too much fun without me."

"Oh, we won't," she said as he went outside. Then she turned to Hazel. "How am I doing?"

"Oh will you just relax?"

"I'm nervous."

"Just be cool."

"Okay. I'll try."

Warren came back with some branches and put them in the fire-place. "This is how you need to arrange them to keep the fire burning. Ivy hand me a match, will you?"

She struck one and gave it to him. "Here you go. Were you a boy scout?"

"Yeah I was. I was the best in my troop at lighting our campfires. Can you give me another match?"

She gave him a second one. "You'll have to teach me sometime."

"Sure." The fire was spreading through the branches and Warren stood up. "Now where were we?"

"Look at this." Ivy gave him a copy of the missing poster from her purse.

Warren held it against the glow of the fireplace. "What a babe."

Ivy couldn't help but feel jealous of the girl that had been missing for a decade. "Yeah. Too bad she's dead. And she died in this house."

"Really?"

Before Ivy could answer, Hazel—who had set the board on the table—said, "How does this thing work?"

"Hold on," Ivy said, "quit fooling around, we have to be precise."

"Yeah. Precise. With a toy. Isn't this from the same people who make the springy dog that you pull on a string?"

"We're gonna contact the girl on that poster," Ivy said to Warren. "I want her to tell us what happened to her."

"Did they ever find her body?"

"No. But we have reason to believe it's in this big old house. Somewhere in here."

Hazel fell over laughing. "Did you just say we have 'reason to believe?' What are you, a cop? Who do you think you are, some nineteen forties detective in Los Angeles or something?"

"Oh shut up Hazel."

"You really think you're on to like, the crime of the century or something. As if."

"Hey, leave Ivy alone." Warren put his hand over Ivy's. "I believe her. And I think this board will help us find out what happened to…" Warren looked at his copy again for her name. "Catherine Blackwell."

CREEEEEEEAK!

The squeal of the gate outside.

They looked out the window and Michelle was coming up the path. Hazel opened the front door for her.

"Hey guys. What did I miss?"

Warren showed her his copy of the missing persons poster. "Ivy thinks this girl died here."

"Far out."

"We're gonna contact her and ask her what happened."

"As if these dumb toys work," Hazel said.

"I did some research after I found this poster," Ivy said. "You know how many unsolved murders there are in the world? On average in one year alone there are roughly about—"

"You guys are totally making me sick talking about this stuff. Can't we get down to business?"

"I think you're scared because you're secretly a believer, Hazel."

Hazel stood at the living room table and put her hands on the planchette all alone. She moved it across the board. "It's speaking! It's spelling something! It says T... O... Y..."

"Seriously?" Warren stood across the table from her.

"See, even your board admits it's a toy."

Ivy put her hands on her hips. "Cut it out. This is supposed to be serious."

"All right, let me try this again. Are there any ghosts here with us?" Hazel moved the planchette again. Then a strong light flashed through the room.

Everyone looked toward the fireplace. The fire had grown significantly.

"What is your name?" Hazel said as she moved the planchette. Again the fireplace flared with Hazel's movements. "T... O... Y..."

"Give it here." Warren put his hands on it.

Ivy joined them. Then Michelle did too.

Hazel backed away from the table and crossed her arms. "You three can fool around with it all you want. I'll enjoy the front row seat."

"Are there any ghosts with us?"

Suddenly the room became a few degrees hotter as the fireplace rumbled. A quick flash of fire spread like a tornado.

"Are there any ghosts with us?" Ivy said. Sparks kept fluttering up from the fireplace and disappearing when she glanced at it then looked back to the Ouija board.

Something in Ivy had expected the planchette to move on its own and her hands stayed in place.

"Why aren't you guys moving it?" Michelle said.

NASSER RABADI

"It's supposed to move on its own, that's what my cousin told me."

"No you're supposed to guide it, aren't you?"

"See, you guys can't even agree on how it works." Hazel leaned on the table. "IF this were real you wouldn't have to argue about how it works."

"Y'know, maybe Hazel is right," Michelle said.

"Oh what, you too? Guess it's just me and Ivy—oh look, it's moving."

And at that moment the flames in the fireplace receded to the brink of extinguishing. With Warren and Ivy pressing their fingertips to the planchette it was guided across the board. Ivy didn't know exactly where it was going and she couldn't tell if Warren was manipulating it or not. Was there really something at work here? Ivy was somewhat torn on her stance—everything that both sides were saying were true. Were they actually being guided now by a spirit or was Warren forcing the planchette? Regardless she didn't try to alter its movements in any way and let her hands slide along it.

"I... W... A... S... K..." Warren repeated each letter out loud as the planchette slid over them, and with every letter the flames in the fireplace returned. Warren stopped with the planchette on K. "Iwask?"

"Maybe it meant Ewok." Hazel laughed.

"No, no, I was 'K.'" Ivy said.

"Maybe it was trying to spell out 'Catherine' but forgot her name started with a 'C.' If I were a ghost trapped in this house for all those years then I'd forget how to spell 'Hazel' too."

"Enough out of you," Ivy said.

Ivy and Warren pressed their fingertips to the planchette once more. It was moving. "I... L... L... E... D..."

"I was killed."

"Ooooooh I'm shaking." Michelle laughed and playfully hit Hazel's arm.

"Hold me Michelle I'm so scared."

"I hope we aren't making the ghosts mad."

"Yeah now they might haunt us forever. Oh nooooo."

"Whatever," Ivy said. "Why did you two even tag along if you don't believe us?"

"I didn't say I don't believe you," Michelle said. "But it's just funny. This is... baby stuff. This is the kind of thing people do when they pretend to be into the supernatural or ghosts or whatever. It's like what Hazel said, it's a toy."

"No, trust me, my cousin said it was real. She had to have her house blessed after using it and everything."

"No offense, but your cousin is totally a liar," Hazel said. "But go ahead, see what it says next. I'm dying to know. First it tells you it was killed here, what's next? It's gonna like beg and plead for you to 'find its body' and 'set it to rest' or something?"

"Well, let's give it a go." Warren's fingers were on the planchette along with Ivy's. He spelled out the letters it landed on: "L-I-B-R-A-R-Y."

"Hey, I stopped by the library this morning when I made the copies of the poster."

"Woah, that means it's a sign," Hazel said, then blurted out a big laugh. "What's it mean? You're on the right track or something, detective?"

"Maybe," Michelle said, "it means her killer was at the library too."

"Come on, you guys are no fun. Don't you want to solve the mystery?"

"There's nothing to solve," Hazel said. "What are we gonna find here that the police couldn't find? I'm sure they searched this place up and down top to bottom."

"What if they didn't search here at all? That's why it's the perfect dumping ground for the body of a dead girl. Why would they search this abandoned mansion?"

"We're just going in circles Ivy. You're looking for something that isn't here."

"Let's try it again," Warren said. "This time I don't want you two sitting out again. I want you to see that we really are getting messages from beyond the grave.

With everybody's hands on the planchette the room warmed up again. Ivy peered at the fireplace and saw that the flames swirled again momentarily into a miniature tornado. The flames were writhing with every movement of the planchette that was now sliding across the board; she hadn't noticed that the others had begun.

"T... O... Y..."

"Stop! I know you're doing that!" Ivy said.

"No it was... 'Catherine.'"

"B... O... O... K..."

"I guess our little ghost likes to read," Michelle said.

"U... P..."

"Book up," Warren said. "Library. Book. Up."

"It's telling us something! A grave message from beyond the grave!" Hazel said in probably what was an attempt at a Vincent Price impression. *"Spoooooooooky!"*

The planchette moved to the top of the board where the numbers zero through nine were written. It landed on the number two. When Ivy looked at the fireplace, it was *pulsing*.

"I think it wants us to go upstairs," Ivy said.

"Therefore the murder happened on the second floor," Hazel said. She and Michelle couldn't stop laughing and whispering little jokes to each other.

"Elementary, my dear Watson."

"I'm gonna go up there." Ivy picked up one of the candles. There was enough light in the living room so that they could see, but she brought it along with her because of how dark it might be further inside of this house. Even in bright daylight it still was difficult for the rays of the sun to find their way into this place. Even the windows that weren't boarded up struggled to take in light…

She went up the stairway. It was a beautiful spiraling stairway, something like out of a gothic castle.

She and her friends came to the second floor admiring it. This was her and Hazel's second time here, and the first time for Warren and Michelle who took it in with all the wonder and amazement that Ivy and Hazel had had a few days ago on their first visit.

The place had a charm to it. Something magical. And something else too—some sense of doing something that was forbidden. This place was a place that existed for them and only them. In a way they were the new owners of the house.

"What are we gonna do?" Hazel said, breaking the sudden silence that had washed over everybody. "Split up and 'look for clues?'"

"Sounds like a good idea. Me and Ivy will go off this way," Warren pointed his thumb down to the right, "and you and Michelle can go down that way. Just holler if you find the library—or if you see a ghost. Whichever comes first."

"Don't bet on it."

Warren and Ivy went off down the right hall and their friends wandered in their own direction with their little laughs and whispers fading with the distance that was put between them, and Ivy thought about grabbing Warren's hand as they walked off but she was too nervous to do so. She looked up at his face in the shadowy hall as a small touch of candlelight writhed its way across his eyes; he looked so mysterious.

"Can I ask you something?" Ivy said.

"Sure."

Nerves grew in Ivy's stomach. "You weren't pushing the planchette where you wanted it to go, right?"

"Of course not. Were you?"

"No I wasn't," Ivy said. She had the urge to tell him something else but wasn't sure what. Here she was alone with Warren on a little adventure—this should bring them closer, she thought. This should spark something, she hoped. Whatever she'd say now was perhaps the most important thing she'd ever say, and she didn't even know which words were supposed to leave her lips. Then she thought about how silly she was for asking Hazel repeatedly if she looked good or not—Warren couldn't even see all the effort she had put into her appearance because of the darkness wrapping around her and concealing her as if she were one of the legendary ghosts that called this old mansion its home.

And she said nothing.

"Let's check out this room."

"Why this one?" It was the only the reply that Ivy could think of in that split second.

"It's as good as any." Warren opened the door.

It wasn't the library room but he stepped inside anyways. A bedroom. A big dusty bedroom. A bedframe without a mattress. A vintage dresser tucked away in s corner with a cardboard box on top of it. The window was cracked open and warm air spilled in accompanied by hints of bright light from outside.

Warren walked over the box. "Let's see what they left behind." He picked it up off the dresser and looked inside. "It's empty."

"What did you expect? This place has probably been picked over already."

Warren shrugged. "I dunno."

Ivy held up the back of her hand to the candle. "Did I tell you I found this ring here?"

When Warren came back over to her he grabbed her hand, looking over the gold ring. "That's beautiful," he said.

"Thank you."

He held onto her hand for a moment longer than he needed to, then he let go. Ivy wished he would have kept holding it. She thought maybe she should tell him that. But then she was too nervous to say anything at all.

"Do you think the others are scared?" Ivy forced herself to say as they left the room and Warren shut the door behind them. "I don't think they're as naïve as they pretend to be."

"I think everyone's a bit of a believer. Hazel and Michelle are just goofing because they don't want us to know they're scared."

"Maybe we should scare them."

"Yeah? What do you have in mind, Ivy?"

She felt her cheeks burning with blood. She was thankful now that she was clasped in shadows so he couldn't see just how red her face had turned.

"Let's scream bloody murder."

"Both of us or one of us?"

"I'll start screaming." Ivy laughed as she envisioned it. "I'll just start making something up. Do you have anything you want me to say?"

"No, no, just do your thing."

Do my thing, Ivy thought. *Easy enough.*

She collected herself, took in a deep breath, then let out a sharp scream. It was hard to keep it up and not laugh when she heard the others screaming in return. Ivy leaned on the wall and was silent for just a moment taking in more breath, then she let out a small series of screams.

"Oh my God! Somebody help me! He killed Warren! Now he's gonna kill me!"

A stampede of footsteps were coming Ivy's way. At that moment, Warren slid behind a corner. Hazel and Michelle were running to Ivy's aid. Ivy was letting out more panicked screams, shouting that somebody was in here with them, and then Warren jumped out of the corner and grabbed Hazel and Michelle who dropped the candle.

The girls screamed and struggled against him before he let go, laughing, and picked up their fallen candle and gave it back to them.

"You assholes," Michelle said.

"I can't believe you guys," Hazel said.

"Hey, I thought you two said there was nothing to be scared of."

"So what? Did you find the library or something?"

"No, not yet."

"You're still shaking," Ivy said.

Warren was smiling. "You did a great job. You should be an actress."

"Yeah," Michelle said, "like it takes talent to fake a scream. I do it all the time."

"So should we just call it quits?" Hazel said.

"What? No way," Ivy said.

"I wanna call it quits too. What about you, Warren?"

"Let's take another look around. You two can split if you want."

"I've got better things to do," Michelle said, "than walk around this gross place looking for a library that doesn't exist. Which way's the exit?"

"I'll help show you to the exit then me and Ivy can find that library," Warren led them through one of the house's mazelike hallways.

SQUEEEEEEAK!

Rusty door hinges that sounded almost like a human shriek.

Warren followed that noise around a corner to investigate, and Michelle asked him where he was going—but the others went after him after a moment's delay and they found the library. Its door was wide open, as opposed to all the other doors in its hall that were all completely shut.

The library was beautiful. A nice desk across the room with stacks of books over it. A window that overlooked the front of the Engstrom House. All the ancient books that anybody of the time could have wanted.

Warren was walking around to the other side of the desk and Ivy followed him over without thinking much about it. He looked out the window at the sky that was streaked with pink. Whippoorwills flew in the distance and sang.

"Nice view," he said.

"Yeah it is."

"See? This is the real shit," Michelle said.

She put a volume down on the desk. There were illustrations of demons in hell. She flipped a few pages over to an exorcism of a woman tied down in a forest and a spirit spiraling out of her mouth. Then there was another grotesque illustration later on in the book of a medieval torture device—Ivy looked away in disgust.

"Look at this one." Hazel held up a book from across the room. A cracked leather cover with faded yellow pages. There wasn't a trace of a name or title anywhere on the cover that Ivy could see from where she stood. "This one's got like, incantations and stuff. I wanna try one."

"Knock yourself out," Ivy said.

"I think we have to draw one of these symbols. Does anyone have any chalk?"

"You think we brought along chalk?" Ivy said. "Who carries around chalk?"

"You could probably use the charred wood I tossed out of the fireplace earlier."

Downstairs Hazel did what Warren had suggested and used a broken piece of charred wood to draw an uneven circle about three feet in length. Within it everybody copied strange symbols they had seen from throughout the book.

"You two should ask it if we're close," Michelle laughed. "Using a Ouija board, yeah right."

"This is a special occasion," Ivy said, and opened her purse for a bag of weed. "Calls for a smoke."

"Oh hell yeah, new girl," Warren said. "Hazel, where have you been keeping her my whole life? All to yourself?"

"Oh, you know it."

Ivy took the first puff of the joint then gave it to Warren. Then Michelle took it while Hazel put the last symbol down.

Hazel grabbed the joint and puffed it between incantations.

"And you two jerks made fun of us," Warren said.

"Maybe I'm pronouncing these all wrong," Hazel said.

"Hey, I never claimed to be a believer," Michelle said. "I only said this was more real than your dumb board."

Warren put Cat's missing persons poster at the center of the circle. "Maybe you were just missing something. Try it again."

Hazel repeated the incantation and then the fireplace abruptly ignited. Despite its heat, the room was chilled. Suddenly a girl was in the center of the circle Hazel had drawn. A pale girl wearing black. Beautiful blue eyes and long dark hair.

It was her. It was Catherine.

The flames spread out of the fireplace and ignited all the symbols that the group had drawn on the floor, yet the wood floors did not burn. Whisps hissed from deep within the fireplace and spread around the hushed room.

"Jesus. I thought you dorks would never figure it out," Cat said, then she pointed at the joint in Ivy's hand. "I'd give anything to be able to hit that joint."

Ivy extended it to her.

"It's not going to work." Catherine's hand passed straight through Ivy's hand and couldn't touch the joint.

"You were killed here. Do you know who did it?"

"Woah, getting pretty personal right off the bat, kid. You remind me of this girl I used to know. What are all of you doing here anyways?" Cat asked.

"We came here to—"

Before Cat could receive Ivy's answer to the question, the whispers in the fire behind her erupted in loud chaos. Groups of unseen voices were speaking from some unknown realm. Cat turned to the fireplace and stuck her head in. "Not now, Ambrose, I'm busy, give me a minute," Cat said. Then she faced Ivy and the others again. "Sorry, you were saying?

"We came to find you."

Catherine laughed. "I'm not that important."

"I have so many things I want to ask you."

"This can't be real," Michelle said. Michelle was trembling and stepping backwards. She was grabbing on to Hazel's arm and Hazel was moving back with her, just as scared.

Warren stepped closer to Cat, looking down at the fire then up to Cat's eyes. "How long have you been dead?"

"Doesn't matter, I'm nineteen forever. You kids look like you're twelve," Catherine said. "Damn I'd really love a smoke."

Ivy blew smoke from the joint at Catherine; it was absorbed into her translucent presence somehow, and she smiled.

"Ahhhh, that really hit the spot."

"I want to know something," Warren said. "Can you tell us—"

But Catherine couldn't answer him because she was fading; quickly becoming transparent. "Oh damn. It's happening already. Hey it was fun guys. We should do this again sometime."

6

Ever since Helen Engstrom and her family died, their old home rested on its lonely hill in Ashfall. Spiders crawled over mountains of dust and spun webs across the corners of each room. Twenty empty years dragged by. The house was a silhouette of its former self; devoid of a family and devoid of any life besides the bugs. And yet it seemed alive.

When three boys gathered at the pathway at the bottom of the hill they halted and pretended not to be nervous, but each must have known what the others were thinking. Billy was cracking his fingers like he always did when he was scared; Samuel's cheeks were deeply red; Edmund's eyes darted all around.

"I heard there's an old witch that still lives inside," Billy said. "She takes the souls of children so that she can stay young forever."

"That isn't true," Samuel said. "You're a liar, Billy."

"No, Samuel, trust me. My sister and her friends were telling me about it after church last week."

"What else did she tell you about? The goblins that live in the back of the candy store?"

"No, really. The family that built this place made a deal with the devil through a coven of witches that lives in these woods."

"Yeah?"

"The witches are a thousand years old," Edmund said. "I heard about them too. The adults don't want us to know about them."

Samuel shook his head. "No matter what you say, neither of you are going to convince me. You both sound like fools."

"If it's not true then I dare you to knock on the door," Billy said. "Go on."

"I'm not going a single step closer to that house."

"Because you're scared? Scared that the witch will—"

"I'm not scared."

"You're scared she'll eat you? Is that it?"

"Nobody lives in that old house."

"Then why won't you knock on the door, Sam?"

Samuel was hesitant. He glanced at the house then back to his friends and said, "Why should I be the one to do it? Why not one of you two?"

"Because we dared *you* to do it," Edmund said. "If you don't do it you owe each of us five silver dollars."

"Yeah, like Edmund said. Five silver dollars."

"I'm only going to do this to prove you wrong," Samuel said. "If nobody answers the door then each of you owe *me* five silver dollars. Do you solemnly swear?"

"Cross my heart and hope to die," Edmund said.

"Stick a needle in my eye," Billy said.

Samuel went up the hill to the Engstrom place; rumors had spread all through town of things that had happened there—things that he could not believe, things that could not have been real, but they chilled him and terrified him anyways.

The gate was open.

He turned back for a moment and looked down at Edmund and Billy. They waved at him. Samuel waved back.

It was the last time he would ever see them again.

He went past the gate, up to the house, and knocked on the door.

Billy and Edmund waited at the base of the hill a little while longer, but Samuel never returned from his trip up to the Engstrom place's front door.

"Where is he?"

"He's trying to scare us," Edmund said. "Well, it won't work."

"Come on, let's get him and go back to town."

The boys went up the hill and to the wide-open gate. Samuel wasn't around, so they called his name a few times but received no response. Instead of passing through the gate they went around it, searching for where he might be hiding.

"We're leaving," Billy said with his hands cupped around his mouth. "We're going with or without you."

"Samuel, come out," Edmund said. *"Where are you hiding?"*

Billy looked at the brooding house through the gate, holding onto a slat in each hand. "He didn't really go inside, did he?"

"That's impossible. The door is locked."

"How would you know?"

"It must be."

"But Edmund, the gate is open."

"Maybe he went down the other side of the hill and is on his way back to town as we speak. He's trying to fool us."

"I think we should check inside."

"Are you crazy, Billy?"

Billy walked around the gate to the opening and passed through. "He must be inside."

"Don't go in there."

Billy didn't stop and kept going forward on the path up to the front door, so Edmund followed him.

"I cannot believe this."

"Samuel? Samuel are you in there?"

When they were both at the front door, Billy wrapped his hand around the knob. "Here it goes…"

The door opened. Billy stepped inside and Edmund reluctantly followed. The boys stood closely together as they entered the front room; all the rumors surfaced again in Billy's mind, and he thought about everything his sister and her friends had explained to him about the witches—the sacrifices that had happened here and the children who had died one by one as offerings to the devil himself. Billy shuddered. The house must have been a gateway to hell itself.

"Samuel? Where are you?"

The boys spoke in whispers calling their missing friend. They stood in the threshold between the front room and the rest of the house; it was a sable portal into another world of vast unreality. It was strange to think that they were inside the place where all the terrible rumors had taken place. They weren't far at all from the rooms where people had supposedly been sacrificed.

"Samuel?" The whisper weakly left Billy's lips. He was so scared he could hardly speak.

Edmund grabbed Billy's arm in a painfully tight grip. "Let's go. Samuel is *not* here."

The boys turned to leave. They were partway to the door when there was a scream from deep within the house that sent jolts of terror ripping through their hearts; the boys stampeded to the door and fled from the house. The gate ahead of them was shut but it shifted open under the desperate clutches of their hands.

7

THE NEXT MORNING, BILLY and Edmund met at the park to discuss what happened to Samuel. They sat at the bench near the baseball diamond. Far away from them some other kids were throwing a baseball back and forth; one kid was chasing a stray pitch that he had not been able to catch.

"I told Mr. Ackerman that Samuel was staying at my house," Billy said. He was holding a baseball in his hands, turned it around in his palms, staring down at it and his feet and not making eye contact with his friend. "How long can we keep up the lie?"

"I don't know."

"What will we tell his parents if he doesn't come home? They'll throw us in prison."

"They won't throw us in prison. We didn't do anything to him."

"Edmund, they won't believe us. We look guilty no matter what we say. Who would believe that he went into that house and never came out? They'll all think we did something…"

Edmund said nothing.

"Samuel vanished because of me. Because I dared him to go inside that house."

"We know at least a couple things for sure."

"Yeah?" Billy finally looked up at Edmund who was disheartened. "What?"

"We know for sure that Samuel was in the house. Because we heard him scream."

"What else?"

"We know he hasn't left that house. So we know where he... must be."

They went to Billy's home and found a burlap sack. Then they went to the shed, where Billy's father, who was a carpenter, kept his tools. They didn't know what they'd need so they filled it up with a bit of everything. The first thing they grabbed was a flashlight that was so heavy Billy thought it would tear the sack in two.

Edmund grabbed two pieces of wood and dumped them into the bag; they were so long that they only partway fit, with the majority of them sticking out of the sack. Edmund then grabbed a third and was putting it in when Billy stopped him.

"What do you think we're gonna do? Build ourselves a treehouse when we get there or something?"

"Sorry I just wanted to be prepared." Edmund put the wood back in its place. "What else do we need?"

"Tools."

"Tools... tools..." Edmund picked up a hammer, and Billy picked up a screwdriver. "What are these for, Billy?"

"We don't know what we're up against..."

Edmund hung his head. "What really happened at that house? Do you think any of it's really true?"

"I hope to God for Samuel's sake that it's not. You know... you know my neighbor? Mr. Carter?"

"Yeah?"

"My sister told me that Mr. Carter has a daughter who was friends with one of the Engstrom girls. She said that after a visit to that house, Mr. Carter's daughter went crazy. I guess she lives in Piedmont Wellness now, and my sister says Mr. Carter goes up to visit his daughter a couple times a year." Billy shuddered. "If you think the Engstrom place is bad, just wait until you hear about Piedmont Wellness…"

"You're not making me feel any better about this."

"Do you have any money?"

"Two nickels."

"Perfect. We'll need Cracker Jack."

"What else are we taking from here?"

"Let's see…" Billy walked around the shed. There was a hacksaw that he picked up and added to the burlap sack. "Okay. This should be good for… something."

"What would we need that for?"

"I don't know. Would you rather go underprepared?"

"Well… no… but…"

"But nothing. Let's go get that Cracker Jack. I think I can get a couple nickels from my mom."

"Do you think we'll be there long, Billy?"

Dark clouds massed over the Engstrom House.

The boys stood in front of the gateway. The burlap sack slipped a little in Billy's sweaty palms.

Edmund gulped. "Here we are…"

"We've got to do this. We've got to save Samuel."

Edmund nodded then stepped forward and opened the gate for Billy to pass through. Then he opened the front door and the boys stepped in.

"Billy?" Edmund said nervously.

"Yeah Edmund?"

"Can I have that Cracker Jack now?"

"No. Not yet. Cracker Jack is for celebrating, now let's go find Samuel." Billy set the sack down on the table in the living room and fished out the flashlight. He pushed the button and the light emerged faint at first then fully developed. Even though it was day-time, the Engstrom House was full of decrepit darkness, as if the unknown was forever chained to this place.

The flashlight cut feebly through murkiness.

The boys stepped through the living room.

They crossed the threshold into the rest of the house.

Up ahead was where Samuel's screams had come from. Suddenly Billy paused then stuck his arm out in front of Edmund for him to pause too.

"What is it?" Edmund said. "Do you hear him?"

"Shhh… quiet for a second."

"What?"

"I said quiet, nimrod."

Billy turned around to face the entrance that they had just passed through to leave the living room. He aimed the light around, then pointed it to the floor. There was dust everywhere, and their footsteps had disturbed it.

"Do you see his footsteps?"

"Which are his?"

"They... they all look like ours..."

Edmund gulped.

Billy said, "Samuel knocked on the door as a dare. Now what compelled him to come in here? To scare us, maybe? Perhaps to prove this house wasn't cursed. But... but why would he need to go past the living room? Did he even go past the living room? Where are his footsteps? If he went further into this house, why did he do it?"

"I don't know."

Billy nodded, saying nothing.

He examined the floor a little bit longer until he decided to move on. He noticed Edmund had taken the hacksaw from the sack and was holding it now in his hand. Terror was spread on his face.

Billy tried to piece it together; Samuel's last moments before the scream that they had heard. Tried to piece together what it must have been like. Tried to put himself in Samuel's shoes, but nothing made sense... unless something had taken him.

That chilling scream played on repeat in his mind. For a minute he thought he actually heard it echoing off the walls in this silent building that had once been a full home. What must that have been like? To live in this house? To become one of its victims... to be in its grip...

"*Samuel?*" Edmund abruptly yelled. "*Samuel can you hear us?*"

"*Samuel?*" Billy yelled too.

They walked through a hallway then turned a corner. They walked around for a little while calling Samuel's name. Where was he?

They passed through a dining room. Billy wondered what the children living here must have thought, must have felt, when they were dying one by one. The rumors were that each child had developed their own distinct and obscure sickness, and each passed in mysterious ways. What truth there was to that, he might never know.

CREEEAAAK! CREEEAK!

Somebody upstairs.

The boys ran out of the room and found the nearest stairway. They shouted Samuel's name on their ascent, and Edmund waved around the hacksaw for reasons that Billy could not determine. They came to the second floor and shouted and shouted; distant footsteps creaked across the floorboards nearby.

They went around corners chasing after the unseen guest but soon the sounds stopped and the boys were still alone.

"Was it him?" Edmund said.

"It must have been."

The boys sat down on the dusty ground for a break.

"Are you sure that Cracker Jack is only for celebrating?"

"Ah forget about it. Help yourself." Billy tossed Edmund a box. "Which card did you get?"

"Looks like... Ward Miller."

"Ward Miller. Ward Miller. I've got a million Ward Millers. Sometimes that's the only card I think they ever printed. But hey, at least I pulled a Honus Wagner the other day."

"Honus Wagner, that's my dream card. You lucky bastard."

Billy shrugged.

"Want some?" Edmund stuck out the box.

"Sure." Billy opened his palms.

Edmund poured some out for him. "So what now?"

"I don't know. And why are you still holding that hacksaw?"

"It makes me feel safe."

"Guys. Can you hear me?"

Billy jumped and Edmund screamed. It was Samuel. He was nearby—practically on top of them. He sounded nervous. Billy looked all around; where had his voice come from?

Billy and Edmund stood up and called Samuel's name.

"Come on, Samuel. Where are you?"

"Samuel? Samuel? Hello?"

"Billy?"

"Yeah?"

"I've got a bad feeling about this."

Elmer Engstrom, the previous owner's nephew, met with Mr. Bloch in the early morning and Elmer unlocked the front door with a key from a gigantic keyring that must have had fifty or more keys on it. Mr. Bloch thought it would take a year to get through them all and find the appropriate key, but Elmer had no trouble getting the door open.

"Here we have a quiet little house tucked away off the main street and as you can see, perfectly harmless looking. While we did have a… tragedy twenty years ago, I assure you that any of the rumors about my family's old home being 'cursed' simply aren't true…"

"Yes, it is a lovely house."

"Five floors, an attic, and a basement," Elmer said as they stepped into the living room. "Out back there's a big shed, a wellhouse, and the family woods. The house comes with all the furniture you see here, as well as the paintings and statues."

"No wonder the asking price was such a large sum."

Elmer laughed a little bit. "Yes, well, I suppose it is a rather large sum. But all the things you'll find in this house are genuine antiques. I bet you'd make a profit if you went through and sold off all these paintings at an auction."

Mr. Bloch ran his fingers over the dusty frame of a beautiful painting of the sea. "Actually I think I'd like to keep all of these around."

Billy and Edmund froze at the sound of distant voices and footsteps; they listened closely and at first the words were audible but formless. Then, ducking behind a corner, they heard the men more clearly. Two men probably in their forties.

"Here on the second floor is my uncle's private library. He was an avid reader. Supposedly he had written a manuscript of his own, but nobody in my family has ever been able to find it. Of course, all the books come with the house as well…"

"What are they doing here?" Billy whispered.

"*Shut up.*"

As the voices slipped back out of earshot, Billy heard the men laughing at a joke...

...then there was a rasping inside the walls.

Billy slammed his hands over his mouth to hold in a scream.

Samuel's sickly voice came from inside the wall.

"Help me..."

When the steps of the two men were coming back in Billy and Edmund's direction, Edmund grabbed Billy by the wrist and as quietly as he could pulled him into a nearby room. Then Edmund hurried to shut the door. Even under the darkness of the room, Billy could tell how red his friend's face had become.

"Billy. Oh no."

"What?"

"I think I left the Cracker Jack in the hallway."

Elmer brought Mr. Bloch back to the main floor. "My uncle was fond of this room here. He hosted quite a few parties here."

The room was large with a fireplace on the far end, a bar on the left, and many old wooden seats scattered around. Mr. Bloch pictured what this room must have been like when the house was full of life, and wondered what had happened to all that people that had last been in here.

"Restock that bar with some liquor, put a gramophone in the corner, and this room would be good to go."

"Most definitely, Mr. Bloch."

"Look, Elmer, I'm probably no more than five years your senior. You can call me Nathaniel."

"Yes sir, Mr. Nathaniel."

The floor above them creaked. Elmer and Nathaniel looked up simultaneously.

"There isn't anybody else in here, is there?"

"No. It's just you and me."

The room where Billy and Edmund were hiding was a big music room with a piano at the center, boxes of sheet music, and old dusty instruments that hadn't been touched for years. They were kneeled over in the corner of the room looking down through the vent where the two men were talking. One of them lit a cigarette then extended the pack to the other man.

Edmund adjusted himself and lost his balance, slipping and making a loud thud on the creaking floor.

Instantly he and Billy moved away from the vent so that the men wouldn't see them.

"What the hell?" Billy said in an angry whisper.

"I lost my balance." Edmund was still red and was nearly in tears. "I have to pee really bad."

"*Help me...*"

It was Samuel again. His voice was coming from inside the walls.

"*Samuel...*" Billy touched his hand to the wall. "We'll get you out of there, but be quiet before you get us in trouble."

"I have to pee… it's killing me…"

"Shut up," Billy said, but when he saw that Edmund couldn't hold it in any longer and wet his pants, he almost lost it.

Billy slipped a hand over his mouth to conceal a sharp laugh that was on the verge of escaping. Edmund, even in the shadows, was turning red as he sat in his own puddle of urine.

"Old floors have a habit of creaking on their own. Happens to me all the time, Nathaniel."

"Yeah, I hear it all the time at my place. Elmer, I've got a question for you," Nathaniel puffed his cigarette, "if all this land's been in your family so long, why do you want to sell it?"

"Me and my siblings and my cousins all live quiet lives. None of us have any desire to fill up such a mansion. So instead of keeping it here collecting dust, we all thought it should go to somebody who might enjoy it. So, now that we've had a look around the house, how about I show you the back yard?"

"Sure."

The men left the room and went outside.

Billy wedged the screwdriver to the seam between two of the wooden boards that made up the walls in the music room and tapped it with a hammer until it came loose.

"How come he's in the walls?" Edmund asked.

"I don't know."

"What could have happened?"

"How the hell should I know? I wasn't there. Your guess is as good as mine."

The wood board popped off. Billy threw it down.

"Get the flashlight."

Edmund found it in the burlap sack then fumbled around to Billy's side and aimed it inside the open wall. There was no sign of Samuel anywhere.

"Samuel?" Billy said. He was dumbfounded.

Edmund gulped. "We should get out of here."

"No way, not without Samuel. We owe it to him. It's all our fault he's gone."

"My uncle was an inventor. He spent many nights in this shed tinkering away at different inventions, but above all, his favorite pastime was crafting toys for his children. Say, didn't you mention you were a bit of a toymaker yourself?"

"Yes sir I am. A man needs hobbies to keep him sane. For me that's woodworking. My daughters have quite a bit of a doll collection, and I'd say I've made about a quarter of those dolls with my own hands."

"Well, you'll have plenty of space and resources here. These woods are practically endless. You know, the family fortune came from selling tobacco that was farmed on this land. This area has seen many overhauls in its time. Complete farmland to complete woodland. There were other houses built here too at different times, each torn down to make way for a new one. I'd say there were about five houses on this ground before the one you're considering purchasing."

Billy tore off two more wood panels.

"Samuel? Damnit Samuel where are you?"

"Billy quiet down. Those guys are gonna hear us."

"I don't care if they hear us."

Edmund set the flashlight down then grabbed the hammer and screwdriver from Billy's hands; Billy wouldn't let go of them and pulled against Edmund. The boys fought with each other over the tools until they both fell down and Billy's elbow slammed into Edmund's gut, causing Edmund to gasp and let go of the tools.

"It's like you don't want to find him."

"Are you kidding me Billy? If I didn't want to help find him I wouldn't be here. We need to be careful is all I'm saying. If those guys catch us we'll be in trouble."

"Goddam it. Where could Samuel have gone?"

"Just calm down for a minute. Breathe."

Billy paced the room back and forth. "It just doesn't make any sense. What's happening in there?"

"Let's take a minute and think things over. We can figure this out."

"Okay." Billy sat down on a dusty box of sheet music. "Let's figure this out."

"I can't think when I'm hungry. I'll go get the Cracker Jack."

Edmund left the room and Billy followed him with the burlap sack refilled with all the tools they had brought along with them for the purpose of finding Samuel. Edmund picked up the Cracker Jack box from the floor and ate a handful.

"Delicious." Edmund stuck out the box to Billy.

"I can't eat when I'm angry."

Edmund frowned. "We'll find him."

"This place is so big. He could be anywhere."

"Do you think…. No. Never mind."

"What?"

"No. I don't want to say it."

"Tell me."

Edmund's frown stretched further. "Well. Does a witch really live here?"

"What? No. None of what anyone says about this house is true. Don't tell me you believe it. Edmund you'd have to be so stupid to—to—"

"You said it yourself that none of this makes sense. What's the explanation? If Samuel was really in that wall we'd have gotten him out by now. How on earth could somebody get lost in a wall?"

Billy kicked the wall. "I don't know. But it's not a witch. Samuel must have made a mistake."

"He walked inside the walls by mistake?"

"Look when we find him we can ask him. After I beat the hell out of him for getting us all into this mess."

"How long do you think somebody could… stay alive in there without water? Or food?"

Billy shrugged. "I don't know. And Samuel won't have to find out. Because we're gonna get him out of there."

CREAAAK! CREEEAK!

Steps above them.

"Did those guys come back in?" Billy asked.

"I didn't think so."

There was a window at the end of the hallway, so the boys went there to see what the men were up to. The back yard of the Engstrom House had a shed and a wellhouse and a large expanse of woods that seemed dark and sickly despite the brightness of morning. There was a bench too where the men were sitting looking at papers. One man had an open briefcase in front of him and was shuffling things around. The other was lighting another cigarette.

"This is trouble," Billy said.

"Why?"

"Didn't you hear what they were talking about? That guy's buying this place from that other guy."

"Yeah?"

"Yeah. So we better find Samuel before we don't have access to this place anymore."

"What," Edmund said, "is he moving in tonight or something?"

"Well I don't know. I don't know how long it takes for somebody to move into a new house. We've lived in my house my whole life."

"I'm sure it'll take weeks. And finding Samuel shouldn't take long. Right?"

"Right," Billy said, but he wasn't sure if he believed that or not.

None of this seemed right. Something strange had happened in the few short minutes Samuel had spent in this house after Billy and Edmund had dared him to go up to it and knock on the door. It was as if Samuel had stepped into another dimension.

A witch. A witch. Maybe it was all real. A witch had gotten him.

Shivers crept viciously on Billy's skin. Everything felt out of joint. Nothing felt like it was right—and nothing felt like it would ever be right again.

"We'll find him," Edmund said. "But now is not the time. Let's get out of here. We can come back tomorrow."

"Okay," Billy said. He didn't want to leave Samuel behind but Edmund was right. It was better to do this when they could have the house by themselves. It would be better not to have to sneak around.

They crept down a nearby stairway to the main floor.

Just then, the back door open. The owner and the buyer entered the house.

"Could have sworn I clipped all the papers together. I'm sure it's in my car, if you'd like to wait here while I retrieve it."

"Sure thing, Elmer."

"Be back in just a minute."

Billy and Edmund snuck around a corner.

"They're gonna find us," Edmund said. *"Where can we hide?"*

There was no way to leave through the back door or the front; one man was still in the house while the other was heading out the front door and sure to come back at any second. They had to wait it out.

Well—there were many rooms to hide in, but when Billy opened the nearest door he found that it led to the basement.

The boys went down. A little light spread through the dense blackness.

Then Billy knew how they were getting out. One of the windows was big enough to climb through.

He pushed it up and open.

"What are you doing?"

"We're leaving." Billy lifted himself up.

"I can't climb. I'm too fat."

"Then see you on the other side."

"Billy no."

"I'll help you."

After Billy was on the other side he looked left then right; out of view of the man who had left to get whatever papers were missing from his car. He stuck a hand through the window for Edmund. Edmund reached but couldn't quite grab him.

"A little further. Come on."

"I can't do it. I can't climb."

"You've got to be kidding me. Find something you can climb on."

"Okay."

There were several tall stacks of boxes. Edmund set down his Cracker Jack then pushed one box over to the window.

"Hurry up."

"I'm coming."

Edmund reached the boxes again then the door opened.

He froze.

The men came down the stairs.

"How could I forget to show you the basement? When I was little this was my favorite place to come. My aunt and uncle kept so many things down here. Things that had been passed down in our family for generations and generations."

"You really feel comfortable letting all this stuff go?"

"Well a lot of the family heirlooms have been taken. Most of the things in here, we really don't need."

"Well, Elmer, if anything in here still catches your eye, you'll be sure to take it, all right?"

"Yes, sir. Although I did pick through the basement years ago."

Edmund stealthily ascended on top of the boxes, praying that they wouldn't give out under him. His eyes darted toward the window but he couldn't quite see outside or see Billy, and he hoped that his friend hadn't left him here all alone.

He wanted to scream.

The men went around the basement making small talk and looking over things. Edmund's arms and legs strained as he kept still in one position for several minutes, holding in his breath as long as he could because he was scared to breathe and make noise. His muscles begged him to move. Sweat billowed down his forehead.

The men came to a stop next to the stack of boxes.

This can't be happening, Edmund thought.

"Enjoy your new home."

"I will. This must be the most beautiful house I've ever seen."

"Well, it's about time I get going. I have to drop off this paperwork so everything can be finalized."

"Of course."

Edmund felt such relief when the men walked away. He shifted his position on the boxes and completely forgot about the Cracker Jack that he had set down at his side. A popcorn and a peanut fell. Although they didn't make a noise, Edmund gasped.

Then the room was suddenly too hot. He was full of worry. Edmund shut his eyes tight and pretended he wasn't here; pretended he wouldn't get caught by these men.

"Did you hear something?" The buyer asked.

"Ha, Nathaniel," the seller laughed, "I guess that must be your first ghost."

8

BILLY DREAMED THAT HE was in the Engstrom House again. He and Edmund were wandering through darkened hallways searching for Samuel. The walls surrounding them had all been torn open in scattered lengths because the boys had spent so much time prying them open in search of their lost friend.

Billy felt tremendous guilt suffocating him so badly that he couldn't breathe. Then he heard Samuel's voice begging for help again, so he and Edmund slammed hammers into the wall and tore it open.

When Billy pulled his hammer back, a red eye stared at him.

"Ah!"

Billy stumbled backwards. Edmund did too.

The boys were silent a moment later when the eye disappeared into whatever lurking hell existed in the walls of the cursed house.

They continued down the hall. The Engstrom place was completely silent. Billy wondered what lay just out of reach behind the walls holding up the house; what abominations existed in that unseen stygian world?

A turn around a corner.

The witch extending her bony hand and laughed wickedly at the boys. Her skin was shriveled and decaying and green and she had a huge wart on her nose. Her teeth were crooked and cracked. She licked her lips.

Everything was changed in Billy's dream, and he and Edmund were in the forest. A coven of insane witches gathered around a cauldron that was boiling over a fire. Billy and Edmund were on their knees with their hands bound behind their back.

There was nothing that either boy could do but watch.

The witches chanted.

Billy wasn't sure how much time passed before two of them grabbed Edmund and brought him to the cauldron. They pressed him against the burning metal edge and he let out a chilling scream that made Billy's guts twist and squirm.

Edmund struggled against the witches but had no strength to use against them. He screamed repeatedly as the boiling liquid in the cauldron bubbled and burned his skin. Behind him, one of the witches picked up a knife from an altar and brought it over.

She dragged it across Edmund's throat and his blood erupted into the cauldron.

Then Billy woke up screaming.

9

BILLY AND EDMUND MET back up to buy Cracker Jack from the candy shop, then they went back to the Engstrom place. All day the dream he had about the witches was on repeat in his mind. He kept seeing Edmund pressed over the cauldron bleeding to death from the gash in his throat.

When they entered the Engstrom House Billy set the burlap sack down on the table and brought out a pencil and a notepad. "I thought of this yesterday. You're gonna map out the house."

"Map it out? Why me?"

"Because you have the better penmanship of the two of us."

"That's why I could never grow up to be a doctor."

"How unfortunate. Anyways you're gonna map out where we heard Samuel and we'll see if we can find any pattern."

"Okay." Edmund flipped open the notepad and wrote. "Let me see..."

Billy's eyes swept the room and took in all the little details he hadn't been able to appreciate last time, like the paintings on the walls and all the photos on the mantelshelf. Hadn't anybody wanted that stuff? Well maybe, he thought, all those things would have been a constant reminder of the horrors that befell the Engstrom family.

The boys wandered the halls.

For a while, Billy forgot which floor they were on. Each level of the house blended together eventually—he wondered how well Edmund was keeping the mapping together. So far they had not heard Samuel yet today.

Billy and Edmund were both depressed. Had they missed their chance? Had yesterday been it? Had yesterday been their final chance to find Samuel?

The boys came to a bay window and took a break.

"We have to get our story straight," Billy said.

Edmund gulped and frowned, staring out the window. "Do you think…"

Billy nodded.

"Do you think he's dead?"

"I hate to say it, Edmund, but how long could somebody stay alive in a wall?"

Edmund said nothing. He kept on frowning.

"Maybe yesterday was our only chance to find him. Goddamn we have to get our story straight."

"What do we say?"

Billy frowned too. "I don't know. I feel so sick about this."

"We can't tell anybody we dared him to go inside the house. If they knew they'd throw us in prison."

"Edmund you idiot they wouldn't throw us in prison, and besides we didn't dare him to go into the house, we dared him to knock."

"We told his parents lies already. What if his parents talked to our parents? What if they—"

"Then we should come clean. Tell them what happened from the very beginning."

"I don't know. There has to be something we can do. I don't know, Billy, I don't know. I don't like this. I don't want to go to jail. I won't survive in there."

Billy cracked his knuckles. "We won't go to jail. We'll just have to think of something…"

CREAAAK! THUD!

Movement in the walls.

"Samuel?" Edmund screamed.

"Samuel is that you? Sam?"

"Samuel? Hello?"

The boys pressed their ears to the wall.

Silence.

"Maybe we won't have to think of a lie at all," Billy said.

10

Nathaniel Bloch and his family moved in on a scorching summer day.

After a little while he went out back and put his tools and supplies into the shed. It was going to take a few trips to bring everything there. He was carrying a big box from his house to the shed when he saw something flash in the corner of his eye; a blur that passed quickly. He turned to glimpse what he thought was two boys running into the woods.

He paused to see if it were his kids, but nobody came out, nobody made any noise, and everything was completely still.

"Boys?"

No answer.

He set down the box in the shed then went to the entranceway into the woods behind the wellhouse.

He traveled down the path. There was a stream of water on his right. The expanse of trees seemed to go on forever and ever. He went further and further, occasionally pausing to take in the beauty of the trees and the birds and squirrels that called them home.

He was going to turn back when he heard a branch snap some-where up ahead.

"Boys, are you back here?"

No answer.

Deep in the woods, Nathaniel went over a slight rise then came to the family cemetery. Nathaniel circled the graves reading any of the stones that were not covered in moss or severely withered. A tiny, tiny tree had sprouted in a corner of the cemetery near a couple graves, but had snapped and fallen over.

Instinctively he picked up the remains tiny fallen tree. It was about four feet tall and three and a half inches in diameter. Maybe he could make something with it, he thought. A creation for his children from the woods of their new home.

Nathaniel dragged it back with him through the woods. When he was back at the shed his daughter Jeanette was in the back yard looking for him.

"Hi Daddy."

Nathaniel set down the little tree then picked up his daughter and kissed her cheek. "Hi Jeanette. How are you liking your new home?"

"Oh I love it, it's so pretty. Daddy what's that tree for?" She pointed. "Are you going to carve something from it?"

"Sure. I'm gonna make something special."

As a gift for his children, using wood from their new forest, Nathaniel Bloch commissioned a dollhouse from a local artist. The artist supplied his own tools and worked away in the attic with the blueprints of the home that Elmer Engstrom had supplied.

The artist crafted an exact replica of the home right down to the smallest details. Five floors. An attic. The exact number of rooms, and the doorknobs placed on the exact side of the door as they were in the blueprints—some on the right, some on the left. Candleholders on the walls. Carpet in some area, hardwood floors in others. The dollhouse mimicked their home's exact details in miniature and there was nothing that the artist left untouched. There was nothing that was guessed upon—if the blueprints did not exactly specify, then the artist himself went down with a camera and took pictures of whatever he needed.

The attic room became the children's toy room. Mr. Bloch built shelves and bins for his children's belongings and put them around the attic. His daughters filled the shelves with stuffed animals and dolls; his sons filled the bins with wooden cars, baseballs, and toy soldiers.

And the centerpiece of the toy room was the dollhouse.

"I spent a long time making this for you," he said to his kids on the day he finished putting together the dollhouse. "It's our new home. And I made these for you girls," Mr. Bloch said, handing them a box.

The girls opened the lid. Inside were new dolls that were small enough to fit inside of their new dollhouse.

Mrs. Bloch and Jeanette and Carrie played with the dollhouse in the attic that day while Mr. Bloch and Franklin and Daniel and Alvin threw around baseballs in the back yard. It was a gorgeous day, the dwindling summer weather still above seventy degrees.

Jeanette had ice cream after dinner then went back up to the attic to play with the dollhouse. A little while later her father came up to check on her. He sat next to her and ruffled her hair; she gave him a kiss on the cheek.

"Father, I love the dollhouse. And I bet you thought it would take us longer to find it, huh?"

"Find what?"

"The secret room. You thought we wouldn't find it so fast but we did."

"What secret room?"

"How many are there? Are there really secret rooms in our new home like there are in the dollhouse?"

"There aren't any secret rooms in the dollhouse, Jeannette. What are you talking about?"

"But there is. There's a secret room next to my room in the doll-house. Carrie found it first. Is there really secret rooms? Since it's supposed to be exactly like our home?"

"Why don't you show me this 'secret room.'"

Jeanette's room was on the second floor—she had picked it out for the view, and for its proximity to the library room—and when she pointed it out on the dollhouse, she moved a small section of the wall back with her finger to reveal a hidden room just as she had mentioned.

Nathaniel plugged his nose.

Inside was rotting meat. Little pieces of moldy rotting flesh.

"Did you put that in there?"

"No, Father. It was already there."

Jeanette moved out of the way so he could look at it closer. The room was structured properly and had been hidden next to Jeanette's room, but there was nothing like this on the blueprints he had been given. Why would the artist do this?

"That imbecile I hired must have done this. Come on now," Nathaniel stood up, "it's time for bed darling. I'll deal with this tomorrow."

"Can't I play a little longer, Daddy? Please just ten minutes?"

"Not with that rotting meat in your toys. Come on, bedtime."

Jeanette wondered what the purpose of the hidden room could possibly be.

She left the attic with her father, leaving all her toys behind except for her favorite new doll, and went downstairs and brushed her teeth. Then Mother said prayers with her, tucked her into bed, kissed her forehead, and left the room.

Jeanette was falling asleep and drifting away into the darkness behind her shut eyes. The world was fading away from existence and she was entering the realm of sleep; the realm of dreams.

There were whispers. Whispers from her new wooden doll.

But she couldn't focus on them. Sleep was too strong. And she drifted fully away into a beautiful dream...

Nathaniel showed up at the artist's house and knocked at the door.

"Mr. Bloch, pleasure to see you," he said. Then, after seeing the anger on Nathaniel's face, he asked quickly, "Is there something wrong?"

"What kind of sick mind do you artists got?"

"What are you talking about? Here, sir, why don't you come in. Is there something wrong with the house?"

"You're damn right there is." Nathaniel tossed him the little bag that was in his pocket. The artist fumbled as he caught it. Then he dropped the bag in disgust.

"What is this?"

"You tell me, you're the one who put it in my house."

"I did no such thing."

"My daughter found it in the dollhouse you created. Found it in a hidden room. What, you thought that a couple little girls playing house wouldn't open every little latch? They were bound to find it."

"I don't follow, sir."

"The hidden room, you imbecile. They found the hidden room."

"What hidden room?"

"The one you put in the house."

"I didn't put any hidden room in the house, sir."

"Don't lie to me, kid. I saw it myself."

"I mean, I guess it's possible there could be a gap between pieces of room that one could constitute as a 'room' but there was nothing added nor subtracted. I followed your instructions precisely, the dollhouse that I built is an exact replica of your home."

"Before coming here I double checked the blueprints. You did follow it all right, except there was a hidden room. So why did you put it there? Why did you leave rotting meat for my girls?"

"Sir, I'm not gonna stand here in my home while you yell at me. There is the door, sir. It was a pleasure doing business with you."

"What kind of artist are you, huh? Leaving little pieces of meat behind hoping the kids might get sick from touching it? Is that it?"

The artist walked up to Nathaniel and grabbed him by the collar. *"Get out of my house."*

Nathaniel smacked him. "I'm not going nowhere til you tell me what other surprises you left for my little girls."

The artist punched Nathaniel in the gut then stepped away across the room and opened a desk drawer. Inside was a gun. He took aim at Nathaniel.

"Now, good sir, I am well within my rights to shoot you, but I don't want to leave your five kids fatherless nor do I want to make a widow of their mother. But if you keep up your behavior today, I might just have to cripple you. Now I'll leave you with this and only this: I don't think you did much research on that house you bought. Maybe you paid it a visit and thought everything checked out. Well that new house of yours has a bit of a reputation around these parts. There's something that ain't quite right with it."

"That's a bunch of balderdash."

"You bought that house now you gotta deal with the consequences. Get out of my house, or I'll be forced to do something that neither of us wants me to do."

11

A FEW WEEKS AFTER finding the ring, Ivy dialed Hazel's number one morning before school.

"Are we still on for tonight?"

"Oh totally. Hey, do you have me on those math answers?"

"Sure, but I don't know if we have enough time before first period. And I'm very sure most of my answers are wrong."

"Oh well, that's fine with me, I don't care if they're wrong. I just want them done."

"If that's the case why don't you just guess on all the answers? Oh and make sure you don't forget to bring—"

KNOCK! KNOCK! KNOCK!

"Ivy are you ready?"

"There's Abigail. See you soon, Hazel." Ivy hung up as her friend was saying bye. *"Come in."*

Abigail opened the door. "Hey, you ready?"

"Yeah." Ivy grabbed her bookbag from the bed of the guest room. She followed Abigail to Henry's Station Wagon parked in the driveway.

Ivy adjusted the radio until she found a station playing The Go-Gos. *Our Lips Are Sealed.*

"So, Ivy," Abigail said, twisting the knob to turn down the volume, "I know things are a little rough on you right now between you and your parents, and I've kind of saved all the speeches for the past month or so you've been staying with us to give you some space, but I guess I just wanted to say if you wanted to ever talk about it… I guess I just know what it's like. I was in your place before."

"Thanks, Abby," Ivy said.

"You get to that age where you start to… well life changes, you're becoming an adult, and that means sometimes you want to—"

"It's okay. Really. We don't have to talk about this."

"I'm sorry."

"No, no, don't be sorry Abigail. It's just I talk to Henry enough about it as it is. It seems like every day he's asking me… wait, is he telling you what I've been saying to him? Did he put you up to any of this?"

"God no. I don't know anything except what you told us a month ago, that your mother found your pot. But I thought maybe you'd want some advice from somebody that's been in your shoes. I don't think your brother's the best person to give advice on this is all. He's always done what your parents wanted or said."

"Sure. He's the favorite."

"Your parents mean well. They love you. They just want what's best for you. I guess I—"

"Look, can we drop it?"

"Sure. Hey that's a pretty ring, I don't think I've seen it before. Did a boy give it to you?"

"No, I found it on the ground."

"Really? Just like that?"

"Yep. It was just there."

They were quiet the rest of the drive to school.

It was a pretty day out, with clear blue skies and golden sunshine as far as Ivy could see. Whippoorwills were singing. Abigail parked in front of Ashfall High then she and Ivy exchanged goodbyes.

Ivy put her bookbag over her shoulder. Most students had gone inside, but Hazel was waiting for her at the entryway with her notebook in hand.

"Quick, where's the math homework?"

"In my bag."

"All right, dig it out."

"Now? But the bell's about to ring. We'll be late."

"Come on."

The bell rang as they stepped inside.

Hazel leaned against the lockers in the empty hallway while Ivy opened her bookbag and fished around. "What's our excuse?"

"Who the hell cares? Let's just say we were helping an old lady across the street."

"Really, Hazel? Mr. Green won't believe it."

"Would you just hurry up? Just how far down in that bag is your math homework anyways?"

"I dunno, I can't find it."

"Ivy, come on, I need those answers."

Ivy took out all her notebooks and textbooks and sorted through them. "You're going to hate me, but I think I forgot it at home."

"I totally hate you."

"Well on the bright side, we're both late and neither of us have the homework. Now you have to show Mr. Green some of your famous charm I'm always hearing about so we can get out of this."

"How did you forget your homework?"

"I don't know. I forgot to put it back in my bag when I was done."

"Whatever."

"Let's get our story straight. So we were helping that old lady across the street, right? What else? Actually maybe we can say we were attacked by an old lady instead and in the chaos we lost our math homework."

"That just might work."

Beverly stood in front of the algebra class she was subbing for. "Hello everyone, I'm your substitute teacher Miss Hoffman. I'm going to be your sub for the foreseeable future so it'll be nice to get acquainted with you all. I recognize a few faces from the classes I subbed last year, but since I see plenty of new students here why don't we all go around the room and introduce ourselves? Why don't we start with... actually, hold on a sec."

Beverly went behind Mr. Green's desk and found the Tupperware of cookies she had baked. She brought it over to the young girl sitting in the first desk on the right side of the front row. "Take one and pass it on. Then we can begin our introductions."

Ivy and Hazel went up to the second floor of Ashfall High and to room two-thirty-seven. Their substitute teacher was already collecting the homework.

"Hey, sorry we're late," Ivy said. "We were, um, helping an old lady across the street."

"I don't know what punishment Mr. Green normally gives for tardiness, but to me it's one hundred sentences, girls. 'I will not be late to class.'"

"Would you believe me," Hazel said, "if I told you my dog ate my homework?"

"Not a chance," the sub said. Then she added: "I'm your sub this week. My name is Miss Hoffman. What are your names?"

"I'm Ivy."

"Hazel."

The girls sat in the two remaining desks at the very front of the class. While Miss Hoffman turned her back to write on the board, Hazel tossed Ivy a note. *Hope you didn't leave the stash out again to get confiscated. Did you remember to bring it or is it on your dresser with the homework?*

Ivy shook her head then pointed a thumb at her bookbag. *"I've got it,"* she mouthed, then looked up at the substitute teacher when she heard her talking.

"Turn in your books to page…"

Ivy tuned her out and wrote down a reply on the note. *Who else is going?* Then she discretely handed it to Hazel when the sub was not looking.

Hazel tossed it back to Ivy when she wrote her reply, but the note fell short of the desk and landed on the ground between them. Since the desk's armrest was on Ivy's right side, she could not quite reach the note without being obvious. She stretched in her seat, shifted around, and moved the note closer with her foot. Then, after a couple minutes, when another teacher knocked on the classroom door and Miss Hoffman went to answer, Ivy picked up the note.

"Good going," she said.

"Well you should have caught it."

"How could I catch it when it landed all the way over—"

Miss Hoffman turned to face the class. "Just because I'm speaking with another teacher does not mean you all have permission to talk. Anyone caught talking will have to write sentences."

"I hate her," Ivy mouthed.

"Tell me about it," Hazel mouthed back.

Ivy read what Hazel had written on the note: *The usual suspects.* Then she wrote back: *Is Warren going?*

Hazel replied: *Uh-huh, and he mentioned you to me.*

This time when Hazel tossed the note, it made it to the desk.

Are you serious? Ivy hurried to write and handed it to Hazel before Miss Hoffman was done with the other teacher.

Hazel wrote back: *Yes. Maybe you and him will have one of those big empty rooms all to yourselves.*

Later on when the bell rang and everybody was dismissed, Miss Hoffman told Ivy and Hazel to stay behind for a second.

"Why were you two late this morning?"

"Well to be honest with you, ma'am," Hazel said, "I didn't do the homework. I wanted the answers from Ivy and she forgot them at home. Don't punish her because of me, we would have been on time if I hadn't held her up for the answers."

"Thank you for being honest with me. Look, things happen, I understand. When me and my friend Abigail were students here, I was always dragging her into something just like you, Hazel, and making us late."

"Abigail Martinez?" Ivy said.

"Yeah, wait a second—you're Henry's baby sister aren't you?"

"Yep, that's me. Wait a second, I've seen you around before."

"I didn't even recognize you—you've really grown up. God I feel so old. Remind me to tell you this story about the time your brother got me kicked out of class for…. Well it's a long story, I don't want to hold you two up." Beverly laughed. "You know what? Forget about any sentences, girls. But if any of your classmates ask, you two still had to do them, okay?"

"Sounds good to me."

"Oh, hey, I almost forgot." Beverly found her Tupperware on Mr. Green's desk and opened it, then extended it to Ivy and Hazel. "I passed these out to the class before you girls showed up. Take some, I baked them."

"Thanks so much," Hazel said.

"These are delicious," Ivy said. "You're a great cook."

"How is Abigail these days? My God I haven't heard from her since…"

"She's good, Miss Hoffman. She and Henry have been busy with some wedding stuff lately. Hey, uh, can you write us a little note for our biology teacher in case we're late? We don't have much time left to get to our next class."

"Absolutely."

When the girls had left the room, Beverly erased the board and was gathering her things when she noticed a folded paper that was forgotten on Hazel's desk. She picked it up and opened it and read what was written:

Hope you didn't leave the stash out again to get confiscated. Did you remember to bring it or is it on your dresser with the homework?

Who else is going?

The usual suspects.

Is Warren going?

Uh-huh, and he mentioned you to me.

Are you serious?

Yes. Maybe you and him will have one of those big empty rooms all to yourselves.

Abigail sat on the edge of the bed and set down the tray, then she shook Henry awake.

"Morning, hun. I made you breakfast."

"Good morning." Henry's eyes creaked open.

Abigail gave him a kiss. "Your clothes are ironed. Lots of wrinkles in your grey suit, you should take better care of it."

"Sure." Henry sipped the cup of orange juice Abigail had poured for him. "What did I ever do to deserve somebody as sweet as you?"

"Hmmm... that is a good question. I know nobody's as perfect as me."

"That's for damn sure."

"And to think that you almost missed out. Dumping me in the eighth grade."

"Ninth grade."

"Of course you remember."

"Come eat some of this with me, I can't finish it all myself. This is enough French toast for three people."

Abigail took one bite. "I tried talking to Ivy today. She just won't open up to me. I feel so bad for her. I just want her to be okay."

"Give her time. You remember how crazy chicks are at that age. Hell it wasn't that long ago when we were that young."

"Ten years. Oh my God, Henry, I'm practically an old maid."

"Darling, you don't look a day over twenty one."

"You're definitely the sweet one. Not me."

"You could be right about that."

Abigail kissed his cheek. "I'd love to stay and fool around but I have to get to work myself. Do you think Ivy wants a ride from Hazel's later?"

Henry shook his head. "Nah. She'll be too embarrassed. I'm sure she'd rather walk."

The final bell rang and school was dismissed. Ivy packed the books she needed and found Hazel.

"Let's go, Ivy Wivy."

"How do I look?"

"Like ten bucks."

After they walked out of school, Ivy checked her reflection in one of the windows. "Is that a zit? Look. See it?"

"No way."

"You're not even looking." Ivy pressed her face closer to the glass. "Oh no, I think it is. What if Warren sees? Do guys notice zits? Do they care?"

"There's totally nothing there."

"Hazel I can feel a bump. My life is *over.*"

"Please if you're gonna drop dead, don't do it in front of me. The last thing I need is a corpse on my hands. Hey, there they are."

Ivy looked up. Warren was parked at the curb. An old Ford hand-me-down with a new orange paint job. Steve was riding shotgun, and Michelle was in the back leaning out the window with her hands cupped around her mouth.

"Hey bitches," Michelle said.

Ivy and Hazel squeezed into the back with her.

"God," Steve said, turning back to the girls, "there's nothing better on this earth than having a car full of beautiful women all to myself." Then he grabbed Hazel's hand and pulled it forward to kiss it. "Oh Hazel, baby, you look delicious as always. Did you dress in those tiny shorts just for me?"

She pulled her hand away laughing. "Yeah. As if."

"Don't play hard to get, baby."

"Show some manners," Warren said. "Hazel, baby, didn't you already reject poor Stevie here the other day?"

"'The other day' for three years now."

"Stevie, don't get rejected by the same girl twice, it's pathetic."

"She knows she wants me. Don't you get it, Warren? Chicks these days always play mind games, it isn't how it was before. Up means down with chicks today. Hell if they tell you the sky's pink you gotta believe them or it's game over."

"Whatever," Michelle said. "You don't know nothing about women. That's why you're still single and nobody would touch you with a thirty nine and a half foot pole."

"Yeah Michelle I know you know your way around a pole. Big Steve's heard all the rumors."

The old Engstrom place brooded on its hill.

Inside the house, Ivy opened her bookbag for the stash of pot.

"Awe hell yeah," Warren said.

"This looks a little short," Michelle grabbed it from Ivy's hands. "Are you sure you didn't smoke without us over the weekend?"

"Sure."

"I never know with you. Every time we come up here I'm worried you're gonna tell us that your mom threw away your stash again."

"That was one time and you weren't even there. That was before I knew you."

When everyone was passing around the two joints on the couches, Warren pulled Ivy aside. He took the blunt from his lips and put it between hers; she grabbed it and inhaled.

"Why don't we go upstairs? Just the two of us."

"Really?"

"What? You don't want to?"

"No, uh, I do. I do. Lead the way."

He took her by the hand. Ivy looked over her shoulder and winked at Hazel. Then they passed through the entryway into the rest of the house, coming upon the huge spiraling stairway. Ivy's heart raced as they ascended. Nervously she grabbed the railing in a tight grip.

"I... I was beginning to think you didn't like me, Warren."

"Well, um, I was too shy to ask you earlier. I always wanted to be alone with you. Away from our friends."

Ivy's heart was racing. "I really like you."

Warren took the joint from his lips. "I *really* like you too."

At the top of the stairs Ivy said, "I'm so nervous."

"Don't be." Warren looked her deep in the eyes then led her to one of the nearby rooms and opened the door. "After you."

Ivy put her hand over his on the doorknob and pushed the door to a close. "Have you ever done this before?"

He shook his head. "No."

Warren set the finished joint on the dresser. Ivy sat on the edge of the bed. Nerves tightened in her stomach as he came across the room and sat next to her. Their fingers intertwined. He leaned in close and kissed her.

Ivy dragged her hands along his body as they kissed; she trembled. Nervous little kisses with her mouth hardly opening.

"I've wanted this for so long," Ivy whispered, then pulled apart from him and walked across to the bathroom that connected this room to the neighboring room.

"What are you doing?"

"Getting more comfortable," she said.

She shut the bathroom door only halfway and looked at herself in the mirror. She made sure after slipping off her shirt that all of her hair was in place—she had to look perfect—and she double checked for pimples. Ivy slid her skirt off then did one more check in the mirror. All good.

Before Ivy could step away the mirror creaked open and behind it was a dusty cabinet with a pocketknife left behind by its previous owner. Engraved on the side of it was the name Helen. For some reason Ivy felt compelled to pick it up, and as soon as she did the knife stuck to her ring like a magnet. She pulled it away with a powerful tug—as though they hadn't wanted to come apart—then she carried it along with her clothes back into the bedroom.

"I thought you'd never come back."

"How do I look?"

"Like a goddess."

Ivy tossed her clothes onto the other side of the bed then rejoined Warren. "Take off your clothes too."

"You don't have to tell me twice." Warren took off his shirt in a hurry.

Ivy unbuckled his belt and helped him slide off his pants. Then she was on top of him, kissing him again, both of her hands intertwining with his. They became lost in each other, and yet her hand moved with a mind of its own, back over to the pile of clothes.

Back to the knife.

Together again, stuck like magnets.

She slammed the blade into Warren's chest then dropped the knife. She halted his screams by wrapping both of her hands around his throat and muting him. Warren's face was stricken with sudden torture and terror and he gasped under her tightening palms. Darkness came over his eyes.

Warren suddenly jolted and fist landed in Ivy's stomach. She let go of him, catching her breath, then the knife was raised up high above her head and she plunged it into Warren's flesh again. While the blade was deep inside of him she twisted it…

And twisted…

And with a maddening fury she repeated the motion over and over all across his body. Blood squirted out of his wounds and covered her. Warren attempted to fight back but all efforts were useless against the power of the archaic knife in Ivy's hands.

He shut his eyes and never opened them again.

Ivy lifted herself off of him and stood over the bed admiring her work. A moment later clarity washed over her. Was this real? Was it a dream? What was she doing here? Was the mangled mess in front of her *Warren?*

12

CREEEEEEEEEEEEEAK!

Something moved above the living room.

"What was that?" Hazel accidentally dropped the joint upon hearing the noise, then looked up at the ceiling. "Did Warren and Ivy go upstairs?"

"What, you think it might be a ghost? Don't be scared, baby, don't worry, if you see any ghosts around this old place I'll take care of 'em. They won't give you trouble with me around." Steve kneeled and picked the joint up then brushed a little dust off the side and put it between his lips. Then he put his arm around Hazel. "And you too, Michelle. Quit sitting all the way over there where I can't see your pretty face."

Michelle was sitting on Hazel's other side and reached over Hazel to get the joint from Steve. "Just hand me that joint."

"Sure thing sweet cheeks." Steve was handing the joint over but then pulled it away from her before she could actually grab it from his hand. He puckered his lips. "Just give Big Steve a kiss first."

"No way, 'Big Steve.' I would rather kiss a pig."

"Do you think it would turn into a prince or something?"

"That was a frog."

Steve leaned forward a little more. "Frogs, pigs, zebras, who cares. Well, my offer's expired. Big Steve needs a little more than a kiss to hand over the pot."

Hazel squirmed out from between the two of them and stood up and put her hands on her hips. "Get a room you two. God, Michelle, you slept with the whole basketball team and this was the one and only guy who would come along with us? This is the best new addition to the group you could find? I'm so glad he was never here before to spoil the fun."

Steve moved over into the open space that had once been occupied by Hazel, and he put his arm around Michelle then blew smoke into her face. "Joey told me about the wild time you two had below the bleachers after the game the other day. He gave you a five-star review, baby."

"Yeah, it's really a wonder that Jessie broke up with you. 'Little Steve' couldn't finish the job."

"Is that what she's sayin'? Truth be told," Steve blew more smoke in her face, "I broke up with her because she wasn't any good in the sack."

"Yeah right, you never stop seeing anybody. She totally dumped your ass." Michelle snatched the joint from Steve's lips. "Gross you slobbered on this thing."

"Hey, hey, a deal's a deal, you owe Big Steve."

"What are you talking about?"

"I told you in order for me to hand over the pot I needed a kiss or a little action. A deal's a deal baby."

"I never agreed to no deal, you lard ass."

Hazel shifted around on a couch. "So Steve, what do you think about your first time here? Does this place scare you?"

"Nah. You think Big Steve is scared of some dusty old house?"

"You know I heard about a couple girls who drowned here in the basement. This house is supposedly filled with restless spirits."

"Ancient history, baby," Steve said to her. Then he took the joint away from Michelle and told her, "You had enough, baby."

"Hey." Michelle tried to snatch it back but Steve held it away.

"I think the rumors are all true," Hazel said. "In fact, Steve, we even met a—"

"No, no, none of it's true. Just think straight for a second," Steve said, giving Michelle back the joint. "I know thinkin' straight can be hard for chicks, they're all so crazy. But hear me out. This is Ashfall. We're in the middle of nowhere. This is a town for small folk and not for the type who'd live in a big fancy mansion. I'm sure when this place was built the family who owned it thought they were like, overseeing some kingdom, but this place blows."

"A couple girls drowned in the basement. At least that's what I heard."

"Now I know that's a lie," Steve said, "how could there be a flood in the basement of a house on top of a hill?"

"'Cause there's this thing underground that catches rainwater. This girl who used to live here went down there playing hide and seek with her friend… and nobody found them for months."

"They make stories like that up to scare kids at bedtime. I bet there ain't nothing down there. And there ain't no ghosts in here neither."

"I wouldn't be so sure about that," Michelle said.

"Oh what, you too? Don't tell me Michelle you're a—a—"

"Do you want to talk to Cat again?"

"Hell yeah, she was the coolest." Hazel walked over to the fireplace.

"What cat are you talking about?"

"Oh, you'll see. Catherine's a new friend of ours. You wouldn't know her."

Michelle gave the joint back to Steve. "Let me give you a hand, Hazel."

"Hey, thanks."

"What are you two broads doing?"

Hazel grabbed the strange old book from the mantelshelf where she had left it last time they were here. "No, you're drawing the wrong symbol. It's this one, let me show you."

Michelle looked at the page Hazel had flipped to. "Gotcha. Thanks a bunch."

"No problem."

"Chicks, man. I don't even know what to say to the two of you. Chicks today are nuts."

"Yeah yeah yeah," Michelle said. "You'll see."

Hazel read from the book thus causing the flames to erupt again, and Cat appeared in the circle they had drawn. She was yawning and stretching.

"Hazel this better be important, you woke me up from my nap. How do you think I stay looking this young forever? Only half of it is supernatural—even in the afterlife you need your beauty sleep."

"*Woah,*" Steve said.

All the eyes turned to him to see his reaction.

"*You're hot.*"

"Sorry buddy, I'm not single."

"Rejected by a ghost," Hazel said. "That's a new one, even for you Steve."

"Even dead chicks wouldn't come anywhere near you Steve," Michelle said. "Two whole dimensions and Steve can't find one girl to go out with him."

"Awe don't be mean to poor Steve, I'm sure he's a good guy. Either of you two single ladies would be lucky to have a guy like him."

"Where have you been all my life?"

"I've probably been dead for most of it."

"They don't make 'em like they used to, that's for sure."

"Haha, thanks Steve."

"Are all ghosts as beautiful as you, uh, 'Cat' was it?"

"Yeah, my name's Cat. But no, I'm sorta one-of-a-kind. You should check out some of those monsters hiding in the basement. That's where all the vicious stuff is hiding."

"What's in the basement?"

"All sorts of things are lurking down there. I'm sorry I can't be more specific, we haven't figured out how to keep me around longer. And my time here is…" Cat was disappearing. "Just about up."

Steve had gone red with terror that he could not hide.

"You heard what she told us, Stevie. I dare you to go down to the basement, and maybe I'll consider giving you a little kiss," Michelle said. "I bet you won't do it."

"Uh, I mean, I would, uh, but I don't even know where it is."

"Course you don't. I bet if we found you the stairs you wouldn't go down alone."

"I sure would. You don't know what you're talking about."

111

"Then let's go."

"Now?"

"You're practically shaking, Steve. That's why I make it with guys like Joey behind the bleachers after games and not you. To tell you the truth I was gonna make a bet out of this that involved us going back behind the bleachers ourselves, but if you're not brave enough to go down into a dark basement…"

"Hey wait just a minute, Michelle, that's a load of—"

Michelle gave him a kiss on the cheek. "I dare you to go to the basement. If you've got the balls you'll do it. I'll give you ten minutes alone with me in one of these empty rooms if you go down to the basement and… and bring us back something."

"Lead the way."

TICK! TICK! TICK!

The glass on Warren's watch was cracked, but it still worked. It ticked away the final seconds of his life.

Ivy stood over Warren's dead body.

Blood leaked from his throat and spread wide. It seemed as if she were watching him from another reality; she wasn't in her body and this wasn't real. This was a nightmare—she was in her dreamscape and any moment she would awaken. But the cracked watch on Warren's wrist was still ticking; ticking away the seconds of unreality.

Ivy shivered; even the chills didn't feel real. None of it felt real.

Then her tears fell. Her body convulsed. She cried and couldn't breathe. She collapsed under the choking weight of her guilt, gathered herself into a ball and sobbed. She swallowed her screams; she didn't want the others to hear. Didn't want the others to know. Didn't want anyone to know. Didn't want any of this to be real. Didn't know how any of it could be real.

I didn't do it. I didn't do it.

Nothing was real anymore.

Ivy looked at the body from between her fingers, hoping that it would be gone and hoping that the blood would vanish, hoping and praying and begging that Warren would be alive again.

When she shut her eyes she could picture him alive again, half-dressed, laying on the bed. She could see herself on top of him, kissing him, dragging her hands along his body, and his hands tracing her back and sides.

Slowly she stood up again. She parted the curtains to let in more light, then found her discarded clothes and set them down on the bed. She looked at Warren's dead body again and it made her dizzy; he was dead, and she could not understand why she had done it. Her actions were replaying in her mind as she dressed herself again; breaking his wrists, impaling him with fractured bones, and the struggle in between. It all felt like it was out of her control; Ivy was a puppet.

Ivy used the window like a mirror to wipe the splatter of blood from her freckled face; there hadn't been a ton of blood on her, but as she tried to clean herself up it only spread further.

What am I gonna do? Oh my God...

She opened the door, then turned back for a final look at Warren.

"I'm sorry."

Steve sneezed at the dust that their steps kicked up. The hallways were darker the further they went through and turned corners; the statues seemed to come to life under that murky layer of tightening darkness and he was certain that the statues had moved subtly in his peripheral. Some of the windows were boarded up; others were obscured by the vines that grew over them outside the building.

Michelle and Hazel opened doors. Most of them led to bedrooms. Some were closets. A few doors were locked and wouldn't budge. None of them so far had led to the basement.

"I hope we don't walk in on Ivy and Warren," Hazel said.

"Yeah right," Michelle said, "I've seen you checking Warren out. You're probably jealous he walked off with her."

"You're totally wrong, I don't like Warren."

"I never said you liked him, I only said you're jealous. There's *such* a big difference."

"Like you know anything about jealousy or liking anyone, going behind the bleachers to make it with a different boy every night."

"Are you a prude or something, Hazel?"

"Um, no."

"Then quit acting like it."

"Even Hazel knows you make it with all my teammates," Steve said. "I'm last but not least, am I right?"

"If we ever find the basement in this place," Hazel tried another door. "Guess you're out of luck, Little Steve—oh damn, there it is."

Steve stood in the doorway looking down. The ancient wooden steps were streaked with a distant glimmer of light from an unseen window. He couldn't make out more than the indistinct outline of objects shrouded in shadows that were even thicker than the ones that covered him and the girls in the house's twisting hallways.

"Don't chicken out, Steve."

Steve put his hands on Michelle's waist and pulled her close to him. "You don't need a funny excuse like this to get a little action out of me, baby. Why don't we quit the games, huh? There's a thousand rooms in this place with our names written all over 'em."

"Nope."

"You gotta be kidding me."

"Bet's a bet, Stevie." Michelle pulled away.

"What are the terms again?"

"Go down there in the dark for five minutes. Bring us back something cool."

"Define cool."

"I dunno."

"Bring us back jewelry or something," Hazel said.

"You really think the owners of this place left all their gold hanging out down there in the basement? And if they did it's all been picked clean by now."

"Oh well." Michelle blew him a kiss. "Better hope we think it's cool. Whatever it is."

"Good luck." Hazel blew a kiss of her own.

"I don't need luck." Steve took his first step down.

Three or four steps later he stopped and looked back at the girls. Each of them gave him a little wave of their hands.

He continued his descent into the abyss of the basement. The subtle splash of light from a nearby window fought weakly against the growing darkness. Steve stepped carefully through to his right. The window was on the far wall.

"You all right down there, little guy?"

"Yes, Michelle. Your big man's all right."

"Hey, want to prank him?" Hazel asked.

"Should we run off and hide?"

Before Hazel could say anything to Michelle, Steve was screaming.

"Oh my God! Help me! Helppppp!"

"Steve?" Michelle gasped.

The girls were frozen. Slowly they turned their heads toward each other and exchanged worried expressions. They crammed through the doorway at the same time and went down the steps hand in hand.

The basement was eerily silent upon their arrival.

The girls whispered his name.

The basement was still.

Hazel's palms were sweating and her heart was beating fast. She and Michelle whispered Steve's name again but he said nothing; he was nowhere to be found. The girls walked over to one of the windows that let in a little bit of light. They stood in its glow and looked around the room.

What happened? Hazel wondered. Where did he go?

"Help me!"

The girls were jolted by Steve's abrupt screams. He was across from them and was partway submerged through an opening in the floor. His arms clung desperately for any way to keep himself above ground.

The girls rushed to help him and grabbed his hands and pulled him up.

"Watch out! It's behind you!"

The girls turned and screamed then realized they were only faced with the basement's thick darkness while Steve laughed and put his arms around them.

"I was just fucking with you two. There ain't nothing down here."

Hazel punched his arm as hard as she could. "God I hate you."

Michelle was laughing. "You're an idiot, Steve."

"So what do you say, Michelle? Let's bail on this place."

"Hmmm... not quite. You didn't find anything cool."

"All right. Well..." Steve reached for the first box he saw. He pulled out a little wooden doll. "How about this? This cool enough?"

Michelle turned it over in her hands a couple times. "Guess it is. A bet's a bet. See you later, Hazel."

"If you want to find us we'll be under the bleachers at the football field. I don't think Michelle minds a... what's it called again? I believe it's... menage a trois?"

Hazel saw them to the door and watched them leave. Then she decided to check on Ivy and Warren. As she came back to the huge spiraling staircase she heard sobbing.

"Ivy?" Hazel whispered.

Hazel followed the distant cries.

"Ivy? Is everything okay?" Hazel said louder this time. "Ivy?"

Cries again. Cries followed by vague sounds that might have been an attempt at words. Ivy was still far away.

"Ivy it's me. Where are you? Ivy? Warren? Anybody? Can anybody hear me?" Then when she was on the second floor, she turned a corner. *"Hello?"*

Ivy was on her hands and knees crying at the end of a hall; her back was turned to Hazel.

"Ivy what's wrong?"

"I didn't mean to hurt him." Ivy forced the words through her sobs.

"What happened?"

"I didn't mean it."

What's gotten into her? Hazel wondered.

Hazel caught up to her friend and sat next to her, then gasped at the blood that Ivy was covered in. She put her hands on Ivy and searched her for any wounds.

"What did he do to you?"

Ivy shook her head and burst into extreme tears.

"Ivy? Oh my God, what did he do?"

"I killed him."

13

I don't know what I'm doing here, Beverly thought. *This can't be what they were talking about in that note.*

School was over, and she was partway to the old Engstrom. She hadn't been here since that terrible day a decade ago when she and Abigail banished the spirit that had corrupted Abigail.

Now all the terrible memories were coming back to her. Everything that happened in the house, the forest, and the hidden cabin.

Abigail had put the knife in Beverly's hands and begged Beverly to cut the demon out of her; and as Abigail had laid on the cabin floor, Beverly had agreed. But that had not worked. The awful words that the demon had spoken through Abigail's lips chilled Beverly as the memory played over in her mind. When she thought hard enough about it, it was like being brought back to another time; another place. The memory was so clear, so formed, and it was like it had a *texture* to it, a certain feeling that only that time possessed.

Beverly remembered running for the cabin door when Abigail was chasing her with the knife, and the couch being in the way. Thinking about how close she came to death, Beverly felt her heart skipping. All that followed—the chase through the cabin, the knife that nearly plunged through Beverly's skin, and Abigail's struggle against the parasitic demon—was brought back to her. It was real again. As real as it had been when she lived through it.

And Beverly's heart was crushed that she and Abigail did not remaine close after it was all over.

She remembered being at the wishing well afterwards at the lake, the one between the farmhouse and the Engstrom place. After the demon had been banished she had put her hand over Abigail's.

Abigail. How did you do it?

Huh?

When you… when you got rid of it. How did you do it? How did you get it out of your body?

Well, it was all because of you. Because you gave me your wish.

Ten years gone in the blink of an eye. Had she used them properly?

She parked at the base of the hill. Another car was parked there. An orange Ford.

Beverly trembled. She stepped out of her car then looked back in at her baby's empty car seat. She had a child to think about now. Should she get involved with this? She had the chance to be happy now—she could leave all the things that happened here with her and Abigail in the past.

I shouldn't be doing this, Beverly thought. *But those kids could get hurt. They could be in trouble. I might be the only one who knows they're here, and if something happens to them it's my fault for not stopping them.*

Beverly went up the hill, following the ancient pathway. The gate was eerily open fully, and gently creaking with each touch of the wind. Beverly passed the threshold, her heart pumping so hard she thought it would break through her chest.

Hazel came off the bottom steps of the spiraling stairway holding Ivy by the hand when the girls heard the front door open. They came to a stop. Hazel glanced at Ivy who was sullen and looking down at her feet; confusion ran through Hazel's mind again about what Ivy had said—she had killed Warren. It didn't make any sense.

Then she wondered who was at the front door. She didn't dare move and neither did Ivy. Hazel had a sinking feeling in her gut; a feeling that somebody was here who should not have been. She took a small step to the side with Ivy.

"Hello?"

A chill crept on Hazel's spine. Was that Miss Hoffman's voice she was hearing?

"Ivana? Hazel? Are you two here?"

The note, Hazel thought. What had happened to the note? Had she forgotten it on her desk? She couldn't remember where it went.

By instinct Hazel moved under the spiraling stairway, and her and Ivy's grip on each other tightened.

Ivy curled into a ball and didn't peek out behind the steps. But Hazel did. Miss Hoffman stepped through the threshold from the living room into the rest of the house.

This couldn't have been real. Hazel couldn't have been hiding Ivy, who was covered in blood, while she claimed Warren's dead body was upstairs, all while their teacher was here at the old Engstrom place to bust them.

"Is there anybody here?" Miss Hoffman said. She stood around near the base of the spiraling stairway. Hazel couldn't see her anymore because she ducked back completely under the stairway.

She listened to Miss Hoffman move onto the first couple steps.

"Anybody up there?"

Miss Hoffman ascended.

"Look, whoever's in here, you're not in trouble. But you need to get out now."

Hazel shuddered. Was she gonna be able to get out of here without their teacher seeing? And what then? How would she get Ivy out of this situation? Her mind was rushing. The house felt too hot and she was getting a little dizzy. She was uncomfortable crouching under the steps so she sat down on the dusty floor.

Ivy was sobbing. Hazel ran her hand over Ivy's and hushed her. Told her it would be okay. They'd figure it out. By then, Miss Hoffman was up on the second floor. Her steps were creaking with every movement she took.

Hazel anticipated screams. Anticipated slamming footsteps. Anticipated Miss Hoffman frantically running down the steps and out the front door. Anticipated the police questioning and how Hazel wouldn't know what to tell them—she had no way to explain the day's events.

None of that happened. The house was quiet.

Then Ivy tugged on Hazel's hand. "Let's go," she whispered.

Hazel and Ivy stood and moved in short quiet steps from under the stairway. They glanced up at the second floor balcony but didn't see or hear anything.

What was going on up there? Hazel wondered.

They took two more steps when the upstairs floor creaked again. *"Ivy? Hazel? Look, I read your note. I know you're here. I'm not gonna tell anybody. But you need to get out of here now. This is urgent, okay? Do you hear me? You shouldn't be here."*

Hazel and Ivy were at the front door when Ivy grabbed Hazel's hand with both of hers.

"We can't go."

"Why not?"

"My purse is upstairs."

Beverly looked through a few rooms and shouted for the girls. There was no response, and all she heard were the natural noises of the house. Were they even here at all? Well, she thought, they had to be. There was an orange car parked outside. Somebody was here… but where?

"Warren, are you in here?" Beverly said. *"I'm not gonna tell anybody anything. I just want you kids to be safe. You need to get out of here now. It's not safe in here. So come out already and let's all get out of here."*

Silence was chained to the house.

"If there's anybody in here, you need to get out of this house. It isn't safe. Listen to me. It isn't safe to be in here."

Beverly was growing more unnerved with each passing second.

Beverly thought about the first day she came here. Standing here with Cat and Abigail. The day that had changed everything was the day Abigail hurt herself after buying the cursed pen—but for Beverly it all became real once they entered the house. That was when their fates were sealed. That was when the grotesque horrors had seeped into their life for good.

Cat. She could still remember her voice. She could still remember how sad her eyes were when they sat in Beverly's dining room and talked. Then suddenly she remembered the vigil they had for Cat's dead baby.

Tears flowed in Beverly's eyes whenever she thought about her friend. Cat was gonna make things right. She was gonna turn her life around. She was gonna change. Things were supposed to be better. And it was all cut short. For some reason it made Beverly feel so guilty as if she were responsible for it all—as if she should have done something different. As if she should have found a way for Cat to live. But it had all genuinely been out of her control.

It wasn't fair at all.

Hazel and Ivy carefully tiptoed down the hallways on the main floor and crept up one of the staircases carefully, pausing whenever they heard Miss Hoffman's voice no matter how distant and wordless it was.

At the topmost step, the girls peeked around the corner of the stairway. Completely empty and silent. Maybe Miss Hoffman was on another floor now.

Hazel wanted to scream at the thought of being on the same floor as a dead body. She didn't want to see Warren's corpse at all. Whenever they would eventually come to the room, she decided right now that she couldn't go inside.

Ivy led the way.

Hazel studied her friend. Ivy was still crestfallen and... and distant. As if she was becoming an imitation of the person she had once been. There was something wrong with her friend—Hazel stared closely at the back of Ivy's head. Was it even the same girl? Was this really Ivy or somebody else? It was getting hard to tell who her friend really was. For all Hazel knew it was an imposter.

The girls froze at the end of a hall. They looked around the corner.

Miss Hoffman at the stairway. She peeked behind her shoulder and the girls moved out of the way simultaneously to avoid her glance. When they checked again, their teacher was ascending to the third floor.

"Warren? Hazel? Ivana?"

She definitely read the note, Hazel thought. What a dumb mistake.

Ivy brought Hazel to the room and let go of her hand.

Hazel stood with her back to the door while Ivy went inside. Tears fell from her eyes and she rubbed them away. How could Warren be dead? How could Ivy have done something like this? She was trying to wrap her mind around it and couldn't for the life of her come to any logical conclusion.

Just a moment later Ivy was out of the bedroom. She was crying too.

Hazel hugged her, trying to avoid getting blood on her clothes as best she could, and ran a hand on Ivy's back. "It'll be okay."

Ivy sobbed.

"Shush. We don't want her to hear us."

Hazel and Ivy went down one of the stairways. The floor above them creaked, and with it came Miss Hoffman's worried voice that made them jolt a step backwards: *"Is there anybody in here?"*

The girls were back on the main floor. Miss Hoffman was descending too, and the girls stood motionless. Then they realized that their teacher's steps were coming right for them.

Ivy rushed to grab the nearest door, and she and Hazel went inside. Coincidentally it happened to be the door that led to the basement; Hazel struggled to think about how just minutes ago she and Michelle and Steve had shared a laugh here when Steve pranked them—and yet now this had turned into the worst day of her life.

The girls didn't shut the door fully for fear that Miss Hoffman would hear it slam under their nervous touch. They left it open a crack and watched.

She passed by the door and kept going.

"Please listen to me, you're in danger. I want to help you kids. Let's go."

Was she ever going to leave?

The steps became more and more detached and obscure the further Miss Hoffman went.

Was she ever going to leave?

Hazel tugged on Ivy's hand to go down the steps. "I have an idea."

In the basement was a window low enough that they could reach it, and big enough so that they could fit through it. Hazel let go of Ivy's hand and grabbed a random box and asked her to grab one too. They set both boxes below the window then Hazel climbed up first and pushed the window open. She crawled out then extended a hand to help Ivy.

Ivy climbed up and grabbed Hazel's hand but in her hurry as she found her footing and adjusted herself she accidentally knocked one of the boxes back and it made a loud thud accompanied by shattering glass.

THUD! SCRASH!

Beverly stopped in the middle of a hall. Was that the kids?

She followed the noises to the door that led into the basement. She was so terrified to descend into the unknown but if the kids were in trouble... if something happened to them... she couldn't handle it knowing she could have prevented it and helped them.

She tiptoed down the steps. *"Hazel? Warren? Ivana? Any of you down here? Anybody?"*

Through darkness there was a little light flowing in from the windows. A little light reflected up off broken glass that was scattered near a fallen box.

14

HAZEL PRACTICALLY DRAGGED Ivy the whole way from the Engstrom place to the lake. Hazel took off her shoes and undressed down to her bra and underwear, then stepped into the cold water with Ivy. Ivy clung nervously to her.

"I can't swim," Ivy said.

"It's not deep." Hazel squinted against the sun as she loosened away Ivy's grip.

Their jaws chattered; the water only seemed to become colder, and their bodies never adjusted to its temperature. Hazel worked fast, cleaning Warren's blood from Ivy's face and hair. It came off and flowed through the water, disappearing under the surface like magic.

The girls climbed out, Hazel redressed, but Ivy knelt at the edge of the lake and scrubbed her clothes with her palms in the water; the blood did not wash out of fabric as easily as it was cleaned from skin, but Ivy was doing the best she could.

When she was finished, the girls sat together in the sun to dry off. Warmth was returning to their bodies. Hazel had so many questions and wanted to be careful with how she asked any of them; she didn't know what was going on in Ivy's head or what had happened between Ivy and Warren in that bedroom.

Ivy broke into tears again. Hazel put her arm around her friend and hushed her. Ivy sobbed quietly into Hazel's shoulder.

"It will all be okay, okay?"

Ivy shook her head. "No."

"We'll get through this. Okay?"

Ivy said nothing.

"Can... can you tell me what happened?"

Ivy was silent.

"I want to help you, but I need to know what happened. Did he hurt you?"

"No." Ivy cried.

"Did he *try* to hurt you?"

"No."

"Did he..." Hazel didn't know how to finish her sentence. "What did he... did he... did..."

There was a long silence only interrupted by the whippoorwills that landed on the ground in front of the girls and chirped then flew away. Long shadows were drawing over them, and sunlight and warmth were dwindling.

"There's something... very wrong with me." Ivy turned her back to her friend.

"We should go now. I think Miss Hoffman's gone. We need to get you home."

Hazel helped Ivy up then led her by the hand. They went back across the open space past the lake and back toward the old Engstrom place. As they approached, Hazel thought she saw somebody in one of the upper windows, but upon closer inspection, there was nobody there. Goosepimples rose on her arms; she thought of the stories again, and what Michelle said she heard about the house. Maybe, Hazel thought, it could all be true...

The girls came to Warren's car.

"Did he leave his keys in here?" Hazel asked.

She opened the front door. No sign of any keys.

"Guess not."

Ivy said nothing.

"We need to get his keys."

Back up the path. Back through the gate. Back up the stairway. Sickening chills wrapped around the girls. On the second floor they went back to the room where Ivy had gotten her purse from.

Hazel was too curious. She had to see him. So she stepped inside.

She hadn't expected it to be so violent.

At first, before she had seen the body, Hazel thought it must have been an accident. She hadn't expected the repeated stabbing. She hadn't expected Warren to be unrecognizable in his dried pool of blood. It was a nightmare that had come to life. A nightmare that had been pulled into the real world.

While Ivy found the keys in Warren's pants pocket Hazel was standing in the doorway staring at the body. She didn't know what she expected the corpse to do but she couldn't pry her eyes away from him.

Would she ever know what happened in this room? Well, she was wasting time here pondering.

Hazel knew the way to Warren's house. She sat in the driver's seat then turned the keys in the ignition and looked down at the fuel gauge. The needle was a hair past empty. There wasn't enough gas left to get them back to Warren's house without stopping.

"Shit."

Hazel expected the car to quit on them at any second. There was a gas station only a couple minutes away if she sped ten or fifteen miles over the speed limit—which she did, praying no cops would stop her. They had to get rid of this car as quick as they could.

Ivy and Hazel both stepped out of the car at the gas station. Hazel found two singles in her purse. "I'll go inside and pay."

Ivy waited next to Warren's car for Hazel; Hazel kept eyeing her from the window inside the gas station, and was a little nervous as she stepped in line and her view of Ivy was obscured. Whoever was at the front of the line—there were three customers between Hazel and the cashier—was causing a commotion, demanding a manager.

The manager came over to help out, and another cashier who must have just gotten off his break took over at the empty register and moved away the little 'CLOSED' sign. He was a pimple faced and lanky teenager. She recognized him from school—his name slipped her, but she had seen him around. He was in one of her classes. Great. The last person she wanted to see. Somebody who might recognize her. There were holes in her story already.

The line was moving.

Soon she had to face her classmate. She set the two dollars down on the counter, practically slamming them. Her hands were shaking.

"Put it on pump number—"

"Hey, don't you sit behind me in algebra?"

"I don't know. I need two dollars on pump two."

"Yeah, I think I've seen you around Ashfall High."

"No you haven't."

"I don't think I'd forget a face as pretty as yours. Hey, I've got a pretty short shift here being part time and all. Want to grab coffee tonight?"

"No thanks. Can you just take my money please?"

He picked up the two bucks. "Which pump again?"

"Two. Two on two. Thanks. Bye."

"Call me. My name's Arnie."

Ivy was pumping by the time Hazel walked out. "What took you so long?"

"Sorry, you wouldn't believe the—oh my God. Oh God," Hazel pulled her aside, trying to shield them away. Abigail was parked at pump three and stepped out of her car. She walked right by the girls toward the building then did a double take.

They had been caught.

"Hey girls, funny running into you here," Abigail said. Then her smile faded a little. "What happened?"

"What do you mean?" Ivy said.

"You're soaking wet."

"We were playing in a lake," Hazel said, hoping to take away any attention from Ivy.

"Yeah? Fully dressed in school clothes?"

"I guess you can say we got a little carried away," Hazel said. "Well, see you."

"Head straight home, girls," Abigail said. She took two steps away then turned back to them just before they could get into the car. "Hey, whose car is this?"

"My sister's," Hazel said. "She's letting me borrow it. See you later."

Hazel couldn't have gotten out of there fast enough. Her heart was racing. Glancing over at Ivy, she saw that Ivy was as red as an apple.

"She doesn't know it's his car," Hazel whispered. "Don't worry. Okay? Okay?"

"Okay. I just want to go home."

"We have to drop off Warren's car first. Trust me, we'll be back at your place soon enough. Okay?"

She parked in front of Warren's home, left the key in the ignition, then she and Ivy left. They hardly were a few steps away when they heard a screen door open and the gruff voice of a man calling Warren's name; the girls were frozen then quickly ran through a random yard, running through to the next block before stopping to catch their breath.

"He didn't see us," Hazel whispered. "I promise."

It was getting dark, but that did not mean all eyes were off the streets in Ashfall. The girls went through alleyways and passed through the night unnoticed, creeping between houses and taking shortcuts and lesser traveled paths to get to Ivy's home.

Both cars were in the driveway. Henry and Abigail were home already.

They went in through the back. The sliding glass door opened under Hazel's soft touch; she tried to move it without making a sound. The back door led into the living room which was adjacent to the stairway. The girls tiptoed in, and Ivy went up the stairs slowly at first then stomped her way up in desperation to get away from her family.

"Ivana? That you?" Henry said from the other room.

"She went upstairs," Hazel said, following his voice into the kitchen. Abigail was cutting some meat over at the counter while Henry was reading a newspaper and drinking coffee. "Hey guys."

"Is Ivy okay?" Abigail asked.

"Uh—uh yeah, she's just a little embarrassed about what happened."

Henry put down his coffee. "What happened?"

"Oh, nothing bad, don't worry. She fell in a mud puddle."

"Is that why she was soaking wet?" Abigail asked. Then, to Henry, she said, "I ran into them earlier."

"I think she was too shy to tell you. She didn't look where she was going and fell in. We tried to clean her off but didn't do such a good job."

"Same thing happened to me once," Abigail said. "I was wearing new jeans and fell into a lake. Are you joining us for dinner, Hazel? I'm making carne asada."

"Oh, no thanks. I'd totally love to but I've still got a *ton* of homework to do. I've got fifty sentences due Friday—your, uh, old friend assigned them to me."

"What old friend? Oh, was it Mrs. Thompson? Is she still teaching there? She *hated* me with a passion and made my last semester of high school hell. It was because my friend Beverly asked her how far along she was, but she wasn't pregnant."

"No, that's who it was. Miss Hoffman. She said you and her were attached at the hip and she was always getting you into trouble, I guess her story checks out."

"Oh *Beverly's* your teacher?"

"Yeah, our sub. Mr. Green's out for a while."

"Hmmm. That's strange. I never thought of Beverly as a teacher. She always wanted to be a baker."

"Um, I'm going upstairs to say bye to Ivy, thanks again for the dinner invite."

"You're always welcome in our home," Henry said. "And if you need a drive back just let me know."

"Thanks."

Hazel went up the stairs to the second floor. Ivy walked out of the bathroom with a towel wrapped around her and went with Hazel to her bedroom. Ivy sat sullen on the edge of her bed.

"Please don't leave me tonight."

"I have to. I'm a mess too. *I stink!* We're lucky they weren't prying and asking questions."

"What did you tell them?"

"That you fell in a puddle of mud and had to shower. You didn't look where you were going. But Ivy… how do I even begin to say this…. We need to… we have to… we have… well we have to get our story straight. Miss Hoffman has that note. She knows we were there. And Warren's family…" Hazel choked as she said Warren's name. "Well he's missing. They're gonna be asking questions. We have to get our story straight."

"Okay."

"Can you tell me why you did it? I'm sorry but I have to know what happened."

Ivy cried without answering; Hazel helped wipe her tears away.

"I don't want you to cry. I just want to know… why… how…"

Ivy shook her head and continued to wipe her tears. "I don't know. I just don't know what came over me. I just… did it."

"I need to know what happened. Ivy, do you understand how much trouble we're already in? Warren's parents are gonna be calling the police any minute. Tomorrow at school everyone's gonna be pointing their fingers at us. We were the last ones to see him alive…"

Ivy pulled on her hair. *"I don't know I don't know I didn't want to hurt him."*

"Stop doing that." Hazel pried her friend's hands open. "And keep your voice down. What if Henry and Abigail hear you? Now look, we have to get on the same page here. We need to figure out our story, okay? So… tomorrow we say that we were at my house, just you and me. You and me and no one else. We were doing homework and I was teaching you how to knit."

"Okay. Sure."

"And if they ask you what you were learning, I was showing you how to patch up a brown sweater I made for my cousin."

"Okay."

"We never went to the old Engstrom place. Not today. Not ever."

"Okay."

"I think it goes without saying, but I love you Ivy. I don't want anything bad to happen to you. My lips are sealed about everything we've done today. But it's going to drive me crazy if I don't know why you did… what you did."

Ivy shook her head. "I don't know."

"Please stop saying that. You two were all over each other. You two went up to that room to have some alone time and only one of you came out alive. The other one is dead and we're covering it up.

I want to help you but I also need to know why I'm doing this. Why did you kill him?"

"There was somebody else there. Somebody made me do it."

"Who made you do it?"

"The voice in my head," Ivy said. Then the girls were silent for a few moments until Ivy sobbed again and said, *"What have I done?"*

"I'm trying to help you," Hazel whispered. *"Just tell me the truth and I can help you."*

"You can't help me. He's in my head."

"I have to get going." Hazel stood up. "Goodbye."

Ivy didn't say a word back to her.

Hazel turned the knob then opened the door slowly. One last look back at Ivy who was sitting on her bed hanging her head. From the hallway Hazel heard Abigail calling Ivy from the bottom of the stairs. Hazel and Abigail exchanged goodbyes as Abigail gave another offer for dinner then to drive her home but Hazel declined. As she left the house, Hazel wondered if her cheeks had looked as red as they felt, and if Abigail could detect the fear, worry, and pain that Hazel had been trying to hide.

She walked home replaying the day in her head.

Nothing made sense.

Hazel had a feeling she wouldn't be getting any sleep tonight.

15

Ivy laid in the grass where she and Hazel had dried off after their dip in the lake. The full moon streaked the surface of the water that rippled from the soft breeze that felt very pleasant against Ivy's skin. It was a beautiful gentle night full of fireflies glowing and crickets chirping and frogs jumping.

She ran her fingers over the golden ring on her left hand, turning it around and around.

TAP! TAP!

CRACK!

Something was approaching from the farm and snapped a tree branch. Ivy turned to face the visitor.

She twisted her ring again. Fireflies passed in front of her, sparkling against the gloomy sable horizon. A frog hopping nearby stretched its tongue out and caught one of the bugs then hopped back to the lake.

The stranger neared.

It was the same black goat she had seen at the convent. She petted it and kissed its head.

"I will do whatever you want," Ivy said, then she slipped off her robe.

The goat led her to the lake. It walked down first, going completely below the surface. Chills wrapped all around Ivy as she followed him through the water deeper and deeper until she was completely submerged in water.

For a moment she thought this was death, then the goat lifted Ivy's head from the water. She gasped as her left arm flung backwards looking for the edge of the lake where she could grab onto and stabilize herself.

But then she looked into the goat's eyes, and a calmness came over her.

Together they came out of the lake. Two flaming branches formed an inverted cross where Ivy had previously been lying. Below the branches was an archaic book that was worn and falling apart; it was open to a page with text written in ancient calligraphy.

The goat poked Ivy's hand with one of his teeth.

She wiped the blood on the page.

"Signed in blood," Ivy said, "and sealed with a kiss."

Hazel was so sick from worry but the nighttime air was refreshing. Michelle hadn't been home when Hazel got back from Ivy's, so she sat in a chair at her bedroom window, keeping an eye out for when Michelle would be back.

It was midnight when Michelle was finally back home. She sat in her back yard and put logs in the firepit, then struck a match and dropped it in.

Hazel left her bedroom and went down the stairway then out the back door without waking her family. There was a length of wooden fencing between the yards that was loose and came off with any pressure whatsoever; Hazel moved it away, nerves growing in her stomach, rehearsing what she was gonna say.

"Oh hey. What are you doing up?"

"I couldn't sleep." Hazel sat in a folding chair next to Michelle. Then she blurted out: "Michelle, do you trust me?"

"Do I trust you to do what?"

"In general. Do you trust me?"

"I mean, I guess I do. But with what?"

Here it goes, Hazel thought. "After school yesterday, you never saw me or Warren or Ivy. You were with Steve the whole time."

Michelle leaned forward. "What are you even talking about?"

"Tomorrow people are going to ask you questions. I don't know what you and Steve did yesterday, but you need to think of something. We never had plans together. We never went to the Engstrom place, we never saw each other since study hall."

"I don't know what you're trying to say. Hazel, what's going on? You're kind of scaring me…"

"I'm trying to say that today never happened." Hazel looked away from Michelle and into the fire. "I can't explain it all. Not now. Please. Just trust me. It's what's best for all of us. Okay?"

"Did something happen? After I left?"

"I can't tell you."

"Why not?"

"I just can't. That's why I asked you to trust me."

"Something's going on here and I don't like it."

"Do what I told you. You never saw us today. In fact, whenever you *did* see us in the past it was at Warren's house or my house or your house. Never the Engstrom place."

"Hazel come on what are you saying? If I'm supposed to trust you then why can't you trust me?"

"I can *trust you,"* Hazel said, tears on the verge of slipping. *"And I totally* do *trust you.* Look, I can't give you all the answers right now, I just can't, and arguing about it won't get us anywhere. Please just do this for me."

"I dunno…"

"I'm going to try and get some sleep." Hazel stood up. "Please just… I'm… please just trust me."

Ivy opened the shed door at the farm near the Engstrom place and found a length of rope that she cut with the knife she had found in the Engstrom House.

She went off into the night, guided by something unseen…

A small house up ahead. Ivy crept through the front yard to the side door. Her hands were shaking with excitement. The voice in her head overtook her own, and a smile widened on her lips. She felt a rush and her heart was racing.

CREEEEEEEEAK!

Although her steps were careful, the floorboards screamed. Ivy paused, listening to the silence of the little house. Nobody stirred.

Everything was dead quiet, except the terribly loud beating of her heart.

CREEEAK!

Another step. The floorboards quieted somewhat.

Through an open door at the end of the short hallway, she saw a woman alone in bed. Ivy tiptoed to the lady's side then peeled the covers back to find it was Beverly Hoffman.

The rope was tied into a noose. Ivy slid it around Beverly's throat and tightened it a little at a time until she heard a baby's awful screaming. It pulled her out of her trance and she was frozen and completely confused why she was here.

Beverly would wake up at any second with that baby screaming; Ivy had to work fast. She loosened the noose and removed it from Beverly's neck without her waking. Then she tiptoed away, and the other voice took over, and she went into the baby's room.

Ivy was seeing her life through a lens; watching her life unfold rather than controlling it. She saw herself putting her hands around the baby. A little girl dressed in pink. She must have hardly been a year old, Ivy guessed.

As Ivy tiptoed out of the room with the baby, the baby cried and Ivy was frozen. Beverly shifted in the other room. Ivy heard the bedsprings but she was too far past the hallway and into the kitchen to turn back now and put the baby away without being seen or heard.

Ivy rocked her slowly until her cries hushed.

"Give Mommy one minute, Ruth," Beverly said.

In her panic, Ivy ducked under the table with the baby to remain hidden. Tears flowed in her eyes. The baby would have been sobbing again if it weren't for the fact that Ivy was holding her left hand over the baby's face keeping its mouth shut and hushing its breath. The baby was clutching Ivy's finger in her other hand tightly—and tighter by the second.

The baby was breathing heavy. Ivy could feel it straining. If she loosened her hand at all then its screams would give her away, and there was no getting out of it. But what good would it do her to have a dead baby on her hands? She didn't know what to do and now Beverly came into the kitchen. Ivy could barely see what was going on through the darkness and through her limited vision from the chairs that were in front of her. Beverly was moving around and yawning.

If this baby did not scream then Ivy surely would.

"Where did I put your bottle?"

Ivy held her breath. She was too afraid to breathe. Afraid of adjusting herself even though her arms and legs were screaming in pain from the scrunched position to stretch and release the pressure on them. Her joints and muscles were stiffening.

The baby was shaking. Shaking hard. Ivy was so nervous that she was trembling along with the baby.

Beverly was quiet for a little while then said, "Got it."

She was making baby formula, humming a song, still completely unaware of Ivy and her baby being under the table. Sweat poured down Ivy's forehead and into her eyes, burning them. Her palms were sweaty too. She wanted to pull her hand away from the baby and let it breathe but… but something inside of her wouldn't do that. Something inside of her wouldn't let herself get caught, even if it meant hurting this child…

Time was running out. Or maybe it had already run out. She couldn't stay hidden forever. She had to make a move. And when she did, what would happen?

Suddenly Beverly's footsteps led out of the room and back to the short hallway. And before Ivy could think much about that, there was the scream—Beverly's hideous scream that shocked Ivy and made her scream too.

Beverly couldn't breathe. Ruth was gone from her crib.

She dropped the bottle of baby formula and staggered away from Ruth's bedroom when she heard her baby screaming and the side door slamming shut. Her heart was going to explode as she ran to the kitchen—a short run that felt like it took an eternity—and there Ruth was on the table sobbing.

Beverly picked up her baby and looked her over; Ruth was fine. No injuries. Nothing. Beverly rocked her baby and cried along with her until both of their cries stopped together. Then Ruth was asleep. Beverly put her back into her crib then wheeled the crib into her room.

She locked the door then dialed the police.

Beverly sat at her kitchen table with one of the police officers who was asking her questions and writing things down in a little pad he pulled from his pocket. The officer's partner was brushing away cat hair from his clothes where Smudge rubbed against him as Smudge walked through the kitchen and climbed up onto the table. Beverly was holding Ruth in her arms even though Ruth was asleep—she wasn't gonna let Ruth out of her sight, not for a single second.

"So what you're saying, ma'am, is that somebody tried to abduct your baby... then left her on the table."

"Yes sir," Beverly said. She couldn't stop shaking. She was almost afraid her jittering would wake up Ruth, but it didn't. "My poor baby. Her face is so red. Just look at her. Oh my God."

"So let me get it straight." He looked down momentarily at his notepad then turned his attention back to Beverly. "You didn't hear anybody come in and out. Your door was unlocked. No signs of forced entry. Somebody—God knows who—came in and grabbed your baby. Then decided to leave without her? Did I get all of that right?"

"Yes sir," Beverly said, still shaking.

"I want to ask you again for the record. Can you think of anybody who would want to hurt you and your baby?"

"No sir," she said.

"The child's father?"

"Sorry, what?"

"Could the child's father have—"

"No sir. I don't, well, I don't know who he is."

"Ah, I see," the officer said. After they were both quiet for a little while, he said, "It's a goddamn miracle your baby is safe. Pardon my French."

"Safe? Do you see her face? Look at those red spots. It looks like somebody was choking her."

"Well, I hate to say this, ma'am, but I haven't got nothing to work with here." The officer looked sick to his stomach. "I'm gonna head back and put in the paperwork. This will all be on file. But there's not anything else I can do for ya."

"Really? Nothing to work with? Somebody snuck into my house and snatched my baby from her crib. Are you joking with me?"

"I understand. But the way things are… there's really not much I can do for you besides filing this report. Besides your case being on record, there's really not much else I can do for you tonight."

"Are you kidding me?"

"Well what would you like me to do? Your baby's just fine."

"I—I don't know. Keep a patrol car in front of my house? What if they come back?"

"They aren't coming back."

"But—but sir. I…"

"Yes?"

"Do you have a family, officer?"

He laughed a bit. "Yes I do, and that's besides the point. Geez, all you people always ask me that. Always ask me what I'd do if this happened to my wife or if that happened to my kid. That's irrelevant. What I'd do for anybody is based on the facts we have and the severity of the crime… and somehow I don't think snatching babies and putting them on tables is a crime anybody would risk jailtime for.

Now, if there's another case of 'stolen baby placed on kitchen table' that comes across my desk then I'll be sure that I reach out to you personally because your testimony could be crucial for us to bring in a repeat offender."

"My baby was snatched from her crib and you're not gonna do anything about it? A stranger was in my house."

"All I can do, really, is to advise you to keep your doors locked." The officer looked at the pad again and this time flipped through two pages. "You said nothing was stolen, right?"

"No. Well I didn't really look around, my main concern was Ruth, but my purse is still where I left it. This wasn't a robbery."

"Then I don't know what it was. It wasn't a kidnapping, it wasn't a robbery… well, I can only think of one thing," he said, and Beverly could not tell if he was trying to hold in the laugh that was slipping through his serious expression or not.

"And what's that, sir?"

"Maybe whoever did this had the wrong house." He stood up and pushed in his chair. "Have a good night, ma'am."

"That's it? Really?"

"Maybe they realized you weren't the person they had intended to hurt. That explains why they didn't touch a single hair on your baby's head. Be glad things turned out the way they did tonight—it isn't always such a… pleasant outcome. Okay?"

16

Even though twenty years had passed since the Engstroms died, Nathaniel Bloch couldn't shake the idea that some essence of them lingered behind. As he went through his new home's hushed dark hallways he looked over his shoulder because somebody was watching him. And nobody was there. Only his imagination.

Nathaniel was the only person awake, but before he could begin any of the projects he was saving for the rare occasion—like now—when he had a free hour, he needed to check on his kids. He opened Alvin's bedroom door. Asleep above his covers and his arms and legs in an odd sleeping position that was laughable. Then he checked on Franklin. Then Carrie. Then Jeanette, who was asleep with the four little dolls he had made; the dolls all shared a pillow between Jeanette and the wall. Then he checked on Daniel. All his children were asleep and well.

One last thing to do. Nathaniel went outside into the starless night to check the gate; it was swinging wide open with fierce winds. He closed it and locked it then went back inside. Little chills carried with him from the nighttime coldness and brought out goosepimples. He rubbed them away. Then, above him, there was a strange noise.

TAP! TAP! TAP! TAP! TAP! TAP! TAP! TAP!

He paused in the threshold between the living room and the rest of the house.

There it was again: *TAP! TAP! TAP! TAP! TAP!*

Nathaniel stepped up the main spiraling staircase. "Who's up past their bedtime, huh?"

But all was silence; no response from any of his children. He went further up the steps and heard the sound again, the eerie tapping that disturbed the quiet house: *TAP! TAP! TAP!*

Nathaniel had a little look around the second floor. Nobody was around. Maybe it was their dog, he thought, although he knew what Lincoln's footsteps sounded like, and those noises were not them. The hallways were all empty and the sounds had vanished, as if he had scared away whatever had been the source of them.

He put it out of his mind and went downstairs. In his study room he sorted envelopes.

CREAAAK!

Scurrying steps.

Lincoln came into the study and up to Nathaniel's side.

"Lincoln, buddy," Nathaniel patted his head, "did I ever tell you how much I despised taxes? I remember the days when an American kept his entire check. This wouldn't have happened under your watch, Abraham. No sir. Hey, what do you have in your mouth? Open up. Come on boy."

It was one of the little dolls from Jeanette's room. Lincoln wouldn't unclench his teeth and his mouth was foaming; an angry growl struggled out of his clenched teeth from deep within his throat. Lincoln swung his head furiously side to side then finally spat out the doll; it was partway torn up from the clutches of his sharp teeth. Before Nathaniel could pick up the doll, Lincoln slammed his paws on it and ripped it fully apart. The dog kept going in a powerful rage until the doll was fully beyond repair; its wooden torso and appendages splintered and crushed and ripped up, its purple dress shredded into thin strands.

Lincoln moved back a step as if admiring the destruction of the toy. He barked madly at it. Nathaniel cautiously approached his dog and petted him. Slowly the barks and growls quieted down, and Lincoln laid down on the floor and looked up to his owner with pleading red eyes. Lincoln had been crying. What was wrong with him? Why had he been so angry?

"What's gotten into you, buddy?"

Lincoln whined.

Nathaniel gathered the remains of his daughter's doll. Lincoln jumped to his feet and barked angrily again.

"Quit it, Lincoln. It's only a toy."

Nathaniel stopped in the kitchen to throw the doll away in the garbage can. Lincoln followed him, continually growling the whole way.

A little bit later, Nathaniel went up to his bedroom and crawled into bed next to his wife while Lincoln hopped onto the foot of the bed and curled up.

Soon Nathaniel drifted into a dream...

Lincoln was about to fall asleep too when he heard the sickeningly familiar noises.

TAP! TAP! TAP! TAP! TAP! TAP! TAP!

He sat up, listening closely. They were near.

He glanced back at his owners, then decided not to wake them. There was no way to make them understand.

Lincoln slid off the bed and crept slowly into the hall. No longer could he hear them, but he had their scent. Lincoln stuck low to the ground, ready to pounce, ready to defend his owners and their family no matter the cost.

Lurking silently through empty halls. Wandering endlessly. Lincoln turned corners in search of the evil that lingered in this house; the evil that refused to leave. Lincoln would search all night if he had to.

TAP! TAP!

Lincoln's lips pulled back to reveal his teeth. Images formed in his mind; he pictured himself sinking his teeth into them, crushing them, destroying them, slamming his paws on them and pulling them apart as he had done to the lone doll he had captured. The other three dolls would meet a similar fate.

TAP! TAP! TAP! TAP!

Lincoln was ascending the main spiraling stairway to check on his owner's children when the sound of the enemies struck again. Suddenly he was overtaken with a panic and rushed the rest of the way up to the second floor, nearly slipping as he fumbled to find his footing. As soon as he was on the second floor he ran.

The three dolls were moving in a hall from one of the children's open doors; Lincoln's tongue licked his lips as he bolted through the hall. Somehow the dolls passed through solid wall and disappeared; somehow they phased through solid matter. When Lincoln was close enough, he inspected the vanishing point. The dolls hadn't phased through the wall, but instead had crawled into a mousehole.

He growled.

He slammed his paws on the wall and tried to tear it open; tried to break it down and find the abominations. He hardly made a scratch. He backed up, lowered his head, then ran again and slammed his right shoulder into the wall.

Still he couldn't make any progress.

Abruptly he heard them again around the corner; that tapping noise of their ugly footsteps. Perhaps they had only hidden in the mousehole as a slight diversion; perhaps they wanted him distracted while they acted out their plan.

Lincoln turned sharp around the corner and followed the footsteps to the center of the hallway. They were above him. Stopping to catch his breath, he was furious at the seemingly never ending chase; he wanted more than anything to clasp his jaws around the demon dolls and kill them.

There was no time to keep sitting there; Lincoln went up the nearest stairway—the house was full with many of them—and went to the third floor. The steps were fainter up here. The enemy was traveling further up. Immediately he thought of the attic room.

He passed briefly through the fourth floor then to the fifth; the dropdown stairs led into the attic. Lincoln climbed up slowly, carefully, as he had seen his owner's children do. His steps made no noise. Once he was at the top of the stairs he peeked in and saw that the dollhouse was open and that the little dolls had retrieved the mutilated corpse of their dead family member and laid it above strange symbols that were drawn with chalk on the floor.

The three remaining dolls had taken hands and were moving around in a circle on around their dead relative.

While they were distracted, Lincoln attacked.

Lincoln opened his jaws as wide as physically possible and stampeded through the attic. The dolls broke off their ceremony and moved away in the blink of an eye. Lincoln came away with the remains of the mutilated doll and spit it out across the room. By the time he changed his momentum and ran after the other dolls, they were fleeing the attic.

Lincoln moved swiftly and jumped through the opening instead of climbing down the steps and landed on his feet. The dolls had just come off the final step when he landed; he faced them in a standoff. Lincoln leaped and each doll went in a different direction; one to the left, one to the right, and one straight past him. He went for the one on the right since it was the one moving slowest. Lincoln's eyes were wide with excitement; his long tongue dangled out of his mouth and dripped with slobber.

The doll looked over its shoulder; its carved expression, which had been a happy smile, morphed into a frown. It knew the end was near.

The doll faced forward again, forcing its legs to move a few more desperate steps, and Lincoln knew he had won. His jaws snapped around the doll and he sunk his teeth deeply into it. He didn't annihilate it yet. He would do that in front of the other dolls so that way they could witness the torture that they would also have to suffer.

He wanted them to know that they could not and would not escape. They were dead.

Going through another hall of the fifth floor, while the doll clinging to life between his teeth was squirming, Lincoln sniffed to catch the scent of the other dolls. The enemies were distant. They had gotten out of there quickly. He caught the scent of nearby mice instead.

Suddenly sharp pain pulsed in his skull as something slammed into the back of his head. Little claws were scratching at him. His jaws opened as he let out a painful cry. Lincoln slammed his unseen attacker off of him and into the wall; then he realized his attackers had multiplied. Two unseen forces were clawing him. He slammed again into the wall until the attackers came free.

Inching back, he saw them. The remaining two dolls were on the backs of mice. Each doll was armed with needles and pins and thumbtacks. The third doll, the one which he had crushed with his teeth, was climbing onto its own mouse.

They were in a standoff again; Lincoln and the three dolls each atop their own mice.

Lincoln pounced.

This time the dolls did not try to run away but were ready to fight. Their mice squeaked and charged. Lincoln knocked two of the mice and doll teams down with a kick while the third crawled up his back and stabbed him with pins and needles. Lincoln attempted to knock the mouse off of his back but the other dolls quickly regrouped and attacked.

The mice—seemingly under the control of the dolls, somehow obeying their every command as if by magic spells—bit Lincoln and gnawed at his flesh. No matter how hard he hit them and broke them away from him, the mice kept returning to fight.

Stabs in every direction; the dolls swung around and climbed up Lincoln's back while the mice anchored their jaws into his joints. Slapping away one of the mice, one of their teeth snapped off and was lodged in Lincoln's flesh. It stung with every subsequent movement.

He had to retreat; there was no winning this if the dolls were armed with needles and as long as the mice obeyed their commands. Even if he was a godlike giant compared to them, he couldn't win the fight.

Lincoln ran aimlessly, moving fast and attempting to shake free the dolls from his back. The dolls never wavered; they lifted their pins and brought them down repeatedly.

TAP! TAP! TAP!

The mice were chasing behind him in fast scurries.

Lincoln's heart sank. He had a bad feeling about all this.

Suddenly he barked—barked loudly in hopes to wake his master, but his master slept on the ground floor, and here Lincoln was on the top floor. His barks must have died out in the space between there and here. He was on his own.

The pain was unbearable; he needed desperately to remove the dolls from his back. He knew he wouldn't last much longer if they kept stabbing him, and if the mice kept biting him...

There was an awful trail of blood. It leaked from the mice's bites and his unsteady steps streaked it across the hardwood floors. His mind was empty. He didn't know what to do.

Lincoln ran, still barking, and came to a stairway. He jumped.

Everything was a dark blur. His body thudded and new pain burned in him with each hit against the steps. The fall seemed endless, and he thought he'd fall for eternity. Then, once reality settled in, and Lincoln was at the landing, he stood on his shaky feet and backed away. Were the dolls still around? The mice? He didn't see them. Had they decided to retreat? Maybe he could make it to the master in time…

As Lincoln descended to the third floor, he heard the sickening steps above him; they were up to something, those damn demented dolls.

It was all a bad nightmare; something that shouldn't have been real, Lincoln thought.

Back on the ground floor he returned to the hallway of his owner's room. The door was shut. He nudged it until it opened.

And somehow the dolls had beat him here.

The doll stood atop of its mouse's head with the pin fully extended in its hands. The doll jammed it into Lincoln's eye.

Nathaniel woke up at the sound of his dog's cry. Lincoln was not at the foot of the bed anymore. He stepped out of bed and followed his dog's distant cries through the hallway. But Lincoln's steps faded with each passing moment.

SQUISH!

Nathaniel looked down to see what he was stepping in that was so sticky. He kneeled. Lincoln's footprints in thin streaks of blood.

17

RUFF! RUFF! RUFF!

Lincoln's cries were heard from all levels of the house but nobody could find him. He was somewhere that the Bloch family was never able to exactly pinpoint or locate. The attempts to find Lincoln all ended in failure.

One morning, when Nathaniel was ready to head into town, Jeanette and Carrie came rushing to find him as he stepped out the front door.

"Daddy wait!"

"We hear Lincoln upstairs! We need your help!"

Nathaniel brought his toolbox to the attic. The barks were coming from the back wall near the window, but that made no sense. The wall was thin—he examined it and couldn't figure out how the dog could be stuck there. But the poor dog was hurt, lost, and confused.

"Can you get him, Daddy?"

"Yeah, can you get him? Can we save him?"

Nathaniel pushed the wood paneling a little bit. It was loose. He used his crowbar and hammer to pry it away. The barks were still coming as he worked.

"Lincoln, boy, I'm gonna get you out of there."

Nathaniel worked carefully. When he removed the first wood panel, the barks stopped.

He reached in for Lincoln; he moved his arm left and right grasping for a dog that wasn't there and came away with nothing but a handful of spiderwebs.

"Where did he go?"

"Lincoln come back."

"I'm sorry, girls. After I get back home from this meeting I'll take another look for him, okay? I promise."

As Nathaniel left the room, he spotted something. It was the dolls he had made for his children, except all four of them were still together. The one that Lincoln had torn to shreds was back and was completely fixed as if nothing had ever happened to it. Except it was missing its clothes.

Jeanette picked it up. *"Oh, and Daddy? Can you make another purple dress for my doll? She lost it."*

"Sure, darling."

A few minutes later when he washed his hands and cleaned the attic dust from his clothes, he was back in the living room heading out the front door again...

...and Lincoln's barks came from the fireplace.

RUFF! RUFF! RUFF!

After a week of Lincoln being lost, Nathaniel called Animal Control. The Animal Control employee arrived, and Nathaniel let him in and gave him a rundown of the situation.

"And we can never seem to find him in time. Somehow he keeps going missing. I've taken apart five walls trying to rescue him."

RUFF! RUFF!

"Hear that?" Nathaniel said. "That's Lincoln."

"Yes sir, I do. Believe it or not, this isn't the first time I've had a situation like this. Cat crawls into a vent and for whatever reason won't get out, and I get called in to find her. But you say your dog's been stuck a week now? Well, I've never seen it last longer than a day or two myself. Seems you waited a long time to call me."

"Yeah I did. But that's because I thought we'd have found him by now."

"Has Lincoln ever done anything like this before?"

"No sir. He seems to have gotten lost in the middle of the night. Maybe he was confused since we haven't been here so long."

"How many walls did you say you took apart again?"

"Five. Maybe six. I took apart paneling, cut holes in walls, but can't find a trace of good ole Abe Lincoln."

"No worries, sir. I'll have him out in no time."

"Great. I owe you bigtime, mister."

Ernest from Animal Control tracked the sounds of the lost dog to the basement. He set down his toolbox, but he didn't need any of those tools for the job because the wall in this room was strange; unfinished with loose bricks stacked in piles. The top of the stack of bricks, behind which the dog was continually barking, wasn't very high above his head, and Ernest pulled away a brick. He felt sad for the poor thing, having been stuck a week in the walls of this vast house—and what kind of owners were these, he thought, that they should let this poor animal be stuck in there for so long before calling for help?

His pile of discarded bricks was growing. He set them aside and as he cleared them away discovered that there was a door behind them, as if all of these bricks had been stacked here purposely in a rush to obscure whatever this entrance led to. When the door was fully exposed he turned the knob and it swung open to a vortex of blinding darkness.

RUFF! RUFF! RUFF!

The dog called from within. Ernest shifted the contents of his toolbox, finding his flashlight that had sunk to the very bottom, then shined its light into the empty void. Darkness ate up the force of the feeble light.

A step forward. Darkness fell over him.

He crossed through the threshold.

Complete and utter silence. Ernest moved his light from left to right and back again.

RUFF! RUFF!

The cries of the dog were still distant. Ernest moved another step deeper, looking immediately back over his shoulder to make sure that the strange door had not swung back shut and that there was still an exit from the interior of the walls. Just how deep were these walls? From the hints of vague details that his light source slithered across, he gathered that the walls were rough and some structures or types of wooden foundations had been laid, but to what extent, he was not sure. They seemed to go on forever and ever in each and every direction. It could have been a maze in here. A labyrinth without end.

RUFF! RUFF! RUFF!

"Don't worry, pup. Ernest here is on the way."

Traveling a few feet further into cavernous darkness there was a structure of rough wall, and Ernest traced his left hand against it as he moved in the direction of the barks. The dog was calling, begging for help, begging for anybody to come rescue it.

"I'm close, pup. Don't worry. I'm gonna get you out of this place."

The wall slipped away from his touch and turned. It led to another pathway; there were two directions he could choose if he were to go forward. The first choice was the direction he was already headed in—straight down. The other direction was the sudden left turn in the structure. Once again Ernest couldn't believe how deep and strange it was in this hidden place, as if the Engstrom place's walls were bigger on the inside than on the outside.

He decided to keep straight. That seemed to be where the dog's cries were strongest. But he wondered what else lurked in this maze, and what else he might stumble across or discover if he went in a different direction…

Poor dog, he thought again, lost, blinded by the terrible wretched darkness, hungry, thirsty, scared. Its cries made him shiver.

RUFF! RUFF!

Louder. Closer.

Ernest followed its calls. Each step unnerved him with thoughts of getting stuck or lost in here…

Perhaps, he thought, it would be better to turn around, hand over the problem to Mr. Bloch, but he was being paid to retrieve the dog, he couldn't refuse to do his job when the dog was within reach.

Closer…

And closer…

SQUISH! PLOP!

Ernest had stepped in something. He braced himself with one hand on the wall, lifted his foot, and shined his light on it. Red and black slop. Some sort of goop. He didn't know what it was. But then, shining his light on the floor, he saw that the dog must have passed through here several times; there were many tracks in each direction.

The pathway Ernest was traveling turned abruptly and he stepped around the corner with it.

His faint light touched the abomination that was stuck to the wall by a pulsing web of flesh. The young boy's sickly face was contorted with fear and pain as he writhed. Strands of strange purplish flesh sank in and out of the boy's torso. He was wrapped in the same red and black slop that Ernest had stepped in.

Then the boy's mouth fell open, and a broken tooth dripped out with his slobber. His tongue licked his lips and he frowned. His eyes swelled with tears. Ernest stumbled backwards in sudden terror that clenched his heart and tightened around it. The boy cried then screamed.

But his screams were not his own. They were the dogs. The boy was barking madly, never stopping even after Ernest ran away. His heart beat so frantically that it was all Ernest could hear, draining out the barks.

Ernest's mind was pounding with the terrifying thoughts that had briefly passed through his head minutes prior; thoughts about being trapped down here, and the horrors he might find.

Then the doorway was in view. It was his escape. His way out of this madhouse. He passed the threshold and was back in the Engstrom place's basement room. He left all his tools in their toolbox then ran up the stairs, out of the living room, and into the company van. He pulled away from the house and never looked back. Even when he was far far away his heart wouldn't stop beating, and the image of that damned monstrosity of a boy within the walls was bound to his mind.

Even as days passed, the boy's cries rang in his ears.

18

Warren was smiling in his black and white picture.

MISSING

HAVE YOU SEEN WARREN TURNER?

When Beverly saw the poster, she retrieved the note from her purse and reread it to be absolutely certain:

Who else is going?

The usual suspects.

Is Warren going?

Uh-huh, and he mentioned you to me

Are you serious?

Yes. Maybe you and him will have one of those big empty rooms all to yourselves.

Ivy was called that morning into the principal's office. Principal Anderson was there with two police officers. Both officers were in their late thirties or their early forties. One was pudgy and one was thin. The thin one was balding.

"Hi Ivy," Principal Anderson said.

"Hi Mr. Anderson," Ivy said, then she nodded at the officers. "Good morning, officers."

"How is everything?" The fat one said.

"Good."

"We're gonna keep this very brief, Ivy," Principal Anderson put a hand on Ivy's shoulder. "The police just want to ask you a few questions. You okay?"

"Yes sir."

"Ivy," the fat officer said, "were you very close to Warren Turner?"

"Yes sir I am."

"What can you tell us about him?"

Ivy paused only for a second to gather her thoughts. She had to be clever with how she presented herself. She said, "He's a very sweet boy and a good student. Do you know if his parents are okay?"

"We've been talking to his parents. They're... holding up. Do you remember the last time you saw Warren?"

"Yes sir. It was on Monday. When we were leaving school."

"Did you go with him somewhere?"

Ivy shook her head a little. "No sir. I went to my friend Hazel's house."

"So," the skinny officer spoke up for the first time, "you're leaving school and you say bye to Warren, is he acting any differently? Did he mention anything you can tell us that might help us figure out where he was?"

"Let me think…. Um, not really. He invited me out to the movies but I told him I couldn't go because I had all this homework to do, me and my friend Hazel were going to help each other get everything done."

"Did you see him leave with anybody?"

"No sir."

"I see… I see…" The skinny officer wrote something down in a notepad.

The fat officer, after a sip of coffee, said, "Well, that's all we wanted to know. If you think of anything, or if you hear something, you'll be sure to let us know. All right?"

"Yes sir, I will."

There was a school assembly that morning. Ivy sat in the back row of the bleachers next to Hazel.

The students packed in tight. Some were whispering about Warren and sharing theories—none of them, Ivy knew, were even close to the truth. There were other students laughing and joking about topics unrelated to Warren and his disappearance. Ivy kept an eye out for Steve and Michelle and Miss Hoffman—all of whom had reason to suspect her.

She felt burning hot with guilt. She felt as if one of them would out her. Did Steve or Michelle or Miss Hoffman have to talk to the police too? Could one of the others have spoken to the police and let something slip? Could they have told them…

Ivy shivered.

"Are you okay?" Hazel whispered.

"Yes. Are you?"

"Uh-huh."

"Do you think the police spoke to the others?"

"I don't know," Hazel whispered even quieter than she had before. "I told them not to say anything."

"I'm more worried about Miss Hoffman. I think she has our note."

Hazel said nothing.

Then, before Ivy could say anything else, Principal Anderson addressed the students and faculty of Ashfall High at the microphone in the center of the basketball court.

"This is the sort of thing that as a teacher and a principal you hope you never have to do. I know you've all seen the posters and you've all been talking about it. Sometime after school on Monday, Warren Turner went missing.

"We are working closely with law enforcement to make sure that Warren comes home safely. A few of you might have already spoken to the police. Well, whether you have or have not, it's important that you tell them any detail you have that could assist us in finding Warren. This morning I was…"

Ivy zoned out of what her principal was saying. Her eyes darted down the bleachers toward Michelle. She caught Michelle's glance then Michelle urgently looked away from her. Was that fright she saw in her friend's eyes?

Ivy looked toward the other end of the bleachers where the teachers had all gathered. Miss Hoffman was paying attention to everything the principal was saying.

Ivy was nervous about the note. She couldn't stop thinking about it. She had to get it back. She should have taken it from Miss Hoffman while she was in her house—but she hadn't thought of it then. Where was the note now? In her purse? Locked in a safe somewhere? Or had it already been handed over to the police?

No, the police did not have it. If they had it then she wouldn't be here right now—she'd be under further questioning somewhere. And the police would have probably been searching the Engstrom House for Warren instead of having come by this dumb little high school to ask around if Warren had clued anybody in that he was planning on running away.

Ivy twisted her gold ring.

"Now," Principal Anderson was saying, "your senior-class president has a few things he would like to address and asked me if he could say a few words. Come on up, Raymond."

Raymond came up to the microphone, and Principal Anderson took a seat in the front row of the bleachers. Raymond was tall and lanky and the basketball team's captain and he was a funny guy that was liked by everybody—when running for senior-class president he hardly had to give any effort since he already knew all the votes would come pouring in for him.

"Hi everybody. Well, um, well, Mr. Anderson was right." Raymond wiped some sweat from his forehead. "Doing something like this is never easy. I asked Mr. Anderson for permission and he said I could do this, so I'd like to lead us all in a word of prayer.

"Dear Lord, I thank You for this day and all You have given me. I pray that You bring Warren Turner back home to his family, and I pray that You give strength to his family during this difficult time. I also pray that You will bless—"

A painful guttural scream emerged from Ivy's lips.

"I pray that You bless..." Raymond looked up in confusion.

All eyes turned to Ivy who was screaming continuously—deep and vicious screams and pulling on her hair.

Then she stepped down the bleachers and screamed at Raymond.

"Who the fuck do you think you are?"

Raymond stepped back across the basketball court, saying nothing.

"He doesn't need your stupid fucking prayers."

"Uh..."

"Fuck you you fucking cock sucker."

"Ivy I was only trying to help."

"You can't help him or anybody."

Ivy caught up to him on the court and pushed him down. Her hands clenched into tight fists and she wanted to wrap her hands around his throat and clench them tighter until he couldn't breathe.

But she fought against that feeling. Not here. Not right now. Not in front of everybody.

She ran out of the gym and felt every last person watching her...

Beverly chased after Ivy.

Ivy collapsed by the lockers and was crying uncontrollably. Beverly put her arms around her and hushed her. Ivy cried into Beverly's shoulder.

"It'll be all right hun. It'll be okay."

"What's wrong with me?"

"Let me help you," Beverly whispered low so that the newly forming crowd of students and faculty wouldn't hear her. Then she addressed everybody else: *"Give her space. There's nothing to see here."*

Beverly stood up and took Ivy by the hand.

Ivy's knees wobbled as she followed Beverly. Principal Anderson was pushing his way through the crowd.

"Miss Hoffman, meet me in my office."

"That's exactly where I was going."

Ivy let go of Beverly's hand then sat down in the chair across from the principal's desk. She crossed her arms on top of it and sobbed.

"Listen, Ivy," Principal Anderson said, "I know how much this must be hurting you, so why don't you go home for the day? Maybe take a few days off if you need to. I know things look bleak but you need to keep a positive attitude that they'll bring Warren home."

"Listen," Beverly said, "Mister Anderson, I went to school with her brother and I'm best friends with his fiancé. I know her family well. Let me sign her out and take her home. I'd feel a lot better about it instead of her walking, and I don't think Henry or Abigail can get away from work at such short notice."

"I'll have to call her brother to confirm that it's all right with him. You know how things are these days. Different times. The world has changed so much in a few short years."

"Yes sir."

Ivy rubbed her tears away. She and Miss Hoffman walked through the halls of the school.

"We just need to stop at my classroom. I need to get my purse."

Mr. Green's room was empty. Beverly unlocked one of the desk drawers and opened it for her purse. There was a Tupperware of mini cupcakes.

"I gave these out today to my class. Want one?"

"No thanks. I can't eat right now."

"We're gonna help you, okay?" Beverly brushed some strands of hair from Ivy's face. "Things will be okay but there are some things you need to tell me first. I want to help you but I need the truth. Tell me what really happened to Warren. Tell me what happened at the Engstrom place."

A small step back. "I don't know what you're talking about. I was never at the Engstrom place."

"Ivy, please, if you really want me to help you, you have to be honest with me. I want to help you but I can't do anything if you don't cooperate."

Ivy said nothing.

"Years ago… a long time ago… me and Abigail went through something. I can't tell you everything right now but that house caused a lot of people a lot of pain. It ended several lives. And it's gonna do it again unless you tell me exactly what happened there."

"I can't."

Beverly was about to say something but there was a knock on the classroom door. A teacher was outside with a stack of papers. Beverly stepped outside to talk to her coworker. As soon as the door was shut again, Ivy knew it was time to get to work—she only had one desperate hope where the note might be.

Miss Hoffman's purse was on the table. Ivy reached in while keeping her eyes locked on the glass window. Her heart slammed madly whenever she took her eyes off of it to look down in the purse—she had no good excuse she could give to Miss Hoffman if she were caught. She just knew she needed the note—it was the only thing tying her to the Engstrom House and Warren's death. If she got rid of it she was in the clear.

It was in a side pocket inside the purse. Ivy hurried to slip it into her pocket, and did so as Beverly opened the door and came back in.

"Ready to go?"

"Yuh-yes ma'am."

When school was dismissed somebody put their hand on Hazel's shoulder. She turned to see that it was the pimply faced teenager from the gas station. Arnie. Somehow his name had stuck with her. He was smiling wide at her and carrying some books under his arm.

"Hey. Told you I saw you around here."

"Yeah, well, that's cool." Hazel walked away.

"Hey wait," Arnie said and jogged a couple steps to catch up with her. "He was your friend, wasn't he?"

Was, Hazel thought. "Yeah."

"I'm—I'm sorry about, you know, about your friend. Hey I don't think I caught your name. I'm Arnie if you didn't remember."

"I remembered."

"So what's your name?"

"Hazel," she said.

"Hazel, that's a pretty name. Pretty name for a pretty girl. Wanna get together tonight? We could sit by the fire."

"No thanks. I'm gonna be real busy. Maybe some other time."

"Like when?"

"A million years from now."

"Great. I'll mark it down in my calendar."

Abigail set down the fabric she needed on the table at Quick Stitch then she adjusted the dial of the radio until she found a station she liked. Her coworker Linda came from the back room and went across the store.

"Hey Abby, I'm going on break. Need anything while I'm out?"

"No thanks, but thanks for the offer Linda. Enjoy your lunch."

"Thank you, I'll be back soon. I'm just going down the street to Valenzuela's."

"Sounds good."

Abigail measured the fabric then cut it with her rotary cutter. Sometimes her hands still shook when she picked up the cutter and she was brought back years ago to the day in the tub; she thought about the blade's cold touch and how much she had loved it.

Sometimes everything that had happened to her and Beverly in the Engstrom place seemed like it was all a dream; sometimes she wondered if any of it was even real. Then she looked at the scars on her wrist and remembered just how real it really was.

The front door opened and the little bell rang.

"Hello, welcome to Quick Stitch," Abigail said, before looking up and see who had entered. Beverly and Ivy. Ivy's face was red and she was rubbing her eyes. Beverly was nervous and biting her lip. "What are you two doing here? What's going on?"

"There was an incident at school today."

"An incident?" Abigail set her things down then stepped over to Ivy's side and hugged her. "Are you okay? Tell me what's going on."

"I hurt somebody. I—I—"

"Abby, you have to listen to me," Beverly said, "it's happening again."

Abigail shuddered. "Don't you dare bring this up."

"Abby listen to me."

"Don't you dare say a word about this in front of Ivana."

"Abby it's happening again. And Ivana's involved."

"You're sick, Bev. You know that?"

"She needs our help."

"No. No. I'm not gonna hear this. And where do you get off taking Ivy out of school? She's not your family, you had no right to—"

"The principal called Henry, Henry said after what happened it was okay to sign her out."

"I don't care, you can't just waltz on into my job and start telling me—oh thank God Linda's on break so she wouldn't have to hear any of this. Oh my God."

"Abigail. I'm sorry. But I can prove it."

"What is Miss Hoffman talking about, Abby?" Ivy said.

"Ivy… why don't you wait over there in my manager's office while I talk to Beverly." Abigail walked her over to a room a few feet away then shut the door.

"Abby just listen to me, listen, I've—"

"Can't you forget about the past? Can't you get over it?"

"Oh my God Abigail, are you blind? You wanted me to help you back then. Why can't you help Ivy now?"

"Because I don't even know what you're talking about. You haven't explained anything since you've been here. And I live with her. There's nothing wrong with her. She's a good girl. You make me sick. Her friend is missing so you barge in here telling me she's involved. You better have a damn good explanation."

"Abigail. Don't make this mistake. We can help her before it's too late. But we have to start immediately."

Abigail hadn't realized tears had fallen from her eyes. She rubbed them away. "What do you know about Ivy?" She tried to ask calmly.

"I found this note." Beverly put her purse on the table and stuck her hand inside. "Hazel and Ivy passed this around on Monday, the same day Warren went missing. I found it on Ivy's desk after class. It says they were going with Warren to the…. Um…"

"Yeah? It said what?"

"It said Warren and Ivy would have a room by themselves at the…" Beverly frantically searched through her purse. "At…"

"Well what does the note say?"

"I can't find it."

Abigail rolled her eyes. "And to think for a second there I almost actually believed you."

"No, no, it was just here. I just had it this morning."

"Beverly for the love of God, it's all in the past. Give it up."

"But…"

"Beverly, you'll always be my best friend no matter how much our lives change and we grow apart. But please this is too much for me."

"I promise you I had the note. The girls were supposed to meet Warren at the house the day he went missing."

"I'm sorry Beverly, but I can't believe you. I saw them both that day at the gas station. They were coming back from Hazel's house. They never went to…"

Both of them were silent for a little while.

"I went up there."

"You went back to the house?"

"Yes I did."

"And were they there? Was Warren there too?"

"I didn't see anybody. But that doesn't mean—"

"Bev," Abigail shook her head, "I think it's best for everybody if you walk out of here and pretend none of this ever happened."

"I'm warning you, if we don't do something now then it might be too late."

"I finally put the past behind me and you're here to dig it back up. Just leave Ivy alone."

"When you needed my help back then, I helped you. Now your own family needs your help and you're unwilling to lift a finger."

"You almost let everything slip right in front of her. I couldn't live with myself if she or Henry knew… what I did. Sometimes I can't even look myself in the mirror," Abigail cried a little. *"I can't forgive myself for what I did to Cat."*

Beverly hugged Abigail. "You'll be okay. You'll be all right."

Abigail hugged her friend back. "I miss you so much Beverly."

"I miss you too."

"Please. Just don't say anything else about this to Ivy or Henry. Ivy's a good girl. There's nothing we can do about Warren being missing."

Beverly frowned. "You'll regret this," she whispered.

19

Abigail was in the kitchen cooking dinner, thinking about what Beverly said earlier that day.

"Need any help?"

"Oh hey Ivy. You feeling any better?"

"Much. Thank you. I think I just needed to clear my head."

"That's good to hear. Can you grab the plates please?"

"Yeah." Ivy set three glass plates on the table, then placed a knife and fork next to each of them. "Oh this smells incredible. Abigail you're such a great cook."

She was such a nice girl. Beverly couldn't have been more wrong, Abigail thought.

"Awe, thank you." Abigail put tortas and rice on each plate. *"Henry, dinner's ready."*

Henry was watching TV in the living room. Abigail heard him turn off the TV then he joined them in the kitchen. "Looks delicious."

"Dig in."

Henry sat down and took Ivy and Abigail each by the hand to pray. "Dear Lord, we thank you for this day and for this—"

"BLEH."

Abigail and Henry opened their eyes. Ivy was leaning against the table, puking over all the food. For a second—or maybe even less—Abigail thought she saw Ivy's eyes turn all black. Henry put his hands on his sister and helped her to sit down.

Ivy wiped her mouth with a napkin, taking deep breaths, her eyes burning red.

"Oh my God," Henry said.

Ivy hit her brother's hands away from her. "Don't touch me," she said, then she locked eyes with Abigail. Her lips were wide with a sardonic smile. *"Does my brother know what you did to the priest?"*

"Ivy what is the matter with you?"

"What priest?" Henry said.

Ivy laughed sickeningly and grabbed the knife covered in puke from her plate. Holding it tight in her left hand she plunged it into Henry's gut. Blood leaked from his body and squirted with each pulse. Abigail was shocked; she moved around the table and shoved Ivy away from Henry, causing Ivy to fall backwards in her chair and bang her head hard against the floor. Ivy didn't move again; she was frozen, and her eyes were shut.

Henry limped a few steps out of dining room and into the hallway when he collapsed. The knife was still submerged through his flesh, and Abigail hurried to turn him over before he slumped forward and sent the dagger any further in. His eyes were closing; fluttering open then closed. She wasn't normally strong enough to pull somebody as big as big as Henry, but with her adrenaline flowing through her body she managed to drag him down to their bedroom.

Abigail slammed her and Henry's bedroom door shut and locked it. As she picked up the phone from the nightstand, there was a banging on the bedroom door and Abigail accidentally dropped the phone.

"Abigail it wasn't me. You have to believe me. I didn't want to hurt him. Help me."

Abigail dialed.

"Help me Abigail please I need your help I didn't want to hurt anybody."

This can't be happening, Abigail thought.

The phone seemed to ring forever until the voice came through the other end of the line. *"Nine one one, what's your emergency?"*

Furious slams on the door.

Ivy begged to be let in.

After the phone call Abigail opened the door cautiously. Ivy had gone pale and was slumped against the opposite wall outside Abigail and Henry's bedroom. She had knocked on the door so hard that her knuckles were torn open.

"Help me." A desperate whisper.

"How?"

"It knows you. It wants me to kill you."

Abigail took a step back. "Who are you?"

Ivy sat up and laughed sickeningly. "You know who I am. And now we're back together again."

"No. No I got rid of you."

Abigail ran one step back toward her bedroom door but Ivy moved impossibly fast in the short distance, and grabbed hold of Abigail in a split moment and yanked her to the floor. Ivy crawled over her, digging her nails into Abigail's flesh and streaking her with blood.

"Let go of me."

"When you rot."

Abigail tried to hit Ivy away, but Ivy grabbed Abigail by the wrist and forced her hand down to the floor.

Ivy's sharp fingernails dragged across Abigail's throat and to her chest. *"I'm going to drown you in the cistern."*

Her nails were so sharp she cut through Abigail's shirt.

Unbearable pain shocked Abigail's body as Ivy's nails sank into her chest. Hopelessly she jolted, twisting herself, attempting to break free.

But then Ivy shielded her eyes, and Abigail was free. She moved out from under Ivy without understanding what was happening. Ivy was recoiling in blinding pain.

It was her necklace. Ivy had brought it out of Abigail's shirt when she tore it open: her silver crucifix necklace.

Abigail crawled a few feet away from Ivy and took the necklace off, holding it straight ahead in one hand.

"Leave this girl alone."

Ivy inched away from Abigail, still shielding her eyes. *"You can't help me."*

"Ivy you have to fight it."

She turned her back to Abigail. "I can't."

"Yes you can. Iv, this is what Beverly was talking about. It happened to me when I was your age. But we fought it."

"Don't bother."

Abigail said nothing.

"I don't want to fight it."

Abigail was coming closer. "Ivy…"

"Save your breath."

When Abigail was close enough Ivy abruptly clawed her nails into Abigail's ankle, then she swiftly pushed her. Abigail's head hit the floorboards hard. Through her momentarily blurred vision she saw Ivy running away. With her new headache forming and spreading, Abigail searched blinding for the necklace that had fallen from her grip.

But by the time she had it again, Ivy was gone.

20

Ivy stopped at a liquor store for water. She reached for her pocket then realized her wallet was in her purse which was back at Henry and Abigail's home. She grabbed a water bottle anyways and made sure she was out of sight from the guy at the counter on the other side of the store when she opened it up and chugged it.

Her stomach growled. She slid two candy bars into her pockets. She looked up to make sure she hadn't been seen by the cashier, and she hadn't been, because he was distracted by the three other girls in the store who had walked in a minute after her.

As she was leaving the liquor store the other girls walked out too. And Ivy recognized them as three of the cheerleaders from school. Bridgette, Beth, and Bailey were coming out with a big score of booze.

"Hey Reyes," Bridgette said. "Want to come along with us? We're gonna get totally wasted."

"No thanks I—"

"It's a shame about Warren," Bailey said. "You two would have been *so* cute together."

"Uh, thanks? I, uh—"

"Come on, don't skip out on us, new girl," Beth said. "We haven't seen you since you completely failed to make cheer squad at the tryouts. Come on."

"No really it's okay I don't want to."

Bridgette was the driver. She unlocked the car then got in. "We aren't gonna bite you, Ivy. Get in. What are you, a nark? You gonna go run and tell that I used a fake ID?"

Reluctantly Ivy got into the car. She sat in the back with Beth while Bailey rode shotgun.

"Did the cops talk to you about Warren?" Bailey asked. "I bet they did, didn't they? Come on tell us everything. Do they have any details? Do they like, suspect you or something?"

"Yeah, spill," Bridgette said. "You gotta tell us."

"Yeah, I did talk to them."

"So what happened?" Bridgette looked back at her through the rearview. She had already pulled away from the liquor store.

"Nothing happened. They just asked questions. It's not as cool as it is on TV."

"Yeah, probably because you had nothing to hide, right?"

"I think it was murder," Bailey said. "And I think you did it. I think you killed him."

"What are you talking about?"

"I think Warren had a secret girlfriend or something, and you didn't like that he was two timing you so you cut off his head. Are you keeping him in your cellar? Is your family in on it? Are they gonna be charged as accomplices?"

"Geez, Bailey," Beth said, "cut her some slack. Her boyfriend just died."

"He isn't dead."

"I loved how you totally gave it to Raymond at the assembly," Bridgette said. "You're so hardcore. I love it. I can't believe you didn't make cheer. If only you had been this cool like a month ago."

"Yeah well he deserved it."

The girls were all laughing.

"So where are we headed?"

"Oh, you'll see," Bridgette said.

"I really have to be somewhere, so I can't stay too long wherever it is we're going."

"But we're gonna have some boys over, and that might help you forget all about Warren. Tell me, where did you hide his corpse? Is it really under the floorboards like Bailey said? What's it like to hide a body?"

"No, I said the cellar."

"In an empty room in an abandoned house," Ivy said. "Where nobody can find him."

"Really?"

"Yeah. And you won't believe this next part. Miss Hoffman almost caught me."

"No way, now I know that's not true. What would Miss Hoffman be doing with you guys? Oh, was *she* who he was two timing you with? That's so scandalous."

"No Bridgette he wasn't two timing me with anybody."

"Then why did you do it?"

"For the hell of it."

The girls laughed again.

"I don't remember you being so funny," Beth said. "I really like the new you."

"Yeah," Bailey said, "you finally developed a sense of humor. This is a totally new Ivy. Now if only you could do something about your makeup skills. Sheesh. When we get to Bridgette's I need to help you actually apply some—"

"Oh leave her alone Bailey," Bridgette said. "Ivy's earned her keep just by beating up Raymond. God I can't get over how cool that was. You know it was about time somebody gave it to 'em."

"I guess we better stay on her good side," Bailey said, "or she'll beat us up too."

"Or kill us like she killed off Warren just for looking at somebody else," Beth said.

"I told you, he wasn't looking at anyone else."

"Geez then you're just really a psycho, huh?"

"Sure."

"So where exactly did you say you dumped the body again?" Beth asked.

"I don't think I told you where. It's up at the Engstrom House. You know, the one by the farm?"

"The *what* house?" Bailey said.

"Engstrom. It's, you know, it's the one from all the stories."

"Ohhhhh. That."

"Geez, Bridgette said, "and they call *me* the dumb blonde."

"Can you like, show us the dead body?" Beth said. "Is that why you got all mad at Raymond? Because he almost blew your cover or something?"

"Blew her cover?" Bailey said. "Beth you know this was all a joke, right? Ivy's not a killer. We're just playing around. Beth I think you officially get the dumb blonde crown out of the three of us, kay?" "Why don't we go? I'll give you guys the grand tour. I practically live up there now."

Bridgette pulled the car over then turned back the other way. "I'd so love to see it. You know, I'm so sorry about when I mocked you in front of everyone at the cheer auditions. I know I humiliated you and you cried about it, but I shouldn't have listened to Beth. It was a mistake to be so mean to you. And to think you ended up having to befriend that *Hazel* girl of all people. What kind of name is Hazel anyways?"

Beth reached over and grabbed Ivy's hand. "I love that ring. Did Warren give it to you?"

"It is beautiful, isn't it?"

"God," Bailey said, "a boy gave you his ring and you still killed him."

"Love's a funny thing," Ivy said.

Suddenly Beth pulled it off of Ivy's finger. "Think it will fit me? What size is this?"

"Give it back."

"Woah, calm down tiger. I just wanna try it on, y'know?"

"No. Give it back."

Beth slipped it on her finger. "Fits like a glove."

Ivy grabbed Beth's hand and yanked her forward, then she twisted Beth's wrist. Beth gasped and pulled herself away.

"Hey! That hurt!"

Bridgette stepped on the break and looked back at the girls. "God, Beth, for a second there I thought she was gonna kill you."

"Give me back my ring. Now."

Beth slipped it off her finger. "There. Happy?"

Bridgette snatched it before Ivy could take it back from her. "But it is *so* cute. I wanna try it on too."

Ivy reached over the driver's seat. "If you know what's good for you you'll give me back my ring."

Bridgette tossed it to Bailey. "Catch." Then she was driving again.

Bailey slipped it on her finger and held her hand far away from Ivy. "Like how it looks? Awe, I wish somebody would give *me* a ring this nice."

Ivy grabbed Bailey by her ringless hand and pulled her forward from the front seat and held her in place, then punched her between the eyes. Blood burst up out of her broken nose and splurted over Ivy and over the seats of Bridgette's car.

Bailey slipped away from Ivy's grip and hyperventilated as blood continued to pulse out of her nose. Bridgette momentarily took her eyes off the road, moving around a parked car, to glimpse the horrors that were going on in the seat next to her. Beth had seen enough herself and was opening her door so she could get out of the car—but at that same moment Bailey slipped out of consciousness and collapsed on top of Bridgette. With the driver confused and distracted, the car swerved.

When Bridgette grabbed the wheel again it was too late. She couldn't stop the momentum of the car—her foot had slammed on the gas instead of the breaks and they were heading off the road and up over a curb, and the impact caused the car to flip over and slam into a sharp stop against a thick tree.

Bridgette and Bailey had been cut up by glass and were contorted in the car screaming in pain. Ivy was miraculously untouched by all that had occurred and reached up front for unfinished business. Bailey was still wearing the ring. Ivy bent back the girl's finger until it snapped then she slid the ring off and put it back on her own hand.

She crawled out of the open door that Beth had been flung from. Beth's skull was cracked open and bones were pressed through the flesh of her legs and arms in jagged sharp lengths. Ivy knelt at the girl's side. Beth's eyes were still open so Ivy shut them.

Ivy walked away.

She was only two steps from the accident when she heard the explosion. One little look over her shoulder and she saw that Bridgette's car was in flames. The smoke rose to the sky accompanied by the screams of the two girls trapped inside who were too mutilated from the crash to crawl out.

21

IVY WENT BACK TO her brother's home. She expected the police to be there, but nobody was. When she stepped inside she called Abigail's name. No response. Completely vacant. Ivy went to the washroom and cleaned off from all the blood that had splattered over her. She then changed into a new outfit, and somebody rang the bell.

Her first thought was Abigail, but Abigail wouldn't need to ring the bell for her own home. She had a key. It was somebody else. Perhaps somebody unaware of what had just happened—unaware of the stabbing.

Ivy peeked from the window. Tess was back.

"Tess. Hey. I didn't expect you back in town so soon."

"I'm sorry I didn't call in advance. I had to leave home right away."

"What is it? What's wrong?"

"I know you and Hazel already did a lot for me and I'm the last person who should be asking for a favor..."

"Don't worry, Tess. I'm your friend."

Tess put a letter in Ivy's hands. "I made a friend when I was at the convent. She needs my help to escape. You don't understand what the sisters would do to her if they caught her. The only reason I was able to escape was because I had her help. I promised her I'd come back for her."

"I see..." Ivy said, scanning the note. She gave it back to Tess. "What do you need me to do?"

Abigail must have gotten a ride with the ambulance because her car was still at the house, so Ivy found the keys and drove to the convent.

"Are you sure Hazel couldn't come?"

"She's busy tonight. I already spoke to her on the phone before you showed up."

"Make sure you have a good view of the front door. Like we said, ten minutes exactly from the moment they let me in."

"Good luck."

"Any longer and things have gone terribly wrong."

"If you're not out by then I'll do exactly what you told me."

"Excellent." Tess stepped out of the car.

"Good luck," Ivy said once more.

Tess banged her fists on the front door until one of the sisters answered. It was Sister Wonderly. Tess faked her cries and fell into the sister's arms.

"I've made a mistake. Please forgive me."

Sister Wonderly patted Tess on the back. "It's forgiven, Tess. It's forgiven."

She led Tess to her old bedroom that she shared with her friend Esther. Sister Wonderly awoke Esther who was sleeping—but Tess knew Esther was only pretending, because tonight was the night they had agreed upon to break out of this place together once and for all. Tonight was the night to make things right, because Tess had always felt guilty for leaving without Esther. They should have had a better plan on the day she originally left, they should have had a plan that included leaving together.

Sister Wonderly left the room, and Tess gave Esther a big hug. They sat together on Esther's bed.

"My friend Ivy is going to get us out of here. She has a car, she's gonna help us get far away from here."

"I can't believe you came back. I—I can't thank you enough. They were preparing to... to..." Esther was crying.

"I know," Tess said, then walked across the room.

"I can't thank you enough."

"We don't have much longer until Sister Wonderly tells the others." Tess opened the door and peeked into the hallway, then she shut it. "Do you have your things ready to go?"

Esther pulled a small bookbag from under her bed. "This is all I can carry with me. This and my purse. The essentials."

"Good. Let's go."

She opened the door again. Ivy was awaiting her with Mother Superior and Sister Wonderly.

"Now girls," Mother Superior said, "you're not going anywhere."

The basement was alive with energy; alive with a green glow that cut sharply through darkness. The fire was burning and lent its glow to the altar against the far wall. A dozen sisters were naked and bowing to the fire—bowing until the first girl was brought in. Tess. She was laid on the altar and her hands and feet were bound by rope.

Mother Superior led the ceremony by carving out Tess's heart while Sister Wonderly held the chalice to collect Tess's blood. It was passed around the room and everybody sipped, even Ivy who was watching it all happen.

The black goat appeared in the room and was at the altar's side, grabbing Tess's limp hand in his mouth and dragging her off of the altar. Then Mother Superior and Sister Wonderly brought in Esther, who was crying, begging, screaming behind her duct taped mouth as much as she could, but it was pointless.

Mother Superior put the knife in Ivy's hands.

"Would you like to do the honors? After all, we couldn't have done this without you."

"Can I use a knife of my own?" Ivy brought out the knife she had found in the Engstrom place from her pocket. The same one she had used to kill Warren.

Mother Superior nodded.

Terror came over Esther's eyes unlike any torture or fright that Ivy had ever seen before. They were pleading and begging for life—even for another five seconds of life. But Ivy wouldn't give it to her. They had to get on with the ceremony.

22

THE OFFICER SAT WITH Abigail in the empty hospital cafeteria at a table in the corner. His hands were constantly cupped around his coffee.

"I was going over the incident report. Your fiancé's sister, you said, is the one who stabbed him. Is that true?"

"Yes sir."

"Do you know why she'd do such a thing?"

"No sir."

"Do you know where she might have run off to?"

Should she tell him?

"Well?"

"I think you have to check the Engstrom place. That's the only place I can think of."

He was holding in a laugh, Abigail could tell. "Sure thing. Right after I check out those haunted tunnels that the miners died in a hundred years ago."

"I'm telling you the truth, sir. That's where she would be."

Abigail revisited Henry before she left the hospital, but he was asleep so she kissed his forehead and left his room quietly. One of the officers dropped her off at home since she had caught a ride with the ambulance. On the trip home she was wondering if the nightmare would ever leave her alone, if she could ever escape into a happy life, and wondering as she always did if all the wrong turns she had taken in life were inevitable. So many mistakes, so many things she was running from, would she ever correct them? Would she ever be forgiven for all the wrongs she had done? And Ivy—oh God, poor Ivy. What was going to happen to her? What had *already* happened to her that Abigail was so blind she had somehow missed? Ivy had changed right under her nose and she had been blind to it all. How long? And what else had Ivy done?

Abigail's head was full of unpleasant thoughts, especially the thought of Henry alone in the hospital. The cut wasn't too severe, the doctors had told her. He was lucky, the doctors had said, and it felt like something out of a cartoon or a movie. The knife had not gone terribly deep. He'd be all right. He'd probably be there for three days.

Unreality washed over her when she walked up the path to her house. How had she ended up here so suddenly? Her whole life had changed in the span of a few short moments she was still trying to comprehend—the past had finally caught up to her. It had caught up to her and had swallowed up Ivy in its power.

She went into the kitchen where she needed to clean up the mess from dinnertime. Ivy was sitting at the table among all the filth.

"Do you know the police are looking for you?" Abigail set her purse on the counter.

"Did you rat me out?"

"Are you kidding me?"

Ivy said nothing.

"Do you hear yourself? 'Did you rat me out?' Well what do you think I told to the police? People don't accidentally fall on knives and get impaled. Of course I told them you did it."

"That's a shame. What am I gonna do now?"

"Well now we have a drink." Abigail walked across to the liquor cabinet. Her hands trembled as she fumbled with her keyring for the littlest key.

"A celebration, huh? I thought you liked Henry."

"After all we've been through I need a drink."

"What are you having?"

"Scotch."

"Excellent. That's my favorite."

"Oh, what do you know about drinking?"

"You know how much goes on in this house under your nose Abigail? You're so oblivious to it it's hilarious. Me and Hazel made a bit of a game out of seeing how much we could get away with without you noticing, like one day we'd—"

"I get your point." Abigail set down two cups on the table. "Ice?"

"Sure."

Abigail put ice in each cup.

"You're a doll, Abby."

"After this drink, you have one night."

"One night for what?"

"To stay here."

"Why?"

"I told you, they're looking for you."

"Yeah, so?"

"They can't find you here, are you crazy?"

"Whatever. Hurry up with that scotch."

Where is it? Where did I put it? Abigail thought as she shifted through the contents of the cabinet. "If the police found you here I'd be in trouble for harboring you."

"Yeah, yeah, I get it. What happens to me after that?"

"Hopefully by then I've been able to help you overcome this."

"You can't help me Abigail. Wanting help means there's something wrong with me, and there's nothing wrong with me. I like this, Abigail. You rejected it because you didn't understand it, you didn't understand how good things could be."

"Oh Ivy you're so wrong and you don't realize—" Abigail accidentally dropped a bottle of alcohol and it shattered at her feet.

"You're a bit jumpy there Abby. Do you have something on your mind?"

"No. Uh. I found the scotch."

"Great."

Abigail came back to the table with the scotch and set it down on the table. Then she popped the lid off the Holy Water she had kept stashed in the liquor cabinet and brought it down over Ivy who pushed her hands up in defense and let out hellish screams.

"I'm gonna help you," Abigail said over the screams. "You don't know what you're saying, you're under its spell."

Ivy sat up on her elbows. *"You're gonna suffer a fate worse than death."*

"Oh, quiet down." Abigail brought down the bottle of Holy Water once more. Ivy recoiled again and inched feebly away from Abigail.

They kept a Holy Bible in the kitchen, and a cross on the wall. Abigail pulled the cross off its hook then kept it aimed at Ivy as she retrieved the Holy Bible from the counter.

"None of that stuff worked on you. *Why is it gonna work on* me? Are you stupid?"

"How would you know what worked on me and what didn't?"

"Because I was *there.* You're not speaking to Ivana any longer."

"What do you want from me?" Abigail neared the table with the cross and Holy Bible in her shaking hands; she struggled to keep them straight and conceal any of the fear that she was certain could be read on her face.

"Oh, I seem to recall you tearing me out of your body. Your body that I deserved."

"I don't understand."

"Yeah, you never did. Well, the good news, Abby," Ivy shielded her eyes when Abigail raised the cross up for her to see—Abigail stood directly ahead of her now, "is I'm not gonna kill you or Henry yet. I'm going to leave you both alive so he can see you suffer unlike anybody in this world has ever suffered before."

Abigail gulped. "I know how you are. It's all talk."

"Was killing Catherine Blackwell talk? How about killing Father Gutierrez? Oh Abigail, I'm much more than talk."

"You're not fooling me."

"I'm going to bring it to light. All of it. I'm going to tell everybody what you did to Catherine. I'm going to tell everybody what you did to the priest. I'm going to tell everybody everything."

"Who's gonna listen to you? Ivy you were six years old back then."

"I told you, you aren't talking to Ivy. You're talking to *me.*"

"You can't prove anything."

"I have your diary, dear Abby. What would the police think of the photostats I made? What would they say to a full confession in your own handwriting?"

"You didn't make any photostats."

"But I did."

"Prove it."

"I don't need to. You wrote your own confessions in those books. So the choice is yours, but no matter what you do, I'm gonna bring everything to light. At best, your only hope is to delay the inevitable—but what would a few days of time get you? Absolutely nothing."

Abigail opened The Bible and read: "Lying lips are abomination to the Lord—"

Ivy's body convulsed. Her torso levitated off the ground; two feet up then three, then four, then five.

Abigail moved two steps backwards, chills slithering on her spine.

"...but they that deal truly are his delight."

The dining room dropped in temperature. The cabinets opened and shut on their own and splintered wood from all the hinges. Abigail was frightened and jolted from the shock, dropping her Bible and cross. She kneeled quickly for them, stood back up, and Ivy was gone.

With her Holy Bible held ahead of her in one hand and the cross held out in the other, Abigail turned the corner of the wall that separated the dining room and kitchen. Her eyes darted through darkness and Ivy was not there. The cabinets had stopped opening and shutting but the house was still freezing cold and perhaps getting even colder.

It was worse than a nightmare—it was a living terror.

There's no escaping, Abigail thought. The reality of the horror was clinging to her more than ever. She had already known that there was no getting out of this, but now it was especially real. And she had to face it herself. Beverly wasn't here to bail her out.

A few tears fell.

"Ivy...?"

Abigail stepped through the house but paused when she heard somebody walking upstairs. Then Abigail went to the stairway and stood at the bottom step calling Ivy's name—Ivy said nothing and all sounds from upstairs had ceased.

"Are you up there, Ivy?"

Silence still. Unbearable silence.

Chills clinging tighter to Abigail's body. Coldness so tangible it had texture to it.

Dizzyingly Abigail ascended a step up the stairway. She stood still for only the briefest moment debating to go up further or not. Should she turn back? Should she run away back to the hospital where she—maybe—would be safe? Should she go beg Beverly for help? No—she could not do that. Beverly had a baby now. Abigail couldn't risk the life a little baby's mother. She had to face this herself. And if she got hurt, she thought, it was what she deserved.

"Ivy please we can—we can—" Abigail shut up and paused halfway up. What more was there to say? That they could fight it? That they could defeat it? What was the point? Ivy didn't want that—the spirit had a strong grip on her and she was refusing to let it go. Abigail hung her head. She burst into tears. *"Ivy please…"*

She felt pathetic.

Another step up the stairs.

"Ivy are you up there?"

Abigail approached the top of the stairway and there was no movement—she wondered what Ivy was up to. She wondered what she could do to help her. Wondered if there was any way to reach her through the spirit that now controlled her and overpowered her.

"Ivy what can I even do?"

Ivy's grotesque face peeked around the corner when Abigail reached the final step—contorted and slickly and streaked with dense black shadows that stretched over her. Abigail nearly fainted and reached for the railing in a hurry so that she wouldn't fall, dropping her Bible in the process. It thudded all the way down on every step.

"Nothing," Ivy said. "Sorry, did I scare you?"

Abigail moved down a step. "Ivy I please I—I—I…"

"I know, I know. You want to help me. You've said it a hundred times, what difference do you think it's gonna make? You're not helping me. I like things this way. For once in my life I'm in control."

"You're not in control. Just look at yourself—look at what it's done to you. It's using you. It needs you. You don't have to let it win."

Ivy's hand wrapped around Abigail's neck and forced her up against the wall. "I know when you killed Catherine you were wondering what her final thoughts were. Now I wonder what yours are, now that you're in the same position as she was. What's on your mind, Abigail?"

"I—I—" Abigail choked.

"Look at you, look how scared you are. Don't worry, I'm not a liar despite what you might think. I'm not gonna kill you, that would—that would just spoil all the fun of what I have planned for you. Then I wouldn't get to see what Henry would think of you when he found out that you killed Catherine, or that you killed the priest. Do you think he'd ask for his ring back, or would he be so disappointed that he'd never speak to you again? Thank God he doesn't have *too much* money invested in this marriage, I mean you guys didn't even buy the invitations yet."

Abigail slammed the cross into Ivy's face. It brought up little puffs of smoke where it met her skin. Ivy let go of Abigail then smacked her across the face. Abigail slipped down a couple steps but broke her fall by snapping her hands around the railing and straining her shoulders from the impact. Instantly every joint in her body hurt.

The cross fell down the stairs past her. That and The Bible, her only defenses against the monstrosity, were both at the bottom of the steps.

"Well, Abby, like you were saying, I can't be seen here. Then you'd be in trouble for harboring me. Thanks for your offer, but I won't be staying here tonight. I guess I'll see you around."

23

"Two tickets to Great Gatsby," Steve said then paid for the tickets.

He and Michelle snuck into a showing of Taxi Driver instead.

He put his arm around her tight, watching the movie, but Michelle couldn't pay attention. Everything from the past few days was on her mind—where was Warren? What happened after she and Steve left the house the other day? The way Hazel had acted, and the way Ivy attacked Raymond at the assembly, she couldn't get any of it off her mind.

A little kiss on the cheek. "What's wrong?"

"Can we get away from here? I want to be alone. Just the two of us."

"You don't want to see the movie?"

"I'm sorry. Maybe some other time." Michelle stood up and left.

"Wait. Hey, wait. Michelle. Wait up."

Steve tripped over other people who were sitting at the end of the row. They rolled their eyes at him as he apologized and crawled away. He caught up to Michelle outside the Neon Theater. He grabbed her by the wrist.

"What's wrong?"

She opened her purse for Warren's missing poster and put it in Steve's hands. "What are Hazel and Ivy hiding?"

"I don't know."

"Are you sure you don't know anything about it?"

"Yeah I'm sure."

"Don't lie to me please. If you know something then tell me."

"Michelle I'm as clueless as you are. Why would I lie to you?"

"I don't know. I just… I don't know who to trust anymore."

"Hey. You can trust me baby."

"I have to know what the others are hiding. I think they hurt Warren. Will you go with me? Will you go back with me to see if Warren is… still in there?"

"I'll go anywhere with you."

Michelle entered the Engstrom place's living room and traced her fingers along the wall. She shivered as her mind jumped to the worst possible conclusion of what might have been waiting in here to be discovered. What Hazel and Ivy might have been hiding…

"Let's go upstairs," Steve said. "I think I remember that's where Warren had taken her to."

"Yeah. Let's go."

Michelle stared into the dreadful darkness through the entryway into the rest of the house. Steve had a flashlight with him that he faced into the house's murkiness, and its light struggled to pierce it. Together they went forward.

"Steve?"

"Uh-huh?"

"I'm scared."

He put his arm over her shoulder and held her close. "You've got nothing to fear. Okay?"

"Okay."

The house was dead quiet as they went up the spiraling staircase. On the second floor they moved straight to the left and down the long hallway. Suddenly a random door creaked partway open. Something writhed in the darkness; something less than human. Michelle was drawn to it and moved forward; Steve aimed his flashlight toward it and a streak of light fell over the mutilated face ahead of them; a bloody hand on a broken wrist curled angrily. For one brief moment, Michelle thought she recognized the monstrosity before her as Warren.

She was frozen. Steve ran and tugged on her hand, and she ran away with him and screamed so loudly that her throat burned with searing pain every time she took a breath. A furtive look over her shoulder; the creature was bathed in blinding darkness again and yet she could see his twisted and mangled outline; a damnably human monster that crept from the other end of the hall.

Michelle couldn't process what she had seen or understand it whatsoever; and she was even more confused when she and Steve were back in the living room and Ivy was there. Her arms were crossed. Her eyes were completely black. She was smiling.

"Good to see you two."

"Oh my God." Michelle put her hands on Ivy's shoulders. "We need to get out of here right now."

Steve grabbed Ivy by the wrist. "We shouldn't be here. Let's go."

"You two have no idea how great things can be." Ivy pulled herself out of Steve's grip.

Suddenly the fireplace was raging of its own will; bright flames cut through the living room's darkness suddenly and spread their warmth. An orange glow of flames streaked against Ivy's blackened eyes. Her smile widened.

"Let me tell you about my master," she said.

Suddenly there were heavy footfalls from the threshold. A black goat emerged from the inner darkness of the house.

Ivy petted his head. "Welcome, my master."

Michelle grabbed Steve's hand and ran with him out of the house.

"Don't leave me tonight," Michelle said, holding Steve tight in her bedroom.

"Okay," he said. "I won't leave you."

As night dragged on, she fell asleep in his arms. He was on the brink of sleep too when Michelle's door creaked open.

Awaiting him was the black goat.

Steve followed it back to the Engstrom place. Ivy was already there in the living room. The flames were raging.

"I knew you'd be back." Ivy took Steve by the hands. "Will you give yourself to me?"

"Yes." He tried to kiss her, but she pulled away before he could.

Ivy shook her head. "No kisses yet."

She picked up the big book that was resting near the fireplace; Steve had not noticed it before. Bound in a strange and ancient material, the pages were fragile.

"I need you to write your name in this book." Ivy flipped through it, then set it in front of the fireplace as close to the flames as she could place it without the book catching on fire. "Kneel down, Steve."

Steve obeyed.

"Show me your hand."

Steve lifted his left hand; Ivy grabbed it in both of hers and brought it to her mouth. Steve's pointer finger traced Ivy's lips. Gently she bit him until her sharp tooth broke the skin and she tasted his blood.

He signed his name in the book.

"Signed in blood," she said, "and sealed with a kiss."

Steve stepped into the night.

He passed between the thickly growing trees on the hill. Branches and thorns scratched up his skin. He wanted to rub the dripping blood on his cuts but his hands wouldn't respond to his thoughts.

When he came down the hill he passed by the lake, and he went a little further and came to the farm, then entered the barn where the cows were sleeping. After he shut the door behind himself he felt every animal's eye find him and linger on him. Steve turned to face them. All awake. All frightened. All crying when he took his first step.

The animals pulled wildly against their restraints, attempting uselessly to break free.

Steve had a lot of work ahead of him. Nearby was a pitchfork. Steve picked it up then rammed it through a cow's neck.

Mr. Feldman and his wife woke up to the sound of shrieking animals going crazy in the barn; Mr. Feldman told his wife to stay put, then he hopped out of bed and put his shoes on. His shotgun was between his bed and nightstand, where he kept it every night. He rushed out of the room then out of the house with his gun loaded and ready for any trouble.

Cautiously he opened the door and stepped in. The lights were off, but a streak of moonlight came in through the back windows and partially illuminated the madness. The cows and horses were all screaming louder and louder, perhaps now a little more excited by their owner's presence, and were trying to break free of their restraints.

He stepped through the barn. "Somebody in here? Come out now or I'll shoot ya."

He stepped a few feet over to the light switches and flicked them on. The chaos had been much worse than he had thought or had been clued into by the briefness he saw under vague moonlight—about half of the barn was dead. Blood was soaking into every inch of the place that he could see. There were footsteps in the blood—bare human footsteps. Somebody was in here with him—a madman.

Mr. Feldman aimed the gun, his finger ready on the trigger. He moved slowly back toward the door. There was a second level to the barn, where there was almost nothing but straw. Somebody must have been hiding in it. Somebody who had done all of this.

"Come down from up there right now and I won't kill ya," Mr. Feldman said. It was a lie, of course. "Come down right now. *Right now.*"

Mr. Feldman fired a bullet after there was no response.

"Come on out ya coward. Show yourself."

Laughter on the second story of the barn. Mr. Feldman stood at the center and looked from every angle, but from the ground it was hard to see completely what was going on up there. Somebody could have been crouching out in the open or hiding in an obvious spot and Mr. Feldman could have missed him because of the angle. He fired another bullet at the direction of the laughter but as the laughter became louder, the animals became wilder, and Mr. Feldman didn't know what to do.

He was scared. For the first time in a long time he was terrified. The barn was a complete bloodbath of massacred animals—it was not a break-in like had happened before, when robbers or kids came on his property. Kids would come in and write with paint on the walls. Robbers would come in looking for money and Mr. Feldman would chase them off with his gun and his dogs. This was different. The person in here didn't want to vandalize or steal money—the person in here had a passion for murder and mayhem and torture.

There was only one thing to do: attack the intruder head-on. The stairs were on the right side of the barn in the front and the right side in the back. If the intruder made a run down as Mr. Feldman made his way up, it would be fine with him—there'd be plenty of openings and he'd be able to put a bullet in the intruder for sure. He walked up the steps slowly, listening to them creak through the strain of screaming farm animals—even the animals outside the barn were screaming too—and Mr. Feldman breathed deeply.

Of all the farms in all the world, this crazy's gotta come into mine.

He was at the second floor. Nothing he could see besides dark shadows that lingered despite the lights he had turned on, and all the straw. Yet that menacing laugh was growing louder and louder. Mr. Feldman wanted nothing more than to put a bullet through the monster's head—that's what he saw when his mind tried to match up the laugh to a face. A monster. Not a man.

"Show yourself." He aimed his gun one way then the other. "You little punk. You little coward. *Show yourself.*"

Mr. Feldman peeked down at the chaos from up on the second story. The animals were furious; their restraints were giving out. Soon they might all be free. He looked away from them and turned back toward the mountains of straw, and a bloodied pitchfork knocked away the shotgun from his hands; it went off and a bullet flew through the opposite wall. The boy in front of him might not have been any older than eighteen or nineteen, he thought. The boy was wearing an Ashfall High letterman jacket and his eyes were completely black. Blood splattered on him from the farm animals he had killed.

Then the boy set the sharp points of the pitchfork under Mr. Feldman's throat.

The boy stepped forward, and Mr. Feldman grabbed the pitchfork with his hands and tried to push it away, but the boy didn't stumble or move. He stayed in place with his eternal grip on the pitchfork.

Mr. Feldman tried to shove it away but it didn't work.

The boy took another step. "Dumb old man."

Mr. Feldman fell on his back as the force of the boy's push on the pitchfork increased. Both his hands were wrapped around the slick metal spikes, trying to push it away from his throat. It was no use. The spikes were bloodied and it was impossible to hold a solid good grip.

Two spikes scraped up the skin on his neck; warm blood flowed, but the spikes had not cut deep at all, they had only gone surface level.

The boy moved the spike away. Mr. Feldman watched him dumbfounded.

Then the boy slammed the pitchfork into Mr. Feldman's stomach; unbelievable pain erupted in his body. The boy dragged him to the ledge and he begged him not to throw him over, but the boy would not listen. He picked up Mr. Feldman and threw him down to the cows.

It was all happening so fast that Mr. Feldman could not process all that was happening, nor could he process all the burning pain coursing through his veins. At some point, and he wasn't sure when, some of the remaining animals in the barn had broken free and were roaming around. They looked down at him and sniffed.

He wanted to say something to them, but his mouth couldn't open.

When the animals started eating him, he couldn't scream.

Steve found the gun near the farmer's corpse. The picked it up, discarded the pitchfork, and went inside the farmer's house.

"Walter?" The scared frail voice of an old woman.

Steve said nothing.

"Walter? Honey? That you?"

Steve followed her voice until he came to the bedroom. He stood in the doorway, holding the gun by the barrel. The old woman sat up in bed with tears in her eyes, and terror scrunched into her face.

"What have you done with my husband?"

"I killed him."

The old lady pulled a gun out from under the covers and took aim. Steve jumped out of the way and she fired a shot that went into the wall. Steve slipped into one of the other rooms, hiding in darkness, joining the shadows, and taking aim with the old man's gun.

From where he stood he could see the barrel of the old lady's gun passing the doorframe. A little bit further and he'd have a clear shot.

Then the lady moved her gun back into her bedroom.

Steve stood up, walking out of the darkened room with the farmer's gun, when the old lady popped out and aimed her own at him. She fired a bullet but Steve dodged it, tugging his finger over his own trigger and firing a bullet that zipped an inch past the old lady's face.

While she was stunned and frozen, Steve ripped the gun from her hands. The old lady bit him on the wrist so he smacked her away with the butt of the gun. Then he aimed both of them at her, one in each of his hands.

"Any last words?"

The lady was silent.

Steve put a bullet in each of her feet. It took him about six or seven shots to do so because she wouldn't keep still. After that it was easier. He put one in her left knee then her right knee. She couldn't move any more. Then he dropped the guns and grabbed her by the wrist. He dragged her down a hallway toward the front door.

"What are you gonna do to me?"

"Do to you? To an old lady?"

The lady was screaming and crying as Steve forcefully pulled her down the two wooden steps in front of the house and across the rocky path leading up to them. He dragged her to the barn and dragged her through the madness. The animals were tearing everything apart and fighting with each other. Their screams never ceased. It was a madhouse.

Steve dragged the old woman to the center of the barn, where her husband Walter lay in a pool of blood. The old woman screamed again and again and banged her fists on the floor. As Steve stood over her, animals gathered around and licked their lips.

24

MICHELLE REACHED FOR HIM but he wasn't there. Sleep draped over her mind again; was she imagining his absence? Everything was a strange haze; the flutter of moonlight from her window, the lingering dream, the emptiness of her bed, seeing Ivy, seeing the monster that might have been Warren. What was real and what wasn't?

She sat up and rubbed her eyes and whispered his name.

Her vision adjusted to the dense darkness of her bedroom. Yes, she was alone.

I should have known better, Michelle thought, *than to trust some-body like Steve.*

As soon as she laid back down there were footsteps in the upstairs hallway. Her bedroom door was slowly opened and Steve came in.

"There you are," she said.

He slid under Michelle's covers and wrapped his arms around her. Michelle slid her shirt off and pressed herself closer against his warm body. She kissed him, then their hands intertwined and she lifted his pointer finger into her mouth. It tasted like blood.

"Are you bleeding?" She asked.

Steve said nothing.

Michelle stood up from her bed, grabbed Steve by the wrist, and led him to the bathroom. Blood leaked through his shirt. Michelle helped him take it off. There were three big scratches across his chest; yet he did not act as if he were affected. He seemed fine.

"Oh my God. What happened to you?" Michelle opened the cabinet looking for the hydrogen peroxide. She popped the cap off then poured it over his chest. Steve never answered her question.

Blood from the shirt seeped onto the countertop. Out of the corner of her eye, Michelle saw the blood was *moving.* She looked closer and saw that the blood was in fact writhing. Her heart skipped a beat. The blood was squirming, moving as if it were *alive.*

She looked from the blood back to Steve. His eyes were completely black.

"Baby." Steve closed the space between them with a big step forward.

Michelle stumbled for a step away from him. "Get away from me Steve."

"Don't act like that, baby." Steve put his arms around her and pulled her in for a kiss. She slammed her fists on him but he didn't break away from her at all.

Michelle woke up alone on the bathroom floor. Steve's bloodied shirt was next to her. Her eyes fluttered open then shut again. She drifted through darkness then her eyes opened again. Michelle licked her lips; they were lined with dried blood. Standing up against the dizziness that burned through her head, she braced the wall so that she wouldn't fall over.

"Steve?" A whisper.

She looked around the cramped bathroom. He wasn't with her. The bottle of hydrogen peroxide was still open on the sink's counter-top. She staggered a couple steps out of the bathroom and into the hallway, then back into her room. It was somewhat bright outside her window, and the sun was almost ready to set.

Michelle sat on her bed. Her vision was blurring. She rubbed her eyes, but that did her no good. Then the phone rang. She stayed in place on her bed for a few moments. Then she reached for the phone on her nightstand and picked it up, the cord tipping over her water bottle.

"Hello?"

"Hi, Michelle, it's me. Mrs. Avery. I was calling because it's almost seven o'clock and I hadn't heard from you yet today." *Seven o'clock,* Michelle thought. *Have I been asleep all day?* "Will you be able to babysit in half an hour?"

"Uh…"

"Listen, if you can't do it, that's fine. It's just going to be a little difficult for us to find somebody else on such short notice, and the kids really like you."

"Um, of course I can. I've just got a little headache."

"Really, if you can't, it's no problem."

"I'll be… I'll be just fine."

"Great. Thank you."

"See you soon." Michelle hung up the phone.

She arrived at the Avery residence a little bit later. They were about four or five blocks down from her house. Mr. and Mrs. Avery were pretty eager to leave, and by the time Michelle walked up to their property they were already heading out the front door.

"There's some money on the kitchen table next to a stack of menus," Mr. Avery said. "That Mexican place Valenzuela's is pretty good, I've had them at least once a week for the entire year. Twice or three times a week sometimes."

"Thank you again for watching our kids, I don't know what we would do without you," Mrs. Avery said. "We've been so busy with everything that we haven't had a night out together in... in who knows how long. We really needed this."

"Yeah, no problem," Michelle said. "Have fun you two."

They exchanged goodbyes and Michelle went inside. The older of the two children was eight-year-old Paul, he was in the living room stacking blocks on the couch while watching some cartoon on TV. As soon as he saw Michelle, he got a big smile on his face.

"Hi Ms. Michelle, can we make smores like last time?"

"Am I gonna get in trouble for giving you candy this late?"

"Smores aren't candy, and it's not bedtime yet."

"Well..."

"Please my parents let me have candy at nighttime all the time."

"Oh all right, we can make some smores. I'll get the firepit ready while you grab the chocolate and marshmallows. Is your sister asleep?"

"Yeah. When she's not crying she's sleeping."

Paul followed her to the kitchen. He climbed on top of the counter to reach the top cabinet where the treats were kept.

Michelle went outside to the back yard and dragged the firepit and firewood and lighter fluid from inside the garage to the middle of the yard where there were some seats. With the firewood in place—one log lying on its side, two others stacked against it to form a triangle—Michelle poured the lighter fluid over it.

Paul came outside carrying paper plates under his arm, a bag of marshmallows, two chocolate bars, and a box of cookies. In one of his hands he was holding a lighter.

Michelle met him near the door and took the lighter from his hands. "Give me that."

"What? I wasn't doing anything."

"Kids shouldn't touch these things, it's dangerous. Here, let me help you carry some of these." Michelle grabbed the cookies and plates. "Cookies? Not graham crackers?"

"Remember last time you made it with cookies because we didn't have graham crackers? I like it best this way."

"All right."

Paul put all the cookies on the plates and stabbed marshmallows with skewers while Michelle lit the fire. As soon as the flames were devouring the wood, Paul stuck the marshmallows into the fire and kept them there until they were burned.

"Make sure you break up the chocolate," he said.

Michelle broke up the bars into pieces and put them over some of the cookies. Paul stuck the burned marshmallows on top of them to make them into little sandwiches, then devoured most his smore in a single big bite.

"Delicious." He stuck it out to Michelle. "Try it."

Michelle bit the other end. "You're right, it is delicious."

Michelle put a marshmallow on a skewer and held it a few inches from the flames so it would golden instead of burn. She was mesmerized by the fire, staring deeply into it.

"I'm gonna get milk. Do you want some too?"

"Sure, Paul."

There were footsteps in the back yard. At the opposite end, a black goat appeared. Chills slithered over Michelle's body despite the heat.

"I won't do it," Michelle said.

The black goat left by the time Paul came back with two cups of milk filled to the brim. Some milk spilled over the edges as he came down the steps. He handed one to Michelle. She drank a sip then set it down.

"I'm going to check on your sister now."

Paul said nothing. He put another marshmallow into the flames.

In the kitchen Michelle grabbed a knife from the rack. She clutched it tight as she pushed the first door to her left open. The baby girl was in the crib in Mr. and Mrs. Avery's bedroom. The girl was fast asleep.

Tears filled Michelle's eyes.

"No, I won't do it. I can't do it."

Michelle picked the baby up with her free hand; immediately the girl was crying. Michelle set the baby down on the Averys' bed and unzipped her onesie.

She poked the tip of the knife into the baby girl's stomach. The baby squirmed, and Michelle struggled to hold the child still. Powerful screams erupted. Michelle tried to hush the baby as she dragged the knife to form a pentagram on her belly.

"Hush, baby," Michelle whispered. "Hush, hush."

CRASH!

It was Paul and another little boy who must have been a neighbor. They were standing in the doorway with smores in their hands. Paul dropped his glass of milk then the boys went running away screaming.

Michelle laughed as she listened to their cries...

Paul and Junior ran down the block to Junior's house. The front door was open. Paul and Junior tripped over the toys that Junior had spread all over the floor in the living room earlier that day.

"Dad! Dad!" Junior screamed.

"The babysitter's killing my sister! We need help!"

Junior's father stepped into the living room when he heard their frantic screams. "What's going on in here?"

Paul grabbed his hand and pulled on him. *"Quick! My sister is dying! Help!"*

Michelle stayed calm. She stayed on the bed and zipped up the baby's onesie. She rocked the baby gently, hushing it, and then there were footsteps in the house. A man saying hello. Michelle ignored him and continued rocking the baby, but those irritating screams kept flooding out of it.

"Hush little baby, don't you cry..."

"Hello?" A man in his late thirties stood in the doorway. Pudgy. A bit of a beard. Smiling. "What seems to be the problem here?"

"Are you a friend of the Averys?"

"Uh-huh. Who are you?"

"Your worst nightmare, mister." Michelle winked. "Did the boys run and get you?"

He stepped into the room over the shattered glass and spilled milk. "Uh-huh. I've got two little boys all alone at my house crying and crying and telling me you were... carving up the baby. I can see now that's not the case."

"You know kids and their imaginations. I think they were telling each other ghost stories. There was one of those horror movies on TV, you know? And the boys got scared."

"Yeah. Yeah I can see that. I had a feeling it was nothing."

"I'm sure the Averys are gonna find a way to flip out on me over this, oh God. Hey, you think you can help me rock her? I just can't get her to stop crying."

"Sure," he said. Michelle set the baby in the man's arms. "My son Junior was louder than she is, believe it or not, when he was her age. Once my... ex-wife was so concerned because he kept on crying that she brought him to the hospital. Of course there was nothing wrong with Junior, kids just like crying. It's in their nature."

"Cool. Maybe if she shuts up I can fix us a drink."

"Hey, sounds good to me, um, I don't think I caught your name."

"Michelle. Any bets how long the boys will stay over at your place before they work up the guts to come and check what happened to you? Oh, they probably think I've carved both you and that lovely baby girl up."

"Not sure. They were pretty startled... I'd guess they'd be there quite a while."

"Uh-huh. Hey, look at that, you're pretty good at that, she's quieting down already."

"Yeah. Just need to be gentle with them, Michelle."

"So you said you were divorced. Mind if I asked what happened?"

"We weren't a good match for each other. That's all."

"A little late to realize that, don't you think? After you've had a baby?"

"Yeah, well, sometimes you don't know things until later in life."

"Do you get pretty lonely?"

"Yeah. Yeah I do. Hey, she's almost asleep. Why don't you get started on those drinks?"

"Sure. What do you want? Me, I like scotch on the rocks. I think they've got some pretty good whisky in their liquor cabinet."

"How's a young lady like you get to know so much about drinks?"

"Hmmm... I've been around the block a few times, you know?"

"Yeah, I know. It's been quite a while since I've been around the block myself," he said, whispering now because the baby was nearly done screaming and was quieting down.

"You look like you could use a trip around the block. Try and keep up."

"A slow trip around the block's better than rushing through."

"Sorry. I didn't realize I was speeding, officer."

"That's all right. I'll let you off with a warning. Why don't you get those drinks? Make me a scotch too, or if they don't have scotch I'll take whatever you're having."

"Sure thing. Be back soon, handsome."

Michelle went down the hall to Paul's room and found his baseball bat. She tiptoed down the hallway back to Mr. and Mrs. Avery's bedroom. The man did not hear her or notice her and she approached him from behind. The baby's blood was seeping through its outfit; the man unzipped the onesie and gasped.

The moment he turned, Michelle slammed the bat against his head.

He fell down and tried to safely hold the baby in his arms and avoid hurting it in the fall; the baby was crying again from the commotion. Michelle brought the bat down again on the man's head and blood seeped down and into his eyes. She slammed the bat on his head again and his skull cracked. Repeatedly she brought the bat down on him until his face was split open and his brains leaked out.

She dropped the bat then picked up the crying baby.

"Won't you ever be quiet?"

Paul and Junior hid in Junior's closet.

"When's your dad coming back?"

"How should I know?"

KNOCK! KNOCK! KNOCK!

The sound came from across the house at the front door. The boys looked at each other; they had each gone pale.

Paul opened the closet door and stepped out.

Junior grabbed his friend's arm. "Don't open. It's her."

Paul pulled himself out of Junior's grasp. "Maybe your dad's back. Come on."

"It's not my dad, he has a key."

Paul left the room; Junior followed him. They went to the living room, where they stood a few feet away from the front door. The knocks were still coming consistently.

"Junior." It was Michelle on the other side of the door, not Junior's father.

Paul reached for the door, but Junior pulled him back.

"I told you don't open it."

"Your dad wants you to come next door and show him what you saw," she said, still knocking.

"Go away," Junior shouted. *"Send my dad back here."*

"Just open the door, she's my babysitter," Paul said.

"No, Paul. As far as I know she's killed my dad *and* your baby sister!"

"My mom and dad are coming home. I can't stay here. Open the door."

"No."

Paul moved past him and unlocked the front door.

Michelle stepped inside. She was smiling. There was blood splatter on her outfit.

"You should have listened to Junior," Michelle said, closing the door behind herself.

On the local news: "A single father raped the next door babysitter and killed three children. The babysitter killed the crazed man and survived."

25

ALVIN BLOCH WAS IN the attic toy room getting his baseball from a box when he heard what he thought was Lincoln's barking. He paused, listening closely, taking careful steps toward the wall. It was coming from the panel of wood his father had removed—and subsequently put back in place—for Carrie and Jeanette the other day. Then, pressing his ear to the wall, he heard that it was not barking. It was a boy.

Shivers traced Alvin's body as he heard the boy behind the walls saying, *"Can anybody hear me?"*

Alvin knocked on the wall. *"I can hear you. Can you hear me?"*

"Somebody help me!"

"Can you hear me?" Alvin asked again, still knocking. Then there was only silence. Alvin knocked, stopped, then knocked again. *"My name is Alvin. Are you all right in there?"*

"Who are you talking to?"

Across the room Jeanette had come up the stairs with her little doll in the purple dress in her hands.

Alvin stood up. "I thought I heard something."

Jeanette raised her doll to her ear as if the doll were telling her a secret, and she turned to the side a little to obscure her doll's whispers. "Miss Penelope says we won't ever find Abraham Lincoln."

Alvin switched his baseball from one hand to the other and left the toy room. "See you, Jeanette. I'm going outside. Have fun with your dolls."

"Miss Penelope is the only friend I need."

"Uh-huh."

"Bye Alvin."

As he came off the steps, he heard his sister laughing with her doll.

He kept thinking about the sounds he heard in the wall. Had he imagined them? Or had he really heard somebody there? He shivered again thinking about it. The words were clear and distinct, and somebody must have really been there. But who? How? It made no sense to him. Nobody could be hiding in the walls—especially when they hadn't had any visitors.

Jeanette opened the dollhouse and set Miss Penelope down in the basement, then she grabbed Miss Penelope's family members from their designated box and placed them around the basement as well.

"What was that, Miss Penelope?" Jeanette picked up her doll and set her close to her ear so she could hear her toy's whispers. "Somebody died down there? Below the floorboards?"

Jeanette took Miss Penelope and her family out of the replica basement and set them around the replica of the kitchen.

"There you go. I wouldn't want to be in the scary basement either if somebody died down there, even if it was a long time ago like you said. Now let's play house. Who wants to sweep the floors and who wants to wash the windows?"

Happily she played with her dolls. They whispered to her and she whispered back.

Alvin opened his piggy bank for two nickels then left home on his bicycle for the candy shop in town. It was his favorite place in Ashfall.

Big signs in the windows for Hershey's goods and Toblerone Swiss milk chocolate. A chalkboard sign on the street for soda candy and cigarettes. Kids gathered around and traded candy and baseball cards. Alvin entered with his bike and leaned it against the counter, then he picked up the red and white box of Cracker Jack.

The poster above the display read: *Cracker Jack Ball Players! One of these handsomely colored pictures <u>Free in each package of CRACKER JACK,</u> "the famous popcorn confection." Complete set has 176 Pictures of "Stars" in the American, National and Federal leagues.*

Start a collection of your <u>favorite</u> players!

Ruckheim Bros. & Eckstein.

Brooklyn, N.Y.Chicago, Ill.

Alvin was hoping to score a Stuffy McInnis or a Honus Wagner.

He paid for two boxes then opened them outside the candy shop as he sat on the curb. In the first box a Les Nunamaker. In the second a Ward Miller. He double checked them in disappointment.

He'd trade anything for a Stuffy McInnis or a Honus Wagner. But he couldn't complain about the gamble, and he needed these two anyways if he wanted to put together the complete hundred and seventy six card set. So far he was up to a dozen with only one double.

He swallowed a handful of Cracker Jack then rode his bike back home.

When he was at his new home's hill he saw there were two boys that had beat him there. He had never seen them before. Two boys about his age. The one in the red shirt was a little taller than the one in the white shirt. He couldn't tell much else about them from the distance between them.

He rode his bike over to some bushes and dumped it there, then went a few feet up and watched them from behind a tree. When the boy in the white shirt looked back over his shoulder, Alvin ducked out of view. He lingered there for a little while until he was sure it was safe to look back out at them—by then, the boys climbed up over the top of the hill and out of sight. They hadn't gone directly straight up from the main path, they had been travelling up through the trees. Alvin knew that the boys were trying to remain hidden as well. Just what were they doing here? What was the big idea?

He crept up a few feet then ducked behind a tree.

A pause.

He ran up to the next tree and hid.

A pause.

Then he repeated it over and over until he came up to the top of the hill.

The boy in the red shirt and the boy in the white shirt walked around the perimeter of the gate and down past the house's side. One boy handed the other a burlap sack that seemed to be heavy with supplies.

Alvin couldn't follow them much because there was a wide open space and he was bound to get caught. He waited until the other boys were far enough away before he left his hiding spot. The others were clearly in the back yard and Alvin was out of view.

Still, despite the distance, despite the fact that all the sounds of his footsteps would never reach the other boys, Alvin kept moving slowly and carefully and quietly. What were these boys from town up to? For a second he thought about running to get his father, but when he peeked into the back yard he saw that the boys were going into the forest. If they were planning to rob them—which was Alvin's first thought—then what were they doing in the woods? Why hadn't they broken a window or tried to pick the lock? What were they up to exactly?

Alvin peeked around the corner of the wellhouse. The boys were too obscured by all the trees and vegetation between them for Alvin to see or hear them. Where were they going? Just what was in the woods? He hadn't explored them at all since moving in. Anything could have been back there. Did these boys know something about his home that he didn't?

He waited five minutes then entered the forest.

All was quiet.

Where had those boys gone?

He traveled just off the path, using the trees as a shield. Soon voices became audible. Still he was too far to hear exactly what they said. When he finally had a glimpse of those other boys he saw them disappearing around a slight rise.

Alvin took his time again, waiting until he assumed there was enough distance between them for him to move again. He went down the rise and saw the ancient family cemetery that sent chills under his skin. He was terrified to think about the corpses buried just out of reach. Morbidly he stared at the cemetery and took in each detail of the sickly trees scattered throughout the edges of it, and the misshapen piles of moss that covered gravestones. Momentarily Alvin wondered when the last time any of these people ever had a visitor was—a real visitor and not a curious passerby like he and presumably the other boys were. When was the last time somebody ever knew one of these dead people and visited? A sick thought to know that day these people had visitors, and then there came a day when nobody ever knew where they were buried anymore.

It took Alvin a while to get his feet moving again.

Maybe, he thought, he had lost them. But when he saw the hidden cabin in the woods he had an idea where those other boys might just be hiding at.

Alvin peeked in through the window. One boy was sitting on a couch dumping out the contents of the burlap sack—Alvin couldn't see them too clearly from the angle, and from trying to be discrete as he peeked in only for two seconds at a time—while the other one was on the floor writing something down in a notebook.

The one with the notebook sat up. "I gotta take a leak. I'll be right back."

"Spare me the details, Edmund."

Edmund. So Alvin had one of their names.

Alvin gripped his baseball tight, and when Edmund came out of the little cabin Alvin snuck up on him and held him with one arm around his throat. With Edmund pinned, Alvin held the baseball up to his head.

"Try anything funny and I'll knock your brains out with this thing."

"All right! All right! Don't hurt me! I have to pee!"

"Fat chance."

"Fat chance of what?"

"No talking!"

Alvin led Edmund back through the door, which was a little difficult because Edmund weighed more than him, but he was easy to command being that he was so frightened of Alvin. The other boy on the couch had jumped to his feet holding a saw.

"I bet this saw can do a whole lot more damage than your baseball. Why don't you let my friend go? Especially before he tinkles all over you, kid."

"It's my property, I'm well within my rights to knock the brains outta you both. What are you doing in my house?"

The boy tossed the saw on the couch. "I was too hasty to threaten you. Just let my friend go and let's talk all these things over like men. All right?"

"How can I trust you?"

"What do you want me to do?"

"I dunno... I..."

"I gotta pee real bad."

Alvin let go of him. "Go do whatever you need to do."

Edmund ran through the door. "Thank God."

"Listen, uh, let's rewind a bit, shall we?" The boy said. "My name's Billy. My friend whose acquaintance you just made is Edmund. What's your name?"

"Alvin."

"Alvin. Alvin, do you know… anything about your house?"

"How do you mean that?"

"I just mean… do you know what happened here a long time ago?"

"What are you talking about?"

"Geez, you don't know. God how have you not heard any of the legends?"

"Are you going to start making sense Billy? And where's your friend?" Alvin turned in the doorway where he hadn't moved from. Edmund was a few feet away shaking. "Why are you just standing there?"

"You scared me real bad, uh, are you still gonna hurt me?"

"No. Now get in here. I think Billy was just getting to the good part."

Edmund walked in. "Thank—thank you, uh, for not hurting me."

"Okay. Now get back to the good part, Billy. What happened in my house?"

"All sorts of things happened here. But I won't beat around the brush. Your home is cursed, Alvin."

"Yeah? How do you know?"

"Everyone around these parts knows about it."

"He's telling the truth," Edmund said. "It's cursed. Our friend went missing here."

"Your friend what now?"

"He's skipping ahead. Just hold on for a minute there, Edmund. Alvin, your house used to belong to the Engstrom family, that's why we all call it the Engstrom place. My sister told me witches lived in the woods behind your house and that the Engstroms made deals with the devil to have prosperity but any deal with the great deceiver ends with trickery. A curse was brought onto the family and they all died."

"They all died in that house? In my new house?"

"One by one. Mysteriously. No one knows all the details because anyone who lived there is long dead now."

"So what happened to your friend?"

"Well to tell you the truth, we were much like you, I mean, we didn't believe anything about the curse either when we heard about it. And one day we wanted to scare Samuel so we told him to knock on your door—I mean it wasn't your door yet, it was a couple months ago. He went inside and he never came out."

"And you didn't tell anybody?"

"No, we didn't."

"So is that why you're here at my house today?"

"Edmund and I came here nearly every day up until you moved in. We'd meet up in this cabin to discuss whatever we found the previous day, and we've kept a whole log of everything. We've mapped out your house and we've kept track of any place where we heard Samuel's voice. I guess I should mention that we've been... hearing him in the walls. And I guess you can call also this cabin our headquarters."

"Headquarters. Right. Well I'll tell you the truth even though I don't think either of you are giving it to me straight—I think you're both liars."

"Everything I've told you is the truth," Billy said.

"I'd put my hand on a Holy Bible and swear to it," Edmund said.

"Yeah? Then how did you hear a boy that's been lost in my house for months?"

"We don't know but that's what we're trying to find out."

Alvin's guts twisted. He thought about the voice he heard that morning, and thought about Abraham Lincoln lost in the walls as well, barking and barking and spending weeks in those walls without ever being found...

"I don't believe you. I've been all over that house and never heard anything but Abraham Lincoln."

"Abraham Lincoln?" Edmund and Billy said at the same time, both boys very confused.

"Our dog. Our dog is named Abraham Lincoln. He got lost in the walls himself and we can hear him barking but we can't find him. He's been like this for weeks."

"What did your folks do about it?" Edmund asked.

"A couple days ago we had a man from Animal Control come by to find Abe Lincoln and he was spooked and ran from our house in a hurry. I don't know what got into that man but I think he found an entrance or something into the walls through our basement."

"You know how to get into the walls?" Billy said. "Hell I'd love to give it a shot."

"Not just yet. We've got to prepare first."

"That's all we've done this whole time is prepare."

"Yeah well you prepared to find him, you didn't prepare to go in looking for him. You don't just rush into battle—you have to be strategic. Who knows what we'd find in there."

"I think we've converted you into a believer after all," Billy said.

"That didn't take much," Edmund said.

Alvin went over to the couch and sat down. He saw the contents of the burlap sack were a heavy flashlight and a hammer and some other tools.

"Looks like you guys were preparing to do some construction. What's all this for? Why did you need a box of nails?"

The boys looked at each other.

"Uh…" Billy said.

"We don't know," Edmund said. "I guess you just never know what might come in handy."

Alvin reached into his back pockets for his boxes of Cracker Jack. "Hey you guys want some Cracker Jack? I bought two boxes today hoping for Honus Wagner or Stuffy McInnis. I didn't pull either one."

"Sure man, thank you," Edmund said as he grabbed one of the boxes from Alvin's hand.

"No thanks, I'm stuffed," Billy said. "You know, I've got two Honus Wagners. I pulled one myself, then the other day my pop comes home from work and had stopped at the newsstand and bought a box, said to my sister she had to split it with me. Well I was asleep, Alvin, and the next morning I saw the box in the trash. I pulled it right out of the garbage can and there he was—Honus Wagner waiting inside."

"I still can't believe that story," Edmund said.

"I've got two sisters," Alvin said, "Jeanette and Carrie, and I'd slug either one of 'em if they threw away a Honus Wagner card. Or any other card for that matter. You got a complete set yet Billy?"

"No, maybe thirty or forty cards. That's a lot of Cracker Jack to eat through to find your way to a total set, but hey, somebody's gotta do it."

"Yeah, that's why I'm here giving it away."

"What did you end up finding?" Edmund asked.

"Les Nunamaker and Ward Miller. Guess it's better than nothing. I needed both of 'em. So, you guys, can I check out that notebook of yours? I'm curious what you've found in my house."

"Sure thing," Edmund said, reaching for it.

"Let me read this book through tonight. Then let's regroup tomorrow. Don't worry about sneaking around, you can just knock on the front door, I'll make sure to leave the gate unlocked in the morning for you."

26

Abigail felt bad for knocking on Beverly's door after midnight, but she didn't know where else to go or who else could help her.

The curtain in the window was pulled back a short length then was set back in place, and a moment later the front door opened and Beverly was there moving a strand of blonde hair from her eyes. She looked the same, Abigail thought, as she had all those years ago.

"Abby? What's going on?"

"I—I should have listened to you." Abigail was crying. Tears flooded her eyes all at once. "Henry's in the hospital. Ivy—Ivy hurt him."

Beverly stepped out of the doorway and grabbed Abigail's hand in the cold night then led her inside. "Oh my God. Come in."

"Ivy stabbed him. I should have listened..." Abigail sobbed. "I should have listened to you. I didn't want to believe you."

Beverly led her to the couch. "Wait here. Let me get you something to drink."

A moment later Beverly returned with a cup of water and gave it to Abigail. She drank it in silence then said, "I missed you, Beverly. I missed you so much."

"I missed you too."

Abigail tried to stop crying but the tears kept coming without end.

Beverly frowned and looked away into the darkness of her house. Abigail thought of the poor baby who must have been asleep in the other room. She thought about how godawful she was for dragging that baby's mother back into this living hell.

"When I came back from the hospital Ivy was waiting for me. She said she was going to tell everything about... about Catherine. About everything that I did back then. Look I shouldn't drag you into this, maybe I shouldn't have come here but I didn't want to be alone."

"No, Abby, it's okay. You're my best friend. You'll always be my best friend no matter what happens to us."

"You're a mother now. Your baby needs you. I shouldn't risk your life over this. I'm sorry I came here."

"Calm down a bit, all right?"

Neither said anything for a little while.

"It's my fault," Beverly said, "that we split ways. Ten years ago... ten years ago we almost died. And I was scared if I were too close to you that maybe you'd hurt me or I'd become possessed or—or something. I was scared. So I did what I thought was right and I pushed my best friend away. Could you ever forgive me?"

"Of course I forgave—I already forgave you without you having to ask."

"I wish I could take it all back. I'm sorry Abby."

"You shouldn't be the one who's sorry. I'm sorry. I'm sorry for being here now and making you part of this. And I'm sorry for everything I've ever done. Especially to Cat. Could Cat ever forgive me?"

"Yes. I believe she'd forgive you."

"What's the point of all this?"

"Huh?"

"Of everything we've been through. Everything I did. Everything that's happening with Ivy. It doesn't make any sense to me."

"Evil doesn't make sense. The demon only wants to hurt people. It doesn't have a plan."

"Yeah? Well that makes everything feel so hopeless, Bev. Do you have any stronger drinks?"

"No, I quit drinking ever since I was pregnant with Ruth."

"Ruth. That's a beautiful name."

"Ruth Catherine Hoffman. Ruth after my grandma, and Catherine after Cat."

"Hey Bev, can I ask you something?"

"Yeah?"

"How come you're a substitute teacher? What happened to your plan for a bakery?"

"My baby is a bastard. My parents cut me off. I'm the family disgrace. At least my sister still likes me."

"I'm so sorry Bev."

"It's okay. It's life. I'll get through it."

Abigail finished the cup of water and put it down on the table. "We can't fix things with just a wish. This feels different than what you and I went through. And I'd know that it would take more than just a wish because I've wished for a million things and none of them have come true."

"Did you make sure to throw a coin down the well?"

"Sometimes."

"I don't know what we can do for Ivy either, but maybe things don't have to be so hopeless and bleak."

They went to the kitchen and Beverly put a kettle of water on the stove. She and Abigail sat at the kitchen table as they waited for it to boil.

"How did you know Ivy was possessed?"

Beverly took a deep breath. "I didn't at first. At first I was hoping I could stop it before it begun. I thought the kids were only smoking pot up there or something. But after her friend Warren went missing... I had a really bad feeling about it."

"It's almost ironic."

"How do you mean?"

"When it was me, everybody saw everything I was up to. You and my parents and everybody knew that there was something wrong with me. With Ivy she was so under the radar that I was oblivious. I didn't keep an eye on her. But should I have? Did I make a mistake by—"

"You didn't make a mistake. You were doing what anyone would have done."

"Yeah. Anyone who didn't know better. Well here's what I know. Ivy went through my journals. She found Cat's poster and she knows what I did."

"What did you do, outline it all in a big confession?"

"She found all my journals. Including the one that used to belong to 'Helen.'"

"You kept that thing?"

"Yeah I did."

"Why on earth would you do that?"

"Well remember we couldn't burn it when we tried? I didn't know what to do with it so I kept it in a box."

"Well… you've got me there."

27

HAZEL WAS GLUED TO the TV that morning before school watching the report again of what had happened to Michelle while she was babysitting. She couldn't believe what she was hearing—she couldn't believe what her friend had been through.

Soon enough she had to get up from the couch to go to school. She grabbed her bookbag and headed out the front door. She paused in front of Michelle's house. Should she go up to it and knock? Should she check on Michelle's parents and see how they were holding up? God what an awful experience to live through, Hazel thought.

She decided not to. They needed space. Maybe in a few days she'd give them a call or stop by. She turned away and suddenly was called by a familiar voice—

"Hey kid."

"Michelle. You're—you're—"

"What's with that look on your face?"

"Well are you—are you… are you okay?"

"Yeah, why wouldn't I be?"

"Because of what I heard on the news… about that man and… you were babysitting and—and—and he—"

"Wanna see my scar?" Michelle said. She was in her pajamas and pulled back her long white sleeve to show Hazel before Hazel could give an answer to her question.

"Oh my God." Hazel reached for Michelle's sleeve and lowered it back over the stitches. "I can't believe… I mean I couldn't imagine… oh my God. Why aren't you still in the hospital?"

"All they had to do was patch me up. But yeah, it was worse for him than it was for me. You should have seen the look on his face when I hit him with the baseball bat."

"Uh…" Hazel looked into Michelle's eyes; they were darkening, in the process of turning from brown to black. They were hellish and looked as if they belonged to a stray bat that climbed out of hell rather than to the young girl who was telling her about a horrific incident.

"It really wasn't so bad. I almost didn't feel a thing."

Hazel wasn't sure what to say.

"Well I hope you have a good day at school. I'm not going, obviously, but I hate to miss. Hell you miss one day and it's like you missed an entire month, doesn't it feel that way sometimes? Care to catch me up on what I missed when you get back?"

Hazel's mind went completely blank. "Um, well, okay. Well I should get go—"

Michelle cut Hazel off by laughing really hard and put her arm tight around her. "Sorry, sorry. I was just thinking of something funny that happened."

"Um. Okay. Well I should get going was what I was saying. Like you said, you miss one day and it's like—"

"Hahahahahaha."

"Uh…"

"Sorry, it's just that those kids I was babysitting totally fell for it. After I killed the neighbor boy's father I went to his house and asked the kids to let me in, and they totally fell for it."

"What are you talking about?" Hazel squirmed under Michelle's arm that was still around her.

"Don't tell me you bought my little sob story I fed to the police. Get real."

Hazel pulled herself away from Michelle's touch. "You're sick."

"I killed those boys. It wasn't the father. Do you want to hear all the details."

"Get away from me."

Michelle laughed. "Whatever, kiddo."

Hazel was frozen for a moment, then she ran.

Looking back over her shoulder, Michelle was gone.

When she came to Ashfall High she saw that most students were still loitering outside. Everybody seemed to be happy; everybody was unaware of the demented horrors that were brewing in Ashfall—everybody but Hazel it seemed.

Some kids were going behind the building to smoke in private. Some were sitting down playing trading card games, and one player in particular was running after some cards that had been blown away by the wind.

She scanned the crowd of students for Arnie. No sign of him out here. She went inside. She went to the lockers and looked from end to end; she didn't know which was his or what his first class was. And with how worried she was right now, she couldn't even remember what her own first class was this morning. But she wasn't gonna go to it anyways.

Then over the speakers came an announcement: "Attention students of Ashfall High. We will be having an emergency assembly this morning…"

What is going on here?

Suddenly a couple police officers walked through the front doors of the school. They went down the hall that led to the gymnasium.

After a couple minutes longer of searching for Arnie she saw some of the cheerleaders in uniform crying uncontrollably. She approached them, opened her mouth to ask what was going on, but she decided against it.

Hazel went to the gymnasium and sat in one of the seats closest to the exit.

"God you look like you've seen a ghost." A hand touched her shoulder.

Hazel jumped a little. It was Arnie. She grabbed him by the. "We've gotta go."

"Go where?"

"Anywhere but here. I'll explain on the way. Let's go."

"Is this about… what happened? Did you know them?"

"What? Those little boys?"

"What little boys?"

"You didn't hear?"

"Apparently you didn't hear either. You know three of our classmates died."

"What? Who?" Hazel trembled. Instantly she thought about Ivy—did something happen to her?

"Bridgette, Beth, and Bailey. They were in a car accident. I guess Bridgette lost control of her car and it flipped over. But there's something strange about it all..."

"Let's talk somewhere else," Hazel said, seeing that the gymnasium was packing in tight with students already.

Arnie led her out of one of the gymnasium side doors and Hazel expected a teacher to see and come after them, but thank God nobody did.

"One of them wasn't in the car," Arnie said, "she was flung out of it. But through an open door. Like if they were driving with the door wide open. One of my friends has a dad who's a cop, he told him everything. I found out yesterday."

"Oh my God, that's terrible," Hazel said.

"What did you want to tell me? What boys were you talking about?"

"I don't know where to begin. Maybe I can't even explain everything Arnie. I need you to trust me and I need your help because I'm scared and I can't do any of this alone."

"Yeah? Well what is it?"

"You have to promise you won't tell anybody. Not your friends, not your parents, not the police."

"Okay. Sure. Tell me."

She pulled him by the hand further away from the school, taking him around the corner of the building where they'd be out of sight from any wandering eyes of any teachers or students. Somehow, Hazel still felt watched.

"I can't tell you unless you swear."

Arnie raised his right pinky finger. "I pinky promise."

Hazel wrapped her pinky around his. "Michelle killed these kids she was supposed to be babysitting," Hazel felt disgusted saying it. "She admitted the whole thing to me to me this morning. I really can't prove any of it but I know it's true. There's something wrong with her—and something wrong with Ivy too. I should've done something, I should—"

"Why can't we go to the police? Are you scared of Ivy and Michelle? Look I'll go with you if that's what's stopping—"

"Don't break your pinky promise."

"Hazel, why can't you go to the police about this?"

"Because it was Michelle but it wasn't Michelle. And Ivy, she…"

"Ivy what?"

"She's the one who… killed Warren."

"What the fuck?"

"They're possessed." Hazel peeked around the corner to make sure they were alone. "They… oh it's so much to explain Arnie. Let's go back to my place. We can figure out our plan from there."

"Our plan?"

"We've got to help them. It's… it's all my fault that this is happening."

They went to Hazel's home and up to her bedroom. She grabbed her shoebox from her closet then sat next to Arnie on her bed. Inside the box were crucifixes, little Holy Bibles, and a bottle of Holy Water she purchased from a church.

Then she slipped her purse off her shoulder and opened it, pulling out more crucifixes, Holy Bibles, and bottles of Holy Water. "I keep this stuff in my purse. You should always keep some with you too."

Arnie picked up the bottle of Holy Water and looked it over. "What are you gonna do? Dump this stuff on them?"

"I really don't know. I'm so scared, Arnie. I don't know how to help my friends. And I don't know what they're gonna do next. But we have to help them, we have to do something. I'm too damn scared to do it alone. So will you help me? Please Arnie, will you help me?"

"I'll help you," he said after a moment of hesitation. "And I have an idea."

28

THE JUNK YARD WAS Arnie's second home practically. Before the job at the gas station, he had spent some summers working here with his uncle under the table. Many nights he would search the mountains of garbage for treasures. Sometimes he'd come away with little unique treasures like a vintage metal piggy bank with a clown on it that could only be open by putting a certain number of dimes in; other times he'd come away with nothing. The coolest thing he had ever found was a Civil War era sword. Among his other finds were a cauldron, a set of strangely shaped keys, an axe head, and a purple stone.

It wasn't much of a junk yard in his opinion but a treasure yard; between the garbage were lost worlds awaiting discovery. He had heard of meteors found by metal detecting in deserts or woods; ancient treasures that had been unearthed by fortune hunters. Metal detecting was a way of joining the past and present together; a way of connecting forgotten times; the best way of bringing back things that had been lost and forgetting.

Whoever was on duty today must have been on lunch because Arnie and Hazel entered the gate unseen. He brought her to the far end of the junk yard where a charred jet ski was collecting dust near the gate. The shadow of a tall stack of garbage spread over it.

"I used to work here with my uncle," he said, "but half the time I'd sneak off and do my own thing. I'd look for treasure or I'd play a game or I'd burn stuff. That's kind of why I don't work here anymore. I burned this jet ski one time. It was an old piece of junk and it had been lying around for a couple years and my uncle didn't want it, so I pulled it down from the top of the heap and set fire to it. I love watching stuff burn."

"How could you work here so long with that stench?" Hazel plugged her nose. "Oh God."

"You get used to it."

"Ew. No. I couldn't get used to this place."

"No really, you get past it. This isn't even the worst I've seen this place smell."

Hazel said nothing.

"So I doused this thing in gasoline and struck a match. Once in a while when I've got a little time I still come down here to burn stuff. I even keep my kit down here." Arnie reached into the remains of the jet ski's hood and pulled up a dinged metal case. He set it down on one of the seats and opened it. Inside were matches, a bottle of gasoline, and several different lighters. "You've got your way of warding off demons, and I've got mine."

"Geez you're some sort of pyro?"

"What of it?"

"I don't know."

"You ever lit anything on fire?"

"No.""Give it a try." Arnie put a box of matches in her hands. "Pick out anything you want, it's all junk."

"Why did you bring me here?"

"To burn something. It helps clear your mind."

"I don't want to burn anything. We need to help Ivy and Michelle…. Oh we're just wasting time here. I should go."

"Wait a second, all right? We're gonna help, don't worry. This is just a way of… well it'll be easier to explain with a demonstration. This is gonna help us, trust me. So come on, let's pick something out. Here, I'll do it for you." Arnie reached into a pile of junk and pulled out an old toaster that was wedged inside a random flat wheel. "Go ahead, light 'er up. I'm starting you off with something small and manageable."

Hazel struck the match. "Just toss it in?"

"Hold up," Arnie said, then he reached for the gasoline in his metal box and poured some into the toaster. "Now go ahead."

Hazel tossed it in. The toaster was devoured in a sudden flare and she stepped back. Arnie stayed near it and grabbed a random stick from a pile of garbage; a long piece of wood sharp at one end like she imagined would be used to mount a sign in a front yard. He set the tip of the wood into the flames and it ignited. As he moved it around, Hazel wondered if it gave him splinters.

"If we had spare shirts with me I'd show you how to make a torch."

"I think I should go now, Arnie. This isn't helping. I should do this on my own. Forget everything I said please."

"Hey, hey, relax for a minute. Quit jumping to conclusions. You can't help your friends if you're being so uptight all the time. Clear your head for a minute. Here." Arnie reached into his pocket for a pack of Luckies. He lit one and handed it to her.

She took it. "Thanks."

Arnie lit one for himself. "You're welcome. So you ready to hear my plan?"

"Yeah."

"We burn it down." Arnie hit the burning wood against the old toaster. "No more house, no more demons."

"Can we do that?"

"Why not?"

"We'd get in trouble for burning down a house. Wouldn't we go to jail?"

"Let me hear a better idea."

Hazel paused. "Well I don't have one."

"Nobody owns that place. It's just collecting dust."

"How do you know nobody owns it?"

Arnie shrugged. "I don't. But who cares. Nobody's gonna miss it."

"We can't be foolish, Arnie. We need to have a plan that we know will work."

"Look, Hazel, all plans head south as soon as they're in motion. Nothing's guaranteed no matter how much planning you do. We'd throw the plan out the window as soon as we begin."

"That's not true."

"Goddamn you're impossible to reason with."

Hazel crossed her arms. "You jerk."

"Look, I'm not trying to be an asshole, I'm only offering you the advice that I think can help, and if you can't work with it, then disregard it, okay?" Arnie tapped the stick of wood on the toaster again.

"If that house is causing so much trouble why don't we just get rid of it?"

"How would we do it?"

"It doesn't take much for fire to spread. You know how much gasoline I put on that jet ski?"

"I don't know. A whole bottle?"

"Nope. Not a drop. I struck a couple matches and threw them in. The whole thing went up in flames in ten minutes. I was here with a couple buddies drinking, and we had placed bets to see how many matches it would take. I bet two matches. My buddies guessed anywhere from seven to a thousand matches. I put in two and that did the job. But we're talking about a house here, not this little jet ski. Well, if you want to rid yourself of demons I'd say we'd pour a bottle of gasoline each, toss in the matches, and make a run for it. That house is in a pretty bad location up on the hill, and I imagine it'll be hell for the fire department to get their trucks all the way up there to put it out. That gives it a lot of time to spread. It's already so far from town that nobody will notice for a while regardless. So I think we can do it rather quick. Arson's an easy job."

"You haven't done this before, have you?"

"What are you talking about?"

"Lighting a house on fire."

"What, me? Never." Arnie laughed a little. "Never, Hazel."

"I just... I don't know. What if this is the wrong choice."

"Then we can stand around doing nothing. Hazel I don't want to be mean to you, I actually... really like you. And I want to help you. But you came to me for help. So if you don't like what I've got to say, I don't know why you came to me in the first place."

"I'm scared, Arnie, you ass. Nothing sounds right right now."

"Okay. Just think on it. But I don't know how much time you've got."

When she finished her cigarette she tossed the butt into the toaster. "What else have you burned? Walk me through how this works."

"Well…" Arnie walked away. "Come with me."

Hazel followed him.

They came to a couch that was halfway sloped down a hill of trash. "Couches burn easier than anything since they're mostly wood, and fire spreads easy on fabric, especially this kind. The jet ski took two matches because there was still some gas left in the tank to be honest, that's how I won the bet with my friends. Now two matches could consume this couch sure but that could take hours. One drop of gasoline on this thing and that fire spreads in a matter of minutes with a single match."

"Okay. I think the ones in the house are just like these."

"Good, although I've never seen a fire-proof couch so it probably doesn't matter that much. Now let's see, once I burned up a car that had its engine and seats removed. There was still some material in the lining of the car that was flammable, but surprisingly it was contained within the car's body and didn't spread outside of it until I added gasoline."

"You just do this for fun?"

"Sometimes it had to be done as part of the job, back when my uncle had me throwing things into the incinerator. But the couch, the jet ski, the car, those were all for the fun of it after a few beers with the boys. Do you drink?"

"No I don't."

"Do you want to?"

"Hell I might need one. Can I have another cigarette?"

"Yeah, sure." Arnie gave her another Lucky. "So are you in?"

Hazel coughed on the cigarette smoke. "Let's do it."

"Now you're talking. Come on, let's get those drinks."

Arnie brought her to the office building; it was a small white building whose inside was cramped with a front desk—currently the 'ON BREAK—BE BACK SOON' sign was out—only two feet away from his uncle's office. One step to the left after entering in brought him and Hazel to the front door. The key was one of a dozen on his keychain.

"I never turned in my spares when he fired me. I told him I must have lost them."

"Do you break in here often?"

"It's not breaking in if I have a key."

"But those keys don't belong to you anymore."

"Yeah well I'm family. He wouldn't be mad I'm in here anyways, we're mooching some booze not forging checks. Unless you wanted to." Arnie opened a cabinet drawer that took some wiggling to pry loose. There was a checkbook inside. "How much do you want? His bank account is practically bottomless. You know how much money a junkyard brings in?"

"No. How much?"

"A lot. If my uncle has grandkids, they'll never have to lift a finger."

"Just put those checks down before we get in trouble."

"We aren't gonna get in trouble. Just relax."

The desk was cluttered with papers, notebooks, manuals, sticky notes, empty coffee cups, a couple boxes, and a typewriter, and on the corner was an ashtray where Hazel put out her cigarette.

"Hey, take that out of there," Arnie said, looking back to her from the mini fridge in the corner. "My uncle doesn't smoke Luckies, he smokes Victories, sometimes Kings. He'll know we were in here if you leave that behind. He's the one that got me hooked on Luckies so I wouldn't take his smokes. But you can always count on good ole Uncle Robert for a couple of Pabst Blue Ribbon."

"Whatever you say." Hazel picked it out of the ashtray. Then she cracked open her beer with the bottle opener that Arnie gave her from the other end of the desk. "Thanks Arnie."

"No problem."

"You kids got one for me too?"

A boy was in the doorway; Arnie recognized him as a jock from school. A guy on the basketball team who was about six feet tall with dark eyes and a fresh scar on his cheek. The boy was cracking his knuckles and leaning against the doorway.

"Steve? What are you doing here?" Hazel said.

"Aren't you happy to see me?"

"What happened to you?"

"Well, would you even believe it Hazel? I…" Steve laughed. "I found religion."

"Look dude, you gotta get out of here, all right?" Arnie said, stepping forward. "Get the hell out."

"Nah, I don't think I will."

"Who is this?" Arnie asked Hazel. "Your ex-boyfriend?"

"No Arnie it's nothing like that."

"Yeah," Steve said, "it's nothing like that. Hazel moved on pretty quick. What, she didn't tell you she had the hots for me since we were kids? Haha. Hey, Hazel, you know why your buddy here is so obsessed with burning things? It runs in his bloodline, half his family burned in an oven in Germany."

Arnie slammed his beer bottle on the edge of the desk then held up the jagged edges to Steve. "Get the fuck out of here or I'll kill you."

Steve laughed. "You and what army, dude?"

In a quick motion Arnie attempted to plunge the broken beer bottle into Steve's stomach, but Steve grabbed Arnie's wrist and twisted it backwards, causing Arnie to scream and drop the bottle.

"Oh, I am gonna have a lot of fun with you, Jewboy."

"Fuck you."

"Tough talk for somebody in your position. Your new boyfriend's got balls, Hazel."

"Hazel, get out of here."

"No, she's not going anywhere."

"Fuck you dude. Leave her alone."

"Arnie I'm so sorry," Hazel whispered.

"Oh, don't be sorry. Seriously." Michelle appeared in the doorway behind Steve. She squeezed past him into the room. "I got so worried about you Hazel, I mean, you were acting weird this morning so I told Steve we should keep an eye on you."

"Please don't hurt us," Hazel said. "You guys please let us go. We won't say a word of this to anybody."

Steve and Michelle looked at each other and exchanged smiles.

"I don't think so," Steve said. "Michelle, why don't you take care of Hazel for me?"

"Sure thing."

"Don't you dare touch her, you fucking bitch."

Michelle rolled her eyes. "Will you ever shut up, pal? Hazel I'm starting to question your taste in men."

By a sudden compulsion, Hazel wound her arm back then slapped Michelle across the face.

Michelle gasped then touched her cheek. "That wasn't very nice."

29

HAZEL COULDN'T OPEN HER eyes.

Then she realized she was in absolute darkness.

Chains jingled at her wrists and around her ankles when she woke up and jolted. Her hands were held up high. She tried to break free of the restraints with the little movements that they would allow.

Somebody else's hand found its way to her arm and curled around her chilled flesh. She gasped and backed away as best she could manage to free herself of the stranger's touch. The unseen person moved with her but the hand couldn't reach her again.

"Shhh, it'll be all right. It's me, it's Arnie."

"Arnie…" Hazel whispered.

"Are you hurt?"

"Nuh-no, I don't—I don't think so. Are you?"

"I'm okay."

"Oh my God… what's gonna happen to us?"

"We'll get out of here. I promise."

"I don't want to die."

"Nobody's going to hurt you as long as I'm here. Okay?"

Hazel nodded a little bit even though she was sure Arnie's vision was as nonexistent in this dark room as hers was. "Okay Arnie."

"One night," Arnie said, "I was in the shower and the power went out. Pitch black. I reached for my towel and accidentally knocked it over the railing in the shower. The way it slid against the outside of the curtain I thought for a split second that there was a person on the other side who was about to reach for me. I was so scared I punched the curtain with both of my fists, and a little soap slid down into my eyes. It stung like hell. After I got the soap out and calmed down I had a big laugh at how scared I was."

"Okay Arnie."

"I'm trying to cheer you up."

"Thank you."

"We've got to keep our spirits up. We won't get out of here feeling sorry for ourselves."

Hazel pulled on her chain. She tugged on it but there was no way it was gonna come loose.

"How come you're not mad?"

"What?"

"Arnie, you don't know me. I dragged you into this. You were nice to me at the gas station and I pushed you away until I needed help. I... I used you. Steve hurt you and it's my fault. Don't you hate me?"

"Do you want me to hate you?"

"What?"

"No, I don't hate you. You didn't use me, I wanted to help you."

"You don't get it."

"Stop beating yourself up. Not everything's like you think it is, not everything is your fault. None of my decisions had anything to do with you. Nor did Ivy's or Michelle's or anybody's."

Hazel said nothing.

"You're a good girl."

"Thank you."

"If I die at least I died next to a beauty like you."

"Oh shut up."

"I want to get to know you, Hazel. After this let's go out on a date. Anywhere you want."

"Do you think now's really the time to be asking me out?"

"If not now then when? I'm not gonna wait around for some other guy to sweep you off your feet. Hell no."

"Arnie you doofus. You are so sweet." Hazel stretched against the pull of the chains and reached over to give him a kiss. Arnie had to stretch against his chains to reach her too. It took a lot of effort and their lips hardly met. It was more of a brushing against each other than a kiss, but under the circumstances it was the best she could give him.

After she pulled away, Arnie said, "I wish we met earlier, Hazel."

"Yeah me too. I wish we did too."

They were in silence for a little while. Hazel wondered what was happening; wondered what Steve and Michelle would do to them. She wondered where Ivy was. She thought of the terrors of this house and how they had corrupted all her friends; were she and Arnie next? Was the house going to overtake them too? Would she cease to be Hazel and become something else?

"I think these chains might be faulty. I think maybe they grabbed them from the junkyard. We might be able to pry them open."

"Do you think they're trying to escape yet?" Michelle's voice was outside the door.

"Well I did a good job locking them in if I do say so myself. There ain't a snowball's chance in hell they can get free," Steve said.

Suddenly a door at Hazel's left opened up and two flashlights shined in. She squinted as the beams crossed her face. From the vague illumination it gave, she saw that the room was empty. Then Steve went across the room and pulled a curtain back; a little moonlight seeped into the big room.

Hazel glanced at Arnie; he was looking back at her with sullen eyes.

"What are you gonna do to us?" Hazel blurted out.

"Well," Michelle said, "we've got a little game we want to play. Don't we, Stevie?"

Steve put an arm around Michelle and pulled her in for a kiss. Then he reached into his pocket and brought out a pocketknife. He pressed a button and the spring pushed the blade up. "This one's a fun one. You two kids are gonna love it."

An uncontrollable scream passed from Hazel's lips.

Steve stepped closer and her screams kept slipping through.

Then Ivy walked in and put her hands on her hips. "Did you two start without me?"

"No, no," Michelle said, "we were only giving them an introduction. Care to tell our guests the rules of this little game?"

Ivy faced Hazel and Arnie. "Hazel, God, I've missed you. Who's this guy?"

"This is Arnie, please don't hurt him. Let us go."

"Hmm… how about we play a game first and maybe I let him go if you win?"

"Ivy please don't do this. I know you don't want to hurt us. You've got to fight it."

"Is that what you think? Well then you're an idiot. Maybe I'm doing this because I like it. Why would somebody need to hold me against my will for me to act this way? Hazel, I *want* to hurt you."

"Shut up," Arnie said.

"Where'd you find this guy? Behind a dumpster or something? He reeks. Actually, don't answer that. Let's proceed with our game, shall we?"

Hazel gulped.

"It'll be okay," Arnie whispered. "I won't let them touch you."

"How you plan to stop us, buddy?" Steve said then kicked Arnie in the side. Then he pressed his pocket knife to Arnie's cheek. "I read a book once where this guy was stranded on an island and had to keep cutting off pieces of his flesh to eat to survive. I know this knife isn't too sharp anymore, but I'd like to test out that same idea. How many pieces can I cut off before you die?"

"Stop it I'm begging you." Hazel cried. Her vision blurred from her tears. *"Oh God let us go."*

"You won't be cutting him up," Ivy said. "Well, not yet. Steve, give me the knife please."

Steve put it into her extended hand. "Here you go."

"Great. Now listen," Ivy held the knife up for Hazel and Arnie to see, "I've marked off this knife a quarter inch from the point. Michelle and Steve are gonna stab each of you little by little to see who can survive the longest. We've worked out the kinks a few times with some stray cats we found. The game's pretty fun."

"Yeah." Steve suddenly extended a dead cat in his hands. It must have been in the far corner of the room. "This one died from a one inch stab. Another one survived after taking a whole three inches but it walks with a limp in two legs. It's like a box of chocolates," he laughed, "you never know what you're gonna get."

"I call dibs on Hazel," Michelle said.

"Hey no problem," Steve said, "I been wanting to stick a knife in Jewboy since I first seen him. Since you called dibs I get to go first."

Ivy gave him back the knife. "Let the games begin."

Hazel was shaking; the flashlights were pointed to Arnie. Arnie was struggling to break loose but Steve kneeled and smacked him, then he raised the knife in front of Arnie's face and Arnie was petrified with fear. Steve cut Arnie's shirt down the middle then moved the flaps aside and buried the tip of his knife into Arnie's stomach.

"See, that wasn't so bad, champ. Your turn, Michelle. Get 'er done."

"With pleasure." Michelle smiled grabbing the knife from Steve's hands.

A sudden scream left Hazel's lips.

"Don't scream, that only makes it worse. I think."

"Don't do this please don't do this."

"Leave her alone you sick bastards."

"Where are your manners, Jewboy?" Steve smacked Arnie. "Show the lady a little respect, you got me?"

Arnie said nothing.

Michelle dragged the tip of the knife along Hazel's forearm, leaving behind a trail of long scratches. In that moment she knew she was a dead girl; there was nothing she could do but sit there and take the pain. There was no getting out of this alive. She hoped it would be quick. She didn't want to suffer.

"Kill me already."

"Where's the fun in that? Stop trying to ruin our game. The cats don't even squirm as much as you do."

The point sank into Hazel's left forearm; icy pain turned into a blaze as it pulsed through her tired body. She held in her scream and shut her eyes. Michelle pulled the knife out then poked Hazel in the eyes.

"Open 'em. I want you to watch." Michelle grabbed Hazel's face and turned it toward Arnie. Steve had the knife now.

"Where do you want it, Kike?"

"Up your ass."

Steve was about to stab Arnie again when Michelle stopped him. "I dare you to go half an inch this time."

"Hey, that's not much of a dare, I was gonna do it anyways. Let's see which one of them can take it deeper in the arm." Steve put it in Arnie's left arm; Arnie gasped at the initial pain. "See? It's not so bad, is it? Now a little more."

As Steve dug the knife deeper, a mist of blood squirted out into his face. Arnie let out a piercing scream.

Steve pulled the knife out. Arnie was breathing heavy, letting out gasps.

"You took that like a champ, bud."

"Hurry up, you're having all the fun." Michelle snatched the knife.

"I bet you couldn't stab her as deep as I did. Chicks don't have the stomach for it."

"Oh yeah, wanna bet? What do I get if you win?"

"I'll give you whatever you want if you win. If I win you give me an hour in the next room."

"Ha, like you really need a bet to get that from me, Stevie."

"Well I couldn't place a bet on nothing else, there's nothing else you could give me."

"Whatever." Michelle rolled her eyes. "Now where were we, Hazel?"

"Please. Oh God please don't..."

"How many times do you have to beg before you realize that saying 'please' won't always get you what you want? We're gonna do this no matter how much you beg or scream. So suck it up, buttercup."

Hazel didn't know what to say. She glanced over at Arnie. He was cringing from the pain. Blood was still dripping from his forearm.

"I apologize in advance for this one. It's gonna sting."

Hazel tried to turn away from Michelle and squirmed but there was no facing away from the demon that had overtaken her former friend. Michelle was enjoying every moment of Hazel's fright and struggle.

Michelle was on top of Hazel and giggling. She put the point of the knife against Hazel's breast.

"Oh this is gonna be fun."

The tip of the knife disappeared beneath Hazel's skin; even worse pain than what she felt in her forearm reverberated into her body. Suddenly the room was too hot and she couldn't breathe. There was an air of finality wrapping around her; her heart was beating fast and she was gasping for breath. This was death; she was never going to see her family again, she was never going to get out of here, her best friends were going to kill her.

She had already been crying, but more tears fell. Everything in her vision was a blob.

The knife traveled further down.

"Kill me just kill me already get it over with."

"You know, begging won't help you but I kinda like it. Keep it up, it might score you some points."

"Kill me…" Hazel wept. *"Kill me…"*

Michelle pulled the knife out of Hazel in a quick motion; stinging steely pain flashed through her flesh. The pain was worse than anything Hazel had ever felt before; her torn flesh kept pulsing, kept burning, kept aching, and it was still so difficult to breathe.

"Calm down a little." Ivy wiped away some of Hazel's tears. "It will all be over soon. You don't want to spend the end of your life crying all day, do you? Huh?"

"Nuh-no."

"Good girl."

"Why are you doing this?"

"You're really asking me this?"

"Ivy what happened to you? How could you do this to me?"

"Things are better this way. It's nothing personal, Hazel, so please understand. I only do what my master wants."

Hazel was startled by Arnie's sudden scream; Steve had stabbed him again, this time in his shoulder. She noticed he was having a hard time breathing too. And his eyes were shutting. He hung his head.

"Stay with me, champ." Steve smacked him a little. "Come on buddy. Don't die on me yet. We were only getting started. Goddamn even the doggies didn't die that fast."

"Arnie. Arnie oh no."

"Relax, you hardly knew him," Ivy said.

"Yeah, Ivy's right," Michelle said, "you shouldn't cry over some random boy. I mean, did you even sleep with him yet?"

"Hey, I don't think he's dead, ladies." Steve felt for Arnie's pulse. "Yeah, he's still got a little life left in him. Game's not over yet. You're gonna owe me bigtime, sweet cheeks."

Michelle had the knife back and was kneeling over Hazel again. She turned the knife the opposite angle and pressed it back into the wound on Hazel's breast. "X marks the spot."

Hazel writhed and screamed. She banged her head into the wall. *"Make it stop make it stop make it stop make it stop."*

"Guys hold her still."

Ivy grabbed Hazel's face and kept her steady, stopping her from banging her head again.

"She's a fighter, isn't she?" Michelle said. "Oh Hazel, there's no point in hurting yourself, honey. We're gonna do that for you."

Hazel cried again.

Her head was heavy. Warmth was pumping out of her wound and staining her shirt. She glanced at Arnie; it was hard to tell anything through her blurry vision. Was he breathing? Was he alive? She didn't know. And she didn't know how long she could hold onto her own consciousness.

Her vision was darkening.

"I think that's the end of round one," Ivy said, letting go of Hazel then standing up. "I've got something else we can do until then. Something I was reading in one of the books up here."

"Oh yeah? What's that?" Michelle asked.

"A little ritual. It involves a baby. And I know where we can get one."

As Ivy, Michelle, and Steve exited the room, Hazel's vision completely faded to black.

30

Alvin Bloch met with his new friends Billy and Edmund at their headquarters—the abandoned cabin behind the Engstrom family cemetery in the woods—bright and early. Each boy was holding a burlap sack in their hands.

"Did you guys bring everything?"

"I think so," Billy said, reaching into his bag. "Father's flashlight. Check. Some spare rope from the shed. Check."

Edmund retrieved his own flashlight from his bag. "And I've got mine. And I've got a knife."

"My flashlight's in the basement, as well as a hammer for protection. Waitasecond, Edmund, aren't you forgetting something?"

"Oh right."

"What's he missing?" Billy asked.

"I gave Edmund special instructions during our last meeting."

"Here you go, Alvin." Edmund handed him a box of Cracker Jack, then gave one to Billy. "We'll need nourishment."

"Come on, Honus Wagner." Alvin tore his box open. "I swear to God Billy if you get a third Honus... oh sweet—Ty Cobb!"

"I'll open mine later." Billy tossed it into his bag. "I'm not hungry."

"No, open it now. Come on."

"It's just a baseball card, it can wait."

"No it can't wait. I need a Honus Wagner."

"Let's just get going, guys," Edmund said.

They went over the plan one more time then left the cabin and went back through the woods. Alvin opened the back door, checked that nobody in his family was around, then let in his friends. Quickly the boys snuck into the basement.

"I swear to God, nobody deserves a third Honus Wagner. If you pull it you gotta trade me."

"All right! Enough with Honus Wagner already. You're freaking me out."

"This is the room," Alvin said and opened the door.

They gathered around the strange door that the man from Animal Control had revealed; each boy shined a flashlight inside and saw nothing within. Alvin clutched his hammer tight. Edmund's knife was ready. Billy's rope was in his hands. They were ready for whatever they might face, whether it was Samuel or Abraham Lincoln or anyone else who might be hiding.

Alvin went through first. Then Billy. Then Edmund behind him. It was a strange world they were entering; a place that Alvin felt should not exist. He had no idea such an irregular structure existed within the walls. Who had designed this? What was its purpose? Where did it lead? His mind was swarmed with questions.

"Which way?" Edmund asked.

"Left," Alvin said, choosing randomly.

"And you say you've never been in here before?"

"We didn't know this door was here until that man found it. Nobody's been inside since."

Deeper into stygian darkness; deeper into the unknown. The last people to travel in these ancient passageways must have all been dead, Alvin thought. Spiderwebs clung tightly to the corners. The boys cast their flashlights into the maddeningly endless path ahead of them. The tunnel curved. There were other passages and tunnels where they could have deviated into, but they kept going straight.

"How far do you think these go?" Billy asked. "Will we come out on the other side of the world?"

"Do you guys know which way we came from?" Edmond halted. "I don't want to get lost."

"We've been walking in a straight line," Alvin said. "We won't get lost."

"Maybe we shouldn't be doing this."

"Do you want to find your friend or not?"

"He isn't alive anymore. Nobody can survive down here. We were wrong to do this."

"Then who did he hear all those times we snuck in?"

"Billy you're stupid."

"Guys quit fighting with each other." Alvin stepped between them. "Knock it off. You had your chances to get out of this, but we're here now and we're gonna find Samuel or Abraham Lincoln or whoever is here."

"Okay…" Edmund walked along with them.

Their pathway twisted some more. Alvin wondered if anyone had ever hidden down here and gotten lost or stuck and never found their way out. Obviously it had happened to the family dog, and it must have happened to Billy and Edmund's friend Samuel, but had it happened before? Again he wondered what the purpose of a hidden structure like this was… and where exactly it was built to lead to. Just how spacious was the inside of the house's walls?

Alvin was lost in thought when he accidentally stumbled down a step and lost balance; instinctively Edmund caught him by the arm and pulled him away, stopping him from plummeting down the earthen stairway but causing him and Edmund to fall over into mountains of dust. The boys coughed and sneezed. Billy helped them up. Then they all turned their flashlights to the stairs. At the bottom was an entryway further into the unknown. Their flashlights couldn't penetrate the dense darkness that slithered upwards.

"No way guys, I'm backing out. I'm not going down there."

"Edmund. Thank you for saving me from a snapped neck. But we must go down there."

"Why 'must' we?"

Billy put a hand on Edmund's shoulder. "I don't know how you can be this confused. We owe it to Samuel."

"Don't chicken out," Alvin said. Then he added quickly, "Fine, go back. But you're walking through the dark all alone. You sure you know the way?"

"Yeah I do. It's a straight line, just like you said."

"See ya." Billy stepped down.

"We'll be back soon." Alvin followed.

"Guys wait for me."

They went down the soft steps that shifted under their feet. They passed through the threshold and into a decrepit bunker. There were blankets in the corner of the room that had deteriorated over the years. Bugs crawled in them and scattered back into darkness when the boys shined their flashlights over them. On the other side of the room were tin cans. A pile of antiquarian books. While Billy went around the room revealing more details with his flashlight, Edmund stuck close behind Alvin who went to the stack of books. He picked up the top book—a blank leather cover that was worn and cracked—and turned it open.

Edmund pointed his flashlights at the pages. There were graphic mutilations illustrated on the pages. Bodies torn open and used for rituals. Smoke uprose from candles drawn in the pictures and turned into devils watching from above the hideous acts.

Alvin shut the book and set it back down. Edmund was shaking. Billy shined his light around the room revealing broken glass in another corner of the room. Alvin went nearer to him. Something cracked and broke under Alvin's step.

It was an upside down crucifix. Alvin accidentally had snapped it in half.

"Your dog's not here. Neither is Samuel. I don't know what happened to either one of them but I don't want to stick around this place."

"I don't get it, what exactly is this room?" Alvin said.

"Look." Billy was facing a section of wall behind Alvin.

Alvin and Edmund turned their attention over toward it. Painted in red was a pentagram on the wall with strange symbols within it.

Goosebumps rose on Alvin's flesh. "Oh my God."

"Look up there," Edmund said.

In a high corner of the room was a miniature tunnel, probably only big enough for rats to travel through. A rope was dangling from it.

"I wonder what happens if we pull it." Alvin grabbed it in his hands.

"No, no, come on, let's go," Edmund said. "We've seen enough. I'm not pulling anything. I'm not touching anything. And I'd advise you to do the same, Alvin."

"It's my house, I can do what I want."

"Okay I'm getting out of here. I should have left in the first place."

Edmund was walking out of the room back to the stairway while Alvin pulled the rope. It came completely out of the little hole in the wall and did nothing. Alvin held up the other end under his flashlight to examine it. It looked as though it had been bitten by mice.

Then there was a screeching from within the walls.

Edmund paused in the threshold and all the boys exchanged nervous looks. The screeching stopped then started abruptly again. Alvin and Billy aimed their lights up at the small hole then a rat came charging out of it. Something was attached to its back; something indistinct at first as it moved its claws swiftly to run into darkness, and their flashlights could never keep up with it.

When the rat paused momentarily and their flashlights found it again, it was clear that it was one of Jeanette's dolls on its back. The doll lifted its arm and pointed. The rat followed its command and charged at Alvin.

Alvin thought that this was a dream, because filthy hidden bunkers and animated dolls riding on the backs of rats only existed in dreams. But he couldn't wake up. Panic tightened around his heart and squeezed tight. He and Billy ran behind Edmund. The rat was coming quickly behind them, scurrying up a wall and charging straight forward and suddenly it was invisible in the suffocating darkness. Alvin was only able to detect it by its squeaks.

He stepped backwards, anticipating its jump. Suddenly he was aware that he had still been holding the hammer that he had brought down here with him; and Billy had his rope, and Edmund had his knife. If the creatures came near enough then they could probably fight it.

The three boys, as if they were all attached to one mind and moving of its accord, directed their flashlights to the clicking sound that the rat made. Its jaws were snapping. Its black tongue licked its lips. Its eyes were bloodshot. The doll on its back curled its hands into fists.

Alvin gulped.

The rat charged.

Alvin stepped out of the way and Billy ran between him and the rat and kicked it away. The rat skidded on its side and became separated from the doll. The doll was running back to the rat's side when Billy picked it up; the doll struggled in his grasp. Alvin dropped to his knees with the hammer, ignoring the pain he felt from the hard floor, and slammed it with both hands at the rat. The rat jumped onto Alvin and its claws pressed into his skin, drawing out blood.

It raced along his arm to his back. Alvin slammed himself into the floor until the rat broke loose with a screech. It ran away somewhere and he didn't know exactly where. He was pointing his flashlight in every direction searching for it until Billy and Edmund caught his eye. The doll was in Billy's long thick hair pulling it up by the roots. Edmund was trying to help him pry it free but failing.

And above them, in another little hole, were more of Jeanette's dolls. The three remaining members of the doll family.

Finally Edmund pried the doll loose and threw it down. He stomped on it, crushing it, and the boys were running away again, leaving behind all the horrors of the underworld. Alvin glimpsed furtively over his shoulder; he couldn't see anything in the dark.

TAP! TAP! TAP!

CLICK! CLICK! CLICK!

The rat's disgusting noise it made with its sharp teeth ready to snap into flesh. Where was it? Alvin was ready to kill it.

CLICK! CLICK! CLICK!

Billy must have heard it too because his flashlight also fell over the creature. It was on the wall of the strange structures at eye-level to Alvin. It hissed and was ready to jump the one-foot distance between it and Alvin. Alvin, with a rush of adrenaline, slammed his hammer on the rat's face.

CRACK!

Brains spilled out with blood. The creature still hissed and wobbled and fell to the floor. It landed on its back, writhing, and in pure curiosity Alvin stood to watch it, completely forgetting about the other dolls that had ascended into the current madness and might bring reinforcements. Then the rat turned onto its feet and raced to Alvin angrily with continual hisses.

Edmund plunged his knife into the rat, pinning it to the ground. It screeched and clawed Edmund with its hind legs causing Edmund to let go, and the rat moved again freely with the knife still lodged in its back.

Was the creature indestructible?

It climbed up the wall and while it was still low, Alvin swung his hammer again, crushing its head from behind. The creature sank lifelessly to the floor and curled up. Its blood was everywhere—all over the walls, all over the boys, all over their clothes. Edmund pulled his knife out of the rat and wiped the blade on his pants.

TAP! TAP! TAP!

Their beams of light merged again on the enemy.

The remaining dolls were each riding on the backs of their own rats.

The boys ran—Alvin was so tired of all the running—and wondered how far they were from the door. It felt as though they should have been there already. Had the door been sealed back up? Was there any way out of here?

Somewhere along the run he noticed that the tapping sound of the running rats had disappeared. They probably had miniature tunnels throughout all the walls and inner structures. The rats could be taking Jeanette's dolls anywhere they wanted to go. It could have brought them through a shortcut to the door Alvin and the boys were currently racing to and sealed it off.

We're going to die here, Alvin thought. *There's no way out.*

Then he saw it. The door up ahead on his right. It was shut but he noticed it under the brush of his light.

He fumbled with his flashlight and hammer to free up one hand and dropped them both as he grabbed the knob. It was locked.

Then the rats descended against the doorway. Alvin and his friends bolted for the other direction and traveled yet again into this unknown world; into this archaic chamber of horrors.

All of Alvin's joints hurt and he felt new bursts of pain with every step. It had taken a lot to kill one vicious rat—what would it take to kill three? Killing just one required him to have total accuracy with his hammer, and to have Edmund's assistance. What if the next time he faced one of those rats he missed? What if he had to fight two at the same time? His mind raced with awful scenarios and he saw himself lost, separated from his friends, facing all the dolls and rats alone with just his hammer and his flashlight. In his mind he saw the rats chewing his flesh, burrowing inside his torso, tunneling in and out like they tunneled through these walls. Alvin was completely stricken with terror.

RUFF! RUFF! RUFF!

Abraham Lincoln was nearby. Maybe he could help.

The boys turned with the pathway and eventually made a hard left when the walls curved. They stepped in something sticky, but there was no time to stop and examine what was on the floor. They kept running and the scurrying of hungry savage rats followed; along with them was the hushed whisper of the dolls.

There were many tunnels and passageways the boys could have chosen; Alvin turned a sudden corner on his right and said, "This way."

Edmund and Billy followed him.

The boys halted and caught their breath.

"We've got to fight them," Alvin said. "We can't run forever."

"Billy, Edmund, help me."

Somebody else was with them.

Nervously Alvin slid his beam of light across the narrow passageway and illuminated the boy at the other end. He was on his stomach with a hand extended. His face was torn and bloody.

"Help me."

Billy hurried to his friend's side. "Samuel, my God, what happened to you?"

"Billy... please... help..."

"Oh my God."

"What are you doing?" Edmund took one step closer. Terror lingered on his face. *"That isn't Samuel."*

"We've got to get him out of here." Billy was helping Samuel up. "Come on, that's it, I got you. Let's go."

"I..." Samuel whispered.

"Yeah?" Billy said.

"I am the rat king." Samuel opened his mouth inhumanely wide and a rat sprang from his jaws and jammed its claws into Billy's face.

Samuel laughed wickedly as the rat tore Billy's face apart, and there was nothing Alvin and Edmund could do but turn the corner and run back to the main pathway where they had been chased by the other rats; but where had those rats gone now? There was no sign of them.

Alvin and Edmund kept moving through the unknown, attempting to escape from the monster that was Samuel. Billy's scream made the boys shudder, and neither Alvin nor Edmund dared peek over their shoulders; they were running faster than they ever had in their lives, retracing their steps through these tunnels back to the doorway they had entered from.

TAP! TAP! TAP!

RUFF! RUFF! RUFF!

CLICK! CLICK! CLICK!

Who else was lurking in this dungeon of impossibilities waiting for them? If he found Abraham Lincoln, would it even still be him? No,

Alvin thought, Abraham Lincoln was dead. And it was foolish to come in here after him, and to come in here after Samuel. He should have left it all alone. He shouldn't have intervened.

The rats were ahead of them. Three rats with three riders. The rats licked their lips then attacked. Two of the rats ran up either wall; one rat was coming straight at them on the ground so Alvin went to kick it and missed horribly, throwing himself off balance and falling on his butt. The rat crawled up to Alvin's face and stared at him deeply; Alvin had dropped his flashlight and it was angled to illuminate the rat's sickly face. It was smiling.

And it wanted payback for its fallen brother.

It raised its claws to bring them down on Alvin's face; Alvin attempted to duck but it scratched his cheek and dug its claws deep into his flesh.

Warm blood trickled down.

Alvin fumbled for his hammer and lost it in the blanket of darkness; that same rat and one of its brothers were clawing at Alvin on his back. Suddenly Alvin's previous vision of terror snuck into his mind again; the rats chewing up his flesh, ripping him apart, burrowing into his stomach and crawling out through a straight tunnel up his throat and out of his mouth.

Alvin stood, wobbled, ignored the pain as much as he could, slamming himself into the wall to get them to break away from him. It didn't work and he let out painful screams; they were biting him, scratching him, and he was blinded by the thick shadows in this unholy place.

Somewhere nearby Edmund was screaming as well; Alvin couldn't see what was happening with him, he was too focused on his own attackers.

Alvin dropped to his knees and all of a sudden somebody was lifting his shirt off of him, taking the rats with them. Through the dense darkness his eyes adjusted to see Edmund holding the two rats prisoner in Alvin's shirt, but their claws were already breaking free of the shirt's barrier—it wouldn't last long. Alvin scrambled for his flashlight, pointed it around until he saw his hammer, then rejoined Edmund.

Edmund held the shirt down on the floor. Alvin brought his hammer down on it repeatedly. He lifted it above his head in both hands and brought it down. Blood leaked through the holes, and the rats were clearly dead, but Alvin couldn't stop himself. He beat the dead bodies of the rats until they were pulp. Eventually Edmund pried the hammer loose from Alvin's hands.

There was still something Alvin wanted to know: where were the dolls?

"Billy," Alvin said, "it's my fault."

Edmund wiped his tears. "It should have been me."

Alvin wiped sweat from his forehead with the back of his hand. It was mixed with blood.

They went back to the doorway. It was still locked. There was no opening it from in here, so with the final strength left in his body, Alvin struck the doorknob with the hammer.

They left Alvin's house for the base of the hill.

"I'm so sorry," Alvin said. And he was. For everything. For Billy being killed. For Edmund's scars from the rats. For putting his new friends in this situation. For putting their lives at risk.

Edmund gave him a hug.

Tears dripped from their eyes.

Back in his home, Alvin had to get to work. The dolls were still out there.

He washed off from the blood and scratches. He put on a new outfit. Then he looked for Jeanette. He had a good guess where she was—up in the attic with the toys. That room had become her favorite place in the house, and she often spent more time there than in her own bedroom.

Carefully and slowly Alvin climbed up the steps. He peeked over the edge of the floor and saw her with the dollhouse open. She was moving her dolls around and talking to them, whispering, laughing, and completely unaware that Alvin was there. The dolls did not move on their own like they had done in the walls.

Alvin wondered how much Jeanette knew.

His hands curled into fists. He wanted to get her away from the dolls. Wanted to keep her safe. She was moments from death any time she picked up one of those living abominations. Nobody in their house was safe from them unless he burned them up and got rid of them.

And what did they want? Suddenly he was dumbfounded. What *did* those little dolls want? Why had they attacked? What was their nature? Whose control were they under? How could pieces of wood glued together have minds, have brains, have feelings and emotions and goals? It was all so unnatural and strange.

"Jeanette," he said, uncertain how he was going to follow it up.

"Oh hi Alvin." Jeanette kept moving her dolls around, playing with them, straightening out their shirts, and incorporating other toys into her games. "Do you want to play house with me?"

Alvin climbed into the attic. "No. We have to get rid of your dolls."

"Huh?"

"Put them down and come here."

"Is this a new game? What is it?"

"No this is not a game. You're in danger. You don't know what they're capable of."

Jeanette raised one of the dolls to her ear. It had a purple shirt. Jeanette laughed. "Miss Penelope doesn't like you."

"Put 'Miss Penelope' down."

"But she's my friend."

"Listen to me right now. Put her down and get out of—"

"Hold on, she's saying something." Jeanette lifted her doll to her ear again. *"She doesn't like this game either. She said you really want to hurt her."*

"Jeanette for the love of God drop the—"

"Don't hurt my dolls."

"I'm not hurting your dolls, they're gonna hurt you."

"No they won't."

"Yes they will."

"Leave me alone," Jeanette said. Then another whisper from her doll. And Jeanette said, "Miss Penelope says sorry about your friend."

"What else has she told you?"

"Miss Penelope tells me all of her secrets. She's my best friend in the world."

Somebody was coming up the steps into the attic.

"Why are you two screaming?"

It was Father.

Alvin grabbed Father's arm. "Jeanette's dolls are alive. She won't listen to me. Please Father, they're—"

Before Alvin could finish or before Father could reply, Jeanette said, "Alvin won't leave me alone, tell him to go away. Miss Penelope doesn't like him. Alvin wants to hurt her and her family."

"Come on, Alvin." Father grabbed him by the hand. "Leave Jeanette alone."

"But Dad…"

"Yes?"

Alvin hung his head. What was the point in arguing? "Never mind."

Father went down first, then Alvin followed him. Alvin went back to his bedroom, where on his bed he found a bloody box of Cracker Jack. It had been chewed up by rats. The crumbs of popcorn dusted his covers. Then he noticed the Honus Wagner trading card that had been the prize in this box. It was ripped in half, and a corner was torn with big teeth marks.

So Billy had gotten a third Honus Wagner after all.

31

Night was falling.

Ivy went to check on Hazel and Arnie one more time before she left the house. Michelle and Steve were still keeping watch over them, taunting them, torturing them.

"You two only have about one minute to make up your mind," Ivy said, then she sat between the two prisoners. "Hazel, you're my best friend. I want you to join us. My life would feel so... incomplete without you here with us. Do you really think your own death would be so much better than what we have to offer?"

Hazel sobbed. *"I don't know."*

Ivy ran her hand through Hazel's hair. "I love you Hazel. I think you should consider our offer before it's too late."

Michelle wiped away Hazel's tears from her cheek using the blade. "Quit crying, I'm not gonna hurt you as long as you accept. Let the master into your heart. Let him get inside you."

"Yeah," Steve said, "that's always been easy for you Michelle."

"Can I borrow that knife?"

"Sure." Michelle gave it to Ivy.

Ivy stuck the tip of it under Hazel's chin. "Well, time's up. So I need a yes or a no. Okay? I'd hate to spend the rest of my life separated from my best friend."

"What…" Hazel choked trying to speak. "What… do I have to do?"

Ivy smiled and lowered the knife. "We've got a little initiation we want to put you through to prove yourself. So… you and Arnie wait right here and we'll be right back. We have to get things ready for your big day."

Hazel and Arnie were left alone in the room again.

She was covered in her dried blood, and the room was getting colder by the second, and her arms screamed with hot numbing pain; they had been raised for so long that she had lost any feeling in them besides searing agony.

Arnie didn't look any better. He had lost a lot of blood too and was breathing heavily.

"Are you really going to do it?" He asked.

"What choice do I have?"

"I don't know."

"Arnie, listen, I don't have to go through with it. I just have to comply," she whispered, "I just have to do what it takes to get out of these restraints so we can make a run for it."

"If it comes down to it, I want you to leave without me."

"What?"

"If you have the opportunity to leave, even if I have to get left behind, I want you to run. I want you to go get the police. It doesn't matter if I'm left here. Don't do anything stupid. Don't choose between me and your freedom."

"Arnie I'd never leave here without you. I'm the reason you're here. You didn't deserve this. They were never after you."

"Just listen to me, all right?"

Hazel said nothing.

Arnie tugged on his restraints again as he had done a few times since they had been here. "It's loose. I can feel it. These throwaways from the junkyard, they aren't that tough. Keep trying and maybe we'll get free."

Ivy and Michelle arrived at Beverly's house. Night was falling faster. There was a little glow coming from a couple of the house's windows; Ivy peeked in for a glimpse of Beverly, but Beverly wasn't in the sitting room.

Ivy tried the front door; when that was locked, she and Michelle went to the side door but it was locked as well. The girls crept around to the side of the house and pushed the window up; it slid open and Ivy climbed in, then she helped Michelle come through.

It was a room with bright white walls, a dresser with some diapers and paper towels on top of it, and in the center of the room Beverly's baby was asleep in her crib. She was lying on her stomach covered in a pink blanket with giraffes on it.

THE CURSE OF ENGSTROM HOUSE

"Where's Beverly?" Ivy whispered.

Michelle shrugged. "How should I know?"

"You stay here with the baby. I'll check it out."

Ivy tiptoed through the small home, moving so lightly on her feet that the old wooden boards that made up the floor made no noise. The bathroom door was open and Beverly was inside turning the shower on. Ivy quickly darted out of sight; Beverly hadn't noticed her. Ivy stayed put for a while until she heard the water running and heard the clang of the metal loops connecting the shower curtain to the rod. Then she went past the open bathroom door and into the kitchen.

She grabbed the biggest knife from the wooden block on the countertop then lightly touched the blade with her fingertips to test the sharpness. Nearby at the kitchen table, Beverly's pet cat was asleep. A black cat with speckles of white. Ivy had an idea.

"Here kitty kitty kitty." Ivy petted its head.

Slowly it was awakened from Ivy's touch. Its eyes opened. The cat remained still and calm as Ivy picked it up, then suddenly it let out an angry hiss.

"Don't be afraid, kitty."

Beverly rinsed her hair under the stream of hot water, clearing her mind, when she heard her pet cat Smudge squeal wickedly. Her eyes opened and she felt somebody was in the room with her; Beverly lingered under the waterfall for a moment, absolutely certain that somebody was about to grab her. Then she turned her head slightly and nervously raised her hand to the shower curtain. She pulled it back to find the bathroom was empty.

She stepped out of the tub and wrapped a towel around herself. She stopped with terror in the bathroom doorway. Smudge's body was cut in half. A message was written with Smudge's blood on the wall: *CAN RUTH COME OUT AND PLAY?*

Abruptly Ruth was crying.

Beverly bolted for her baby's bedroom and listened to Ruth's distant cries that were fading away from reality.

Ruth's crib was empty. The window at the other end of the room was open; its curtain billowed with a chilling breeze. Next to it was another message in Smudge's blood: YOU SHOULD HAVE KEPT YOUR MOUTH SHUT!

Beverly's screams never ended.

Abigail came to the hospital tonight to visit Henry. Visiting hours were almost up but they let her in. He was lying in bed staring up at the TV that received such bad signal—couldn't they get something better for their patients?

"Did they find her?" Henry said.

Abigail shook her head. "No. They haven't got a clue. But uh..." Abigail sat down at the chair she pulled up to the side of his bed. "I'm ready to tell you everything."

"Yeah?"

"Yeah."

Then heavy silence. Both of them shut up and watched each other.

"A long time ago I tried to kill myself. You know about that and you've seen my scars but what I didn't tell you was I tried to kill myself because I was possessed. It was the demon's way of entering my body." Abigail paused to see if Henry wanted to interject. He said nothing. She continued: "While that demon was in control of me I did terrible things. I wasn't myself and I didn't want to do these things, but I hurt my friends and my family. I killed people, Henry. I killed Father Gutierrez, do you remember him? The priest from when we were kids. And then I killed my friend Catherine. Beverly saved my life. She was the only reason I survived. She helped me get rid of my demon…"

Henry stared at her. She couldn't tell what he was thinking.

"I've kept it a secret all these years. Nobody knows but you and Beverly. Not even my parents. How could I tell anybody else? I did terrible things but it wasn't me. I didn't want to do those things. But I'm still responsible, aren't I? Because maybe I could have done things differently. Because maybe if I made better decisions I could have avoided it. And for the last decade of my life this guilt has been tightening around my throat. Sometimes when I think about what I did, I can't breathe.

"I understand if you hate me, Henry. When I think about it I hate myself. I wish I could go back and change things but I've had to live with this guilt for so long. And Ivana, well, it's happened to her too. Except it's different because she told me… she told me she didn't want help. She likes it.

"I'm not a good person, Henry. I've always wanted to be. But I'm not. I'm sick. I'm twisted. I've done bad things. I should have been a better person. I was always a brat. I never took responsibility for my actions, and I took Beverly for granted. But I want to change. I want to make up for the past. I want to help Ivy, even if I don't know where to begin."

Abigail went back to Beverly's place and heard screams before she was even in the driveway. She put the car in park but didn't bother taking the keys out of the ignition because she was in a hurry to see what was happening.

Her guts were sinking. She had an awful feeling.

She pushed open the front door.

"Beverly? It's me. What's going on?"

The screaming stopped but Beverly was still crying. She came into the living room and collapsed into Abigail's arms. Beverly's cheeks were blood red and her eyes were strained from crying so much.

"They took my baby. They took Ruth."

Arnie pulled furiously on his chains with his last remaining strength and his right hand popped loose. At first he thought it was a hallucination, but as he lowered his arm slowly and felt stinging pain through the numbness, he knew it was real. His circulation was fixing itself; the strange and ugly pain in his arm was receding.

Hurriedly he adjusted his body so he could swing his arm over and reach his other hand that was still imprisoned. He opened the latch and was both happy and panicked—he was excited he was free, but scared as hell because escape meant facing those devils that had captured him in the first place.

He loosened his feet. He was completely free.

Hazel was asleep. He unlatched her hands and she woke up in the process screaming. Arnie covered her mouth with his hands and it took her a few moments to calm down and realize it was him, she wasn't being hurt, she was safe.

"You're okay, okay?" Arnie moved his hand from her mouth.

"How?"

"I broke one of my chains. It was rusted," Arnie said as he freed Hazel's feet.

It was torture stretching them and having feeling return to her limbs. Then they stood up, staggering a little to the door.

"We're going to get out of here. I promise you."

"Oh Arnie…" Hazel wrapped her right arm tight around his body as he led the way. He opened the door and Steve was smoking a cigarette with his arms crossed.

"You two idiots think we'd leave you alone unsupervised?"

Hazel had no words to say; the begging hadn't worked when she was a prisoner, and it sure wouldn't work now that she had broken loose from the chains. Arnie didn't say anything either; instead he charged at Steve and punched him in the gut.

Steve put Arnie into a headlock. "You gotta try harder than that, buddy."

"Steve? We're back." Ivy called.

Steve smiled. "Let the fun begin. Welcome to the family, kiddos."

32

ABIGAIL AND BEVERLY CAME to the police station.

As soon as they stepped inside Beverly jumped at one of the officers and Abigail had to hold her back from hitting him.

"*I told you and you did nothing!*"

"Calm down a minute woman."

"*Ivana kidnapped my baby! You need to do something!*"

"Hold up, hold up, who is Ivana?"

"*Get me back my baby!*"

The officer brought them into one of the interrogation rooms and sat them down and asked them questions.

"But you didn't actually see this girl you're accusing in your house, did you?"

"Well—well no, but—"

"Miss, you haven't given me one solid reason why this girl would have taken your baby, or why you're speculating that it's her."

"*I am not speculating. You have to go get her.*"

"I'm not gonna get her. And I know exactly where she is. Not long before you two came in I had a call from one of the other investigators on the case, I think you talked to him before Miss Martinez." He nodded toward Abigail. "You two might not believe this, but this

'Ivy' girl is at the hospital right now visiting her brother. Her brother says that the whole ordeal with the stabbing was an accident. She's in the clear. And furthermore, before we sat down in here I put in a call to the hospital to confirm something. This girl you're accusing does not have a baby with her—so I am afraid there is nothing I can do."

The woods behind the Engstrom place were even sicklier at nighttime. Each branch seemed to be an arm that was grasping to reach out and touch you. The moon was full and spread its thin light over the treetops; waterlike it seeped down between them to grant vision. The Engstrom Family Cemetery's gate was decrepit and rusted, and the chills that ran over Hazel's skin was like the fingers of lingering ghosts tracing her body. The fire that was burning in the makeshift firepit that Steve had put together brought her no warmth. It felt as if she were stuck in some sick unreality; some demented nightmare that she couldn't break herself free from.

She was on her knees. In front of her was an ancient wooden altar with strange symbols carved into it. There was an old book on one end—a cracked leather cover without any words, and the edges of its pages were yellowed—and on the other end was a knife. The same one that Steve and Michelle had cut her and Arnie with earlier.

Steve pushed Arnie down next to Hazel. He kneeled with her at the altar. Then Steve handed her a water bottle. Hazel took it from him but didn't drink it.

"Go ahead. It isn't poison. Drink up. You look parched."

Hazel obeyed him. She hadn't realized how thirsty she was until the water touched her tongue. Her mouth and throat were so dry that it stung at first. She would have finished the whole thing if it weren't for Arnie; she chugged half of the water bottle then gave it to him.

There was the cry of a baby at a distance; it became more distinct as Michelle approached from darkness. In her hands was a little bundle. Hazel's eyes darted to the knife on the altar and back to the baby. She was going to be sick.

"There's no going back," Michelle said.

She put the baby on the altar. It wiggled and cried.

Hazel and Arnie looked at each other in disgust.

"You sick fuckers," Arnie said. "It's a damn baby, leave it alone."

"Whose baby is this?" Hazel cried. When there was no answer right away she screamed her question again louder: *"Whose baby is this?"*

Michelle put her hands on her hips. "Beverly Hoffman's. You know, our substitute teacher? The one who got knocked up and doesn't know who the father is?"

"I'm not doing anything to hurt that baby. You guys are sick. You need help. Stop this right now before it's too late."

Michelle kneeled next to Hazel. "Ivy thought you'd get like this, so she gave me a bit of a message to relay to you Hazel. Listen, you made an agreement. A verbal contract. And the master heard it all. You have to hold up your end of the bargain… or else. Understand?"

"No I don't understand. I'm not doing anything to this baby. I can't do this. *Fuck no.*"

"Well you have until Ivy gets back to fully decide."

"No. I'm deciding right now that I can't do this. I won't do this."

"Steve. Knife."

Steve walked around the altar to give Michelle the knife. "Here you are."

"We all had to do something. Ivy had to sacrifice Warren. Steve had to sacrifice the farmer. I had to sacrifice a baby myself, along with a couple kids and a creepy old man, but three of those four were just for fun. We aren't asking much here."

Abigail and Beverly were let into the hospital despite visiting hours being over. A cop escorted them up under the circumstances, then he disappeared off into the hospital somewhere when Abigail and Beverly stepped into Henry's room and shut the door. Ivy was at his side in one of the extra chairs and if anybody had looked right at her they would have seen a beautiful girl, a nice girl visiting her brother in the hospital, not a girl who was possessed, not a girl who had stolen a baby.

"Hello," Henry said.

"Hi," Ivy said. "It's good to see you two."

"I suppose you two heard…" Henry sat up a bit. "I told the police it was an accident."

"It wasn't an accident," Beverly said, stepping forward, restraining herself from screaming. "Ivy, where is Ruth? Where did you take her?"

"What are you talking about?" Henry said.

"Your sister stole my baby."

"She did no such thing."

Ivy burst into tears. Abigail had no way of telling if they were real or fake. She pushed her chair away from Henry's bed then turned to face the window.

"I'm so sorry."

"Ivy? What did you do?" Henry asked.

Beverly ran but Abigail grabbed her arm and held her back.

"Give her back or I'll kill you! I'll kill—"

"Hazel made me do it."

Everybody in the room went silent suddenly.

"Hazel made you do what?" Henry said. "Ivy please…"

"She made us steal the baby." Ivy still was turned away and wasn't looking anyone in the eye. Abigail wondered if Ivy was too ashamed to look at them, or if she was just unable to hide the lies that must have been written on her face. "But I know where you can find her."

The Engstrom House's gate was open and they entered. Ivy was first. Abigail held Beverly's hand.

The house was quiet. No signs of anybody. No cries of Beverly's baby. No sign that anybody was ever here.

The darkness was disorienting. There was a little moonlight coming in from a distant window, just enough to give the living room some visibility.

"I'm so sorry for what I did." Ivy turned to face them. "Please you have to forgive me. You have to help me."

Real tears were forming in her eyes. Her sadness was genuine, Abigail thought for a moment, but then she remembered what she was dealing with. Demons are deceitful. Play along but be cautious.

"Ivy it's okay just help me get my baby back."

"I don't know what's taking Ivy so long," Michelle said, "but maybe we should just get started."

Hazel was trembling. She thought she was going to faint. Dizziness spread through her head and body and she didn't know what to do—she couldn't make a run for it because she was outnumbered and she was going to stumble and fall on her face after one step with how... *sick* she felt.

Oh God, it couldn't be real, Hazel thought.

Her heart pulsed with fear. Sweat rolled her down her forehead and gathered in her palms. She eyed Arnie; he was just as frightened. Then she turned her attention back to Michelle who kept the knife held out for Hazel to take.

"What do you... want me to do?"

"Hazel, don't do it," Arnie said. "Don't."

"A deal's a deal."

"*Hazel.*"

"*Yes?*"

Arnie lowered his head. He didn't say anything, he only wept. Wept for that poor baby on the altar.

Hazel wept too. As she grabbed the knife her eyes swelled with tears. There had to be a way out of this. A way to save the baby. Again a wave of unreality flashed through her; she couldn't believe she was actually here with her friends forcing her to...

"Well," Michelle said, "we want you to cut the baby's throat. Steve, can you hand us the chalice?"

Steve picked up the bronze cup on the altar.

"We need its blood."

Hazel let out a cry. "What happens if I can't do it?"

"Then I'll kill it. Then I'll kill you."

"Don't make her do it," Arnie said. "Give me the knife instead. Hazel I won't let you be responsible for taking a life."

"Nuh-uh, Hazel can do this, she's a big girl. We've got other things for you to do, Arnie."

"I'm not doing anything for you, I never agreed to nothing."

"Oh Arnie." Michelle stood up. "Even the most strong-willed men have their breaking points. You're so tough now but I know that faced with even the littlest amount of pain you'd cave in. Why don't we test it out."

"Go fuck yourself."

"Do you kiss your mother with that mouth?"

"Yeah and I'll kiss *your* mother's too."

Steve had started approaching Arnie but Michelle put up her hand to halt him. "Don't worry about it, Stevie, I want to handle him myself. He needs a little lesson for the blatant disrespect he's displayed here."

Michelle pressed the knife to Arnie's neck as she grabbed him by the collar and helped him up. "Come with me."

Michelle walked him a few feet away and pushed him intp an empty grave that had been dug recently. Perhaps, Hazel thought, her friends had dug it just for her and Arnie and were looking for an excuse just to use it.

Steve handed Michelle a shovel without Michelle having to ask; it was as if they had rehearsed this. Michelle dumped some dirt back into the grave.

"A lot of people think drowning is the worst way to go out. You could probably hold your breath for like three minutes until your muscles give out. But to me that's easy, death would only be a few seconds away. It would kind of me a quick death actually. Well, being buried alive is so much worse, Arnie. You know how bad it is?" Another shovel of dirt down into the grave. "You can survive for hours under dirt. From what I gather you might get about five hours under there, because you can still catch some air along with all the dirt. But eventually your lungs will fill up no matter how badly you try to avoid it. So instead of three quick minutes under the ocean, you're looking at five maddening hours under the ground."

Arnie said nothing.

"You still alive down there? Gee, I'm not so used to guys giving me the cold shoulder."

Arnie was either stupid or stubborn, Hazel wasn't exactly sure. But the baby's cries made her wonder if Arnie actually had a plan—the baby would have been dead a couple minutes ago if her friends had gotten their way. Now Michelle was distracted and Arnie had bought

Hazel a little time. Now what was she going to do with it? Stay here on her knees and waste it?

She went over it all in her head. Michelle was shoveling dirt a few feet away into the shallow grave. Steve was standing near the grave too, looking in and taunting Arnie. In the distance behind Steve she could see the eternally open gateway—the fence's gate had broken off a long time ago and nobody had ever fixed it or replaced it.

If she grabbed the baby and interrupted the whole *ritual* then what could she do to get the baby back to its mother? If she took two steps toward that gate then Steve would intercept her.

Well... there was only one way to find out.

Hazel trembled as she stood up then grabbed the baby from the altar. In that brief moment she was free of Steve and Michelle because both of them were speaking to Arnie.

"Pretty soon you you'll be completely covered," Hazel said. "I'm honestly shocked you haven't caved yet. Well, everyone has their breaking point. Maybe after an hour in the dirt we'll dig you up and see if you've changed your mind. Just to be clear it doesn't matter to me one way or the other if you survive, but I know Hazel's sweet on you, so we might keep you around just for her sake. So consider yourself lucky I'm going easy on you. Anybody else would be dead by now, but we've given you chance after chance and you've thrown each and every single one of them away."

Hazel didn't know what she was doing or planned to do, but she held the baby tight, and in one hand held on to the knife as well. Sweat billowed down her forehead and seeped into her eyes and stung them. She still felt lightheaded and weak from the blood loss and the stabbing. She didn't know if she could make it past any of them but she had to try.

A couple of the metal slats of the gate were rusted and halfway fallen off. Suddenly Hazel was running towards them based purely on instinct, and didn't stop to think too much about what she was doing. The world seemed to move in a blur as if life were a video tape that was set to fast forward.

She pushed one of the slats until it was completely broken off; she gasped for breath and didn't have a moment to push the other one off because Steve was headed her way. Michelle, in the brief second Hazel glimpsed her, slammed the shovel down. Whether this was all part of Arnie's strategy or not, Hazel did not know, but she was glad he made the diversion.

There was no pathway for her in the woods. She ran through them, hitting low branches, wrapping her arms around the crying baby to protect her.

Please stop crying so we can be safe, Hazel thought. *Please, baby, please.*

The baby's cries drifted into the night. Hazel's heart pounded faster with each painful movement between the trees over the rocky soil. Somewhere behind her were the others; whether it was only one of them or all three of them she couldn't be sure, all she knew was somebody was chasing her. Somebody was with her.

The woods felt so alive tonight, Hazel thought, as if life was drifting all around her, as if there were many others here with her and her friends and the baby; as if eyes were all around burrowing into her skin, watching her, anticipating what would happen to the baby.

Chills slithered over her spine. Her head was heavy. At any moment she thought she was going to faint. She did not dare look back over her shoulder, because if she saw a glimpse of one of the others she didn't know what she was going to do.

The baby was still crying, but Hazel realized she hadn't heard her friends for a minute or two.

She stopped to catch her breath.

Where she was, she had no clue. She hoped she had been going back in the direction of the house so that way she could attempt to find a way out, but she wasn't sure. For all she knew she had accidentally taken them even deeper into the woods and they were far away into the wrong direction.

Poor baby, you don't deserve this, Hazel thought. *And poor Arnie. Oh my God.*

There was a cluster of trees just up ahead whose branches were tightly interlocked. Hazel had to sort of crawl to enter the vague hideaway they created. She was in a small, tight clear space where she could sit at the base of a big tree and be shielded from view from anybody. She cradled the baby in her arms. The baby was crying, and snot dripped from her nose.

Hazel wiped the baby's mucus and wiped away her tears. She rocked the baby gently. She had no clue what she was doing, but the baby was slowly calming.

"You're a beautiful little girl. Please don't cry. Please. If you keep crying they might find us. Come on, hush, that's it. Hush little baby don't you cry... hush, hush. There we go."

The baby's tears cleared up. It stared up at Hazel with sad blue eyes.

"You miss your mommy, don't you?" Hazel whispered. "I'll bring you back to her, I promise you. But for now we need to be careful. All right?"

The baby wrapped its fingers around one of Hazel's and smiled. It was as if she understood her.

Hazel gave her a kiss on the forehead.

Oh Arnie. I hope to God you're okay."

As Hazel shut her eyes for a second, there were footsteps in the woods. Hazel froze, carefully opening her eyes little by little. She held her breath. Any small movement, even if it were noiseless, was dangerous. Footfalls were passing on either side of her. She darted her eyes to the baby quickly and then side to side. It was so dark that she couldn't see anything; if Michelle or Ivy or Steve or even Arnie were looking at her right now, she'd have no way of telling somebody was there.

"Hazel?"

It was Michelle's voice. It sent chills down Hazel's spine.

"No sense in playing hard to get. You made a contract and we're going to give your soul to our master one way or another."

Hazel shut her eyes as she listened to the footsteps reach further and further away from her. She prayed to God she'd get this baby back to her mother.

Ivy led Abigail and Beverly through the Engstrom House to the back door.

Abigail was brought back to the day that she had come through here with Beverly when running away from the reanimated Cat creature. She could feel that same terror that had engulfed her back then as if recreating it from memory. She could still feel the coldness of the house from back then, the hopelessness, the sick feeling that she and Beverly would not survive the night—the longest night on earth.

Perhaps that eternal night had not ended.

There was a fire far away in the woods. The smell of smoke carried over to the back of the Engstrom House.

"Looks like they might have had a little trouble without me," Ivy said.

"My baby." Beverly screamed, and she ran into the woods.

Abigail ran after her.

The trees tightened all around. The woods were as detestable as Abigail remembered it. This place had ruined her life and she wanted to be free of it already. She hoped the fire would expand once Ruth was safe. She hoped the fire would overtake the house. She hoped that one day all that would be left of the Engstrom place would be its charred remains.

33

Michelle had thrown enough dirt on top of Arnie to cover him entirely, and she had been right that it was possible to both choke and breathe under the dirt. He couldn't stop it from filling his lungs and sliding down the back of his throat; he coughed and tried to spit out the dirt but even doing that managed to bring little bits of filth past his lips.

His body burned in all the places where Steve had stabbed him; the cuts had not been terribly deep but he had lost blood and he was weak. And he kept thinking about Hazel and the baby running away, leading all of Hazel's friends after her in a chase. There was no way she could outrun them for long, he thought. There was no way Hazel could keep herself and the baby safe. They both needed him; he had to do something… but his muscles strained under the weight of the dirt and the way his body was angled so that he was face down in the grave.

Arnie's hands clenched into fists. He had to help Hazel. She needed him. He had to do something. He pushed his arms through the dirt with desperation and a sudden burst of anger. The dirt above him seemed to weigh five hundred pounds; it was like trying to fight his way up through a block of solid metal. Arnie's body burst with fresh new pains as he pushed against the dirt; he had no way to tell if he was making any progress. His arm was so week in the forearm from where Steve had stabbed, and any movement strained him even worse.

In his mind he saw Hazel and the baby surrounded by Steve and Ivy and Michelle in the woods. He saw Ivy and Michelle grabbing Hazel while Steve pried the baby away from her. He saw Steve cutting the baby open, and Hazel was next—it was all part of their sick ceremony.

He couldn't let it happen.

Arnie clawed at the dirt, moving with determination. Any pain he felt in his stab wounds was ignored. He choked as he moved, terrified that he might suffocate to death before ever being able to help Hazel. As he climbed out of his grave he felt his right arm go completely numb; it wouldn't move.

I'm coming, Hazel, he thought.

Arnie pushed through the dirt with his left arm. He clawed and forced his way up out of the grave. And in a few moments he saw the sky; he was almost there. Then his right arm found a little feeling again; Arnie continued his fight out of the grave.

When he was above ground he spit out dirt.

"Hazel…"

Arnie climbed completely out of the grave. Nobody was around. Then he noticed the red can of gasoline that had been used to start the firepit, and next to it was a box of matches. He picked it up to find that the five gallon can was mostly full.

He popped it open and went around the woods splashing gasoline. Just like he had told Hazel, they needed to burn it all down. It was gonna be hard enough to get a firetruck to the house, and it was gonna be near impossible to get a firetruck back here behind the house.

The tip of a match struck against the ignition strip; a little blue and orange flame.

Arnie threw it into the gasoline-soaked grass.

The baby was asleep.

Hazel's crossed legs were numb so she stretched them, moving as slowly as she could so the baby wouldn't wake up crying. It was already blindingly dark outside but somehow it was getting even darker, and the air was chilling, and Hazel hoped that keeping her arms wrapped around the baby was enough to keep it warm. She needed to get this baby out of here immediately, but she was so scared to move. She had worked up the bravery to run away from the ceremony and through the broken fence, but now she was frightened that she wouldn't get so lucky again. Any movement and any of the others, if they were still around, would hear her. And if she ran the baby would wake up and scream.

"Hazel? Hazel? Hazzzzzellllll?"

Michelle at a distance.

Hazel was frozen.

"Come on out. Let's get this over with."

Just then, the baby cried.

Arnie ran through the woods; it was eerily silent, and he didn't know where anybody else was or how much time had passed. He coughed again, pressing forward, searching for Hazel, softly whispering her name because his lungs were too clogged with dirt for him to yell.

"Hazel... Hazel..."

He wandered until he heard the baby screaming. Instantly he was running toward the noise which seemed to be quieting down as quickly as it had begun. Arnie passed through closely packed branches and Hazel let out a scream.

"Hazel, it's me." Arnie was still struggling to speak without choking.

He entered a tight clearing where Hazel was rocking the baby and whispering to her that everything would be okay and that her mama would be here soon.

"We've got to get you out of here," Arnie said.

"Oh my God," Hazel said, her voice straining to be louder than a whisper. She was too scared to speak much. Her eyes traced him up and down, and Arnie thought she must have been processing what it was like to be buried alive.

Arnie collapsed next to her at the base of the tree.

"Arnie... we need to get you to a hospital."

"We need to get you and the baby out of here first."

"Not much chance of that happening, you know." Steve stepped into the small clearing. He was twirling a knife in his hand.

313

Arnie jumped up and stepped in front of Hazel and the baby. "Leave them alone."

"How many holes do I gotta poke in ya before you quit trying to be a hero?" Steve held the knife out. "You're gonna get yourself killed for some dingy broad? Really, buddy? I knew you were a Jew but I didn't think you were stupid or nothing."

"*Hazel run.*"

"Not so fast." Steve grabbed Arnie in a headlock. Hazel had hardly taken a step or two before she paused. The baby awakened and cried. "Hazel, you move one inch and he dies, then the baby dies, then you die."

"To be fair, that might all happen anyways," Michelle said from nearby. She pushed through branches and extended her hands for the baby. "Now come here baby girl."

Hazel held the baby close to her chest. "Stay away from her."

"Hey Arnie, I think this bitch really wants you to die." Steve laughed. "I told you she wasn't worth it. You still gonna risk your life for her?"

"Fuck you, Steve."

"Arnie my man you'll figure out chicks one day."

The baby was screeching loudly, Michelle was taking a step closer, her fingers were within inches of the child. Then Hazel moved a step back.

"Now what did I tell you, Hazel? No moving or I'd kill Arnie and the baby then I'd kill you. So I'm sorry Arnie, but I gotta do what I gotta do," Steve said as Michelle snatched the baby from Hazel's hands. "Do you have any last words?"

"No," Arnie said. "Just that you can go fuck yourself."

"Goddamn, it almost hurts me to do this…" Steve put the knife to Arnie's throat. "You make me laugh, bud. You're a good kid. Even for a Jew."

Arnie laughed a little.

"Steve, no," Hazel said. "You can kill me, but don't kill Arnie or the baby."

"Hazel what the hell are you doing?" Arnie said.

"Woah," Steve said, "she'll do just about anything for you except put out, won't she, Arnie?"

Arnie hit Steve as best he could manage, despite knowing it wouldn't have any effect on him.

"You know, maybe I should keep you two alive for a little bit. Ivy might get mad at me if I make any decisions without her."

34

THE FIRE HAD SPREAD and devoured many trees. The treetops touched and their flames were spreading across each other. It was what these cursed grounds had always deserved.

Abigail wiped sweat from her forehead. The temperature was constantly rising. Her mouth was dry. A shudder clawed at her skin when she remembered the skeletons that had been dragged up by the vines all those nights ago. The cemetery was just as hideous as she remembered; dead grass, rocky soil, gravestones that had been withered by time or covered by moss so that most of the names and dates were indecipherable. And soon it would all be gone. Soon it would all be burned up.

The altar was new. There was an ancient volume on it with a wordless cover that was streaked with flashes of light from the fires. Up ahead was a shovel tossed to the side, and dirt that had been thrown in every direction. Footsteps led away from the grave as if… somebody had crawled right out of it.

"Where is she? Where is she?" Beverly collapsed on the ground and cried.

Abigail kneeled and put her hands on her friend. After taking a brief glimpse over her shoulder in a bit of a search for Ivy, who had eluded them, Abigail said, *"We'll find her. They won't get away with this."*

"Here, let me hold her."

Voices were coming from the right.

Three figures in darkness; the light of the fires touched them, illuminating Ivy and Michelle and Hazel. Ivy was holding Ruth, and Ruth was crying. Michelle was making a funny face at Ruth to try and get her to stop crying. Hazel's head was hung and she was frowning.

"Ruth!" Beverly stood up and screamed and ran.

Ivy held Ruth up over her head in both hands. Ruth was writhing and screaming. "No, no, no, one more step and it won't be pretty what happens to your baby, okay?"

Beverly stopped from Ivy's threat.

A smile crawled across Ivy's face. "Ruth is such a pretty name for a baby. I like it. Does Ruth have a middle name?"

"Cath-Catherine," Beverly choked as she said it.

"Ruth Catherine Hoffman. Pretty girl." Ivy lowered her then rocked her. Then she looked at Michelle. "Where are the guys?"

"They were right behind us. I think Steve wanted to give Arnie a little scare. But it looks like Arnie got the head start on us himself. Look at that fire. Do you think we have time to finish he ceremony before it spreads too far?"

Beverly fell on her knees. *"Just give me back my baby, I'm begging you. I'll do anything you want, I'll give you any money you want, I won't say a word to the police, just give me my Ruth back."*

"Hmmm..." Ivy said, stepping past her to the altar, setting Ruth down on top of it. *"I don't think so. We really need her."*

"Please... please..."

"Ivana…" Abigail took a step forward. *"We want to help you. Stop before it's too late. I know you don't want to do this."*

"Why not? What if I do want to do this? It's my life, not yours. God, do you really think I'd be doing this if I didn't want to?"

"You don't know what you're saying. You're not yourself and we want to help you."

Ivy laughed. "Help me. Yeah right."

Abigail moved another step closer. "Give her back her baby. We need to get out of here before the fire gets even worse."

"Please…" Beverly cried again. *"Don't hurt her."*

"Don't move again, Abby, or I might have to kill this baby in front of her mother, and I don't totally want to do that, okay? If you stopped interrupting me we could just get this all over with already." Then she looked past them to Abigail. "Abby this is what you were meant to do but couldn't. There were so many plans that the master had for you, and you threw them all away. So maybe think of all this as a little payback, payback for not doing what you were supposed to, and a little payback for Beverly's involvement in stopping my master's plan. Is that fair?"

"Ivy," Abigail said, unsure at first how she planned to continue. "Look I know it feels good. But no matter how much you think you want this, I know you don't. It's messing with your head. You're a good girl. But there are some other things you can't come back from. Give Beverly back her child, and let's all get out of here. It's not too late to change things."

"Why does everyone keep saying this like I'm some kinda idiot or something?" Ivy put her hands on her hips. "I know exactly what I'm doing. I want to do this. Nobody's forcing me. As soon as my master told me his plan I couldn't say no. He told me all about what he wanted to do for you Abigail, and now I get to have what you turned away. Abby, I'm going to be his bride."

"His what?"

"You see, Abby, the real reason I ran away from home was because I was pregnant and didn't want to tell my parents. I didn't only sign away my life, I signed away my baby's life as well. I will be the devil's bride and my baby will be his child."

Before Abigail could say anything, Michelle grabbed Hazel by her hands and threw her down at the altar, then she put a knife in Hazel's hands.

"You remember what I told you to do, right?"

Hazel cried, not responding.

Michelle tapped Hazel's shoulder. "Hazel."

"Yuh-yes."

"You know what you have to do, right?"

"Yes... yes... oh God..."

"You need to complete the ceremony. It's what the master wills. You have to join us, you made an agreement."

"I can't do this. I need out."

"Well Hazel," Ivy said, "that just isn't possible."

Abigail felt a chill then a burst of heat—she had to do something, she had to intervene, but she was dealing with pure uncontrollable evil which was even worse than the surrounding fires. What could she do that wouldn't put the baby in immediate danger? Maybe it didn't matter what she did, because it was either act now or be burned alive, and burning alive was coming for them all within moments.

Abigail ran and grabbed Ivy and pulled her away from the altar. Beverly was at the altar in a heartbeat; she reached for Ruth but Michelle was faster and grabbed the baby a split second before Beverly could.

An impulse brought Abigail's hand into her shirt and she pulled her crucifix necklace out and held it up; Ivy and Michelle were immediately blinded. Beverly snatched her baby away from Michelle and ran into the forest.

Ivy had gone pale under the flash of firelight. She collapsed from the sight of the necklace. *"Get that thing away from me."*

Ivy slid out of Abigail's arms and Abigail stood over her with the necklace dangling inches from Ivy's face. She was hyperventilating.

Abigail glanced at the entrance to the family cemetery. The flames were spreading wickedly, writhing as they pressed closer and closer and swallowing anything in its path. Trees and grass in each direction were ignited and passing along the oncoming destruction.

Was there even a way out by now?

Then the world spun.

Abigail thought the ground beneath her feet had split open, but then she felt Michelle on top of her digging her fingers into Abigail's flesh. Abigail screamed as Michelle tugged on her hair in handfuls, lifting Abigail's head and slamming it down.

Michelle moved Abigail onto her back then ripped her necklace away from her. It burned Michelle's flesh and a little smoke rose up. Michelle threw it a few feet away into the fire that was inching nearer and nearer to the gate. There were screams somewhere around them, and Abigail wanted to see what had become of Ivy and Hazel and Beverly and Ruth, but she couldn't see anything at the angle. Michelle's grip on Abigail's face tightened, and she felt her head about to pop.

"Michelle. Please." Abigail strained to speak. The fire was edging nearer. If she were able to fully extend her arms right now she would have been able to touch it.

"Begging right up until the end. I love it. But it's not enough to get me to change my mind.

The fire was an inch or two away from her scalp; Abigail could already feel it burrowing its way into her skull.

Both of her arms were pinned but her left arm had a better chance of prying free; Abigail panicked and used all the strength she could find in her body to pull out from Michelle. Her left arm became momentarily free before Michelle grabbed her hand and bent her wrist backwards.

The flames licked her scalp. Abigail's body jerked forward to create space, and Abigail felt an obscure compulsion to grab the tree root that her fingertips brushed against. She yanked it out of the ground and jammed it into Michelle's throat and a mist of blood spurted out of the wound. Michelle recoiled and Abigail slid out from under her then pinned Michelle down.

The flames touched Michelle's hair and instantly caught fire. Her screams melted into the night.

Abigail backed away horrified but could not break her gaze from the agony on Michelle's face as the flames spread and overtook her body. The screams worsened, and Abigail's heart skipped a beat.

Then she was aware of the tears falling in her eyes.

35

THE BLAZE OF HEAT coiled around Beverly.

Ruth kept screaming.

Smoke swirled above them. Beverly had to move carefully through the available paths that were not burning, but every few steps she'd come across a wall of flames and would have to reevaluate the way she was going—it was dizzying, and the course of the fires seemed to push her further back toward the unknown regions of the forest rather than closer back to the Engstrom House, thus sealing her away from her one exit back into town. She had no idea how deep the Engstrom House's forest might go, or where it came out, or how to get to town from its depths.

As she hushed her baby, terror was all she could feel. She saw herself becoming trapped and dying in the flames with her arms protectively clinging to Ruth. Nobody deserved to die this way, least of all Ruth—she was a baby, she was innocent, she was kidnapped and dragged into this whole damn situation.

Beverly cried for her child—she would have given her life for Ruth to get out of this safely if there was a way to offer a fair trade.

How much time did she have left before the whole forest was engulfed and there was no way out? Minutes? Seconds?

Beverly stepped over fallen branches. Ruth's strained cries quieted down a little bit. Beverly forced the awful thoughts from her mind and tried to think positively. She maneuvered below some branches and turned around a tree. There was a clear pathway up ahead; she followed it and prayed that God would bring them out of these cursed woods one way or another.

As flames closed in on Beverly and Ruth, and any direction to maneuver through was becoming scarce, she prayed that Abigail was okay wherever she was. She prayed that nobody would have to get hurt. She wanted all of this to just end. She would forgive everybody just to get out of these cursed grounds.

A flaming branch fell in front of Beverly and she abruptly stopped and pulled Ruth back. Ruth let out little cries—she was so tired that she could hardly even cry any longer.

"It'll be okay," Beverly whispered. "Everything will be just fine."

Beverly stepped around the fallen branch, and another dropped from the tree behind her after she passed through. Nowhere was safe in these hellish woods. But she would not be in them for long.

Up ahead was the hidden cabin brooding as it had done so many years prior. Its front door couldn't stay shut because the lock was broken, and it swayed open and shut here and there with each touch of the wind. Her memories of the night she was here flashed quickly in her mind, and she brushed them away.

Her body ached on her ascent up the hill. The flames had not reached this area yet, and an obscure nighttime chill cooled her and calmed her aching burning lungs. Beverly quickly opened the door then slammed it shut after she stepped in. It was warm inside the cabin because across from her the fireplace was raging.

Somebody had been in here recently.

She moved two steps further in and saw that beer bottles had been thrown all over the place, and there were empty cartons of cigarettes tossed around. There were some blankets in front of the fireplace. The kids hadn't limited all their time together to the Engstrom place, they had come here too.

Beverly sat near the fireplace and adjusted Ruth in her lap.

"It's okay Mommy. We'll get out of here soon."

But Ruth was crying a little, some snot dripping from her nose. Beverly wiped it away with her sleeve. Together they sat quietly in the cabin.

Beverly had no idea how she was going to get out of here, through the burning woods, and past the chaos and madness that this cursed night promised. Back through the Engstrom House and safely on the other side, down the hill, and to the car—it all seemed unthinkable and impossible... but she would get out of here. She would find some way.

She'd get out of here for Ruth.

Michelle reached a desperate hand in agony toward Abigail before she died.

Abigail backed away from Michelle's remains.

The fire had partway overtaken the Engstrom family cemetery. Abigail left through the broken part of the fence. Smoke was captured tightly beneath the treetops and choked her. Her eyes burned.

The air was so hot it was painful to breathe. Burning branches fell now and again. Abigail pressed on through the torture of traveling through a forest on fire. She walked until she collapsed.

Abigail stood up a little bit then fell back down. The smoke was suffocating her. The heat was torturing her body. It was all closing in on her. She wanted to push through; her eyes shut against her will.

She laid there a little while, and when the hand grabbed her and lifted her up, it was like a dream.

The door opened and Beverly screamed before she even saw who was with her. Her whole body tensed. Nervously her eyes swept across the cabin to the door; Steve dragged Arnie in. Arnie's face was cut up and bruised. As Steve tossed him into the middle of the room, Arnie grunted.

Following the boys were Ivy and Hazel. Ivy had an arm around Hazel with a knife to Hazel's throat.

"Good, you're here," Ivy said. "And you've even brought that adorable little baby girl of yours. I appreciate your sacrifice, Miss Hoffman."

Beverly stood up, moving in small steps with Ruth sobbing in her trembling arms.

"Go ahead. Run away if you want. But where are you realistically gonna go? Face it, you're beat, hun. You go out the back hallway and you can't outrun us to the door. You manage to get out of this cabin somehow and you're bound for endless flames. So it's best you don't struggle and don't get hurt more than necessary. We can make this whole thing pretty painless if you cooperate."

"You can kill me," Beverly said with another step backwards, "but don't touch my baby. I'm begging you. Please don't hurt her."

"Well…" Ivy let go of Hazel and took the knife away from her throat. She moved closer toward Beverly. "No, I can't really do that. But I could spare you having to hear her cries. I could spare you by…" Ivy was within an arm's reach away. She lifted the knife so that its tip touched Beverly's throat as Beverly gulped. "Taking your life first. What do you say?"

"Hold on just a second, Ivy, if I may say something," Steve said, stepping over Arnie and coming on his way over to them. "Why let her go to waste? At least let me have some fun with her. There's plenty of empty rooms upstairs. I get her for a few minutes while you set up down here. I'll be quick… depending on how much she cooperates. I dunno though, I love a good game of cat and mouse."

"Sure." Ivy rolled her eyes. "You've got fifteen minutes and not a second more, starting now."

Steve glanced at his watch. "Right on."

Beverly ran and was about four steps through the hallway when Steve grabbed her in an abnormally powerful grip. She carefully held onto Ruth and didn't resist Steve's pull so that her baby wouldn't fall or get hurt in the commotion. Ivy had come down the hall too and pried Ruth from Beverly's hands; a giant scream was stuck in Beverly's throat.

She could not fathom what was happening, couldn't think, couldn't move.

Steve lifted Beverly over his shoulder and carried her up the stairs. It was happening so fast that she couldn't think or breathe or feel anything.

"Be back soon."

"The clock is ticking. Don't forget, you're only at about thirteen minutes now, kay?"

"Kay."

Upstairs, Steve kicked open the door to a random room. Beverly's fists landed on him but caused him no pain. He threw her on the mattress in a corner of the room; aside from that and the window, there was nothing else in here. Beverly trembled under his touch as his hands weighed heavily on her.

She spat in his face.

Steve wiped it away then smacked her.

"For a whore you're such a prude."

"Get off of me."

"Nah."

We're all going to die, Hazel thought. Sick thoughts kept repeating in her mind: There's no way any of us will make it out of this alive. We're all going to burn. We're all going to die. We're all going to die.

"Okay, first thing's first," Ivy said, "Hazel, I need you to understand something. You got lucky there in the cemetery. If it weren't for that fire and for Abigail's necklace then I'd have had to kill you. So now I want you to understand that you're going to die if you don't cut this baby open. All right? Nuh-uh, don't open your mouth, quit crying, let me speak." Ivy cut off Hazel before she could even begin saying anything. "Now I don't want to hear any begging, I don't want any pleading, I don't want any crying, and I especially don't want to hear any half-assed negotiations offering up your soul in place of the baby's. Is that understood?"

Hazel weakly nodded, although she did not actually agree to any of that on the inside.

"And as for you, Arnie, same rules apply. That is, if you really do want to join us. So have you decided yet?"

"I'll join you," Arnie said without hesitation, coughing up a little dirt as he spoke. Hazel wondered if he meant it or not; she couldn't tell.

"Both of you kneel at this table."

Hazel and Arnie did so.

"Excellent. Let the ceremony begin."

Steve lifted Beverly's shirt off of her. She shuddered. She slid her hands up and down his body as he kissed her neck so that she could calm him, relax him, distract him for the single moment she needed to slip out from under him. She made a run for the door but he was so quick—so damn quick, and she was in his grasp again.

"Let go of me you psycho."

"You're just making me want you more when you do this."

His fingers curled so deeply into her flesh that she thought her skin would pop open. Steve dragged her through the room and slammed her into the wall then kissed her; his mouth forced its way over hers. She wanted to scream, wanted to hit him, but his hands had pinned both of her wrists to the wall.

Beverly thought of Ruth downstairs, and the knife in the hands of those savages. Whatever the baby was about to go through was worse than anything Beverly could imagine Steve would do to her up here.

Her heart nearly stopped when she thought about Ruth's ripped open body waiting for her downstairs. It couldn't be real—it just couldn't be.

One of Steve's hands left Beverly's wrist and traced down her back to her butt. She had never been more disgusted or violated in her life. Then she noticed that they were near the room's single window. Her free hand was nearest to the pane of glass.

Her first banged against the window glass; Steve wasn't paying attention to what she was doing, he was only focused on her body. Beverly's knuckles stung even though the punch she had thrown at the window pane was weak. The thought of the dwindling moments she had left to see her child alive panicked her, and her second punch was strong enough to violently break the glass and viciously split her hand open; blood poured out of her knuckled and her flap of open skin but she did not stop to think about the pain. Steve broke away from the kiss with confusion on his face.

Beverly did not hesitate. She pulled up a loose shard of glass that cut up her palm and slammed it into Steve's throat. The glass plunged effortlessly into his body. Beverly pulled it out and Steve gulped. Blood spilled not only from the wound but also from the corners of his mouth.

His hands reached for Beverly. She shoved him onto the bed then crawled on top of him and raised the shard of glass above her head. She brought it down into his chest and repeated the motion—she lifted the glass above her head and brought it down as hard as she could until he stopped moving. Then she did it again and again, getting covered in endless splatters of dark red blood.

Her hand hurt as it unclenched from the glass. Little shards were caught in her flesh. She pulled them out mindlessly as she walked over to where her shirt had been tossed into the center of the room. She picked it up and put it back on, then walked out of the room and downstairs into her continuing nightmare...

36

THE FIGURE IN DARKNESS helped Abigail stand.

It helped her through the thickening clouds of smoke. Its arms held her against its body.

Little by little Abigail could breathe again; smokeless air returned to her lungs. But her body still trembled. She still felt her whole body burning. She coughed as she breathed in clear air.

Her hands dizzyingly lifted from her sides as if she had to learn to control them again, and they reached up to her face and rubbed her tired eyes. Her knees buckled and she collapsed; the arms of the stranger caught her and helped her down on the ground.

Abigail's eyes completely opened. It was Cat.

"Cat? How?"

"The cabin," Cat said.

Cat helped her up again, led her a few steps away, and then she faded away with the fire's billows of smoke.

And Abigail wondered if Cat had really been there at all.

Ruth had cried so much that night that it seemed to Hazel that the baby could not cry any longer. Her small pretty blue eyes were red, and dried tears were glued to the baby's face. Snot dripped down her nose. The baby lifted its hands up to Hazel; Ruth must have wanted Hazel to hold her.

Then Ruth grabbed Hazel's left pinky finger.

Hazel cried and looked from the baby to the knife in her right hand. She glanced at Arnie and he was crestfallen. Neither of them wanted any part in this. But they had decided to go along with it until they could find a way out. And now what were they going to do?

Perhaps their luck had all run out now. Hazel had been lucky that Arnie had created a distraction earlier, and had gotten even luckier with the forest fire. Now what? Here with the baby in front of her and the knife in her hand, what could she do? Attack Ivy? Attack her best friend whose soul had been taken over? Could Ivy not be saved?

Any way she looked at it she was sick. Hurt Ruth or hurt Ivy—either way she could not live with herself if she had to do something like that.

She went over the scenario in her head. Steve and Beverly were upstairs. Who the hell knew what happened to Abigail and Michelle. And Ivy was standing on the other side of the table that now sufficed as their altar.

CREEEAK! CREAAAK! CRRREEEAAAKKK!

"Steve," Ivy said, "I was beginning to think we'd have to do this without you. And look at you, coming back with a minute or two to spare."

But it wasn't Steve who came down the stairs, it was Beverly all covered in blood. Her eyes were wide and angry. As soon as Ivy saw her coming off the final steps Ivy reached for Ruth but Beverly put her hands around Ivy's throat before Ivy could do anything to the baby.

Beverly slammed Ivy's head into the wall. In all the commotion, Hazel picked up Ruth to protect her and backed away into the corner of the room. Arnie went with her. As Beverly struck Ivy hear into the wall a second time, she heard Ruth's screams, and her attention turned to the corner of the room.

"Give me back my baby."

"Here—here," Hazel said nervously and stepped forward. Her eyes darted to Ivy who was slumped in the corner.

Beverly grabbed Ruth from Hazel in a hurry and hugged her baby.

Abigail pushed open the cabin door and staggered inside. When she saw Beverly and Ruth she gave them a hug.

"Oh my God. I'm so glad you two are okay."

"Abby, oh my God, I was so worried about you. How did you know where to find us?"

Before she could mention anything about Cat, there was a shrieking cry in the corner of the cabin, and every eye in the room was turned to Ivy.

"I don't know what's wrong with me," Ivy cried. *"I need your help."*

"We all want to help you." Abigail moved closer over to Ivy. "We all want to help you, okay? Ivana we can—"

Ivy sat up and laughed. *"I'm just fucking with you, you dumb bitch."*

Abigail reached into her back pocket. She had come prepared. Her hand curled around the bottle of Holy Water as she watched Ivy stand up and come nearer to her at the other side of the table. Abigail gave a brief glance at the others in the room as she popped the cap off the vile and brought the Holy Water down across Ivy's face. Her flesh was seared where it splashed her and brought up little clouds of smoke.

Ivy screamed and the cabin rattled. Abigail slipped backwards. Her eyes immediately darted toward Beverly and Ruth instead of Ivy, and Beverly was cradling Ruth on the ground. The baby was all right.

The rattling continued as Abigail scrambled to grab the vile of Holy Water that was spilling onto the floor. There was only a tiny bit left in it, perhaps less than a quarter full. She squeezed it tight in her shaking hands and turned to face Ivy who had silently moved beside Abigail and smacked her across the face with the back of her hand.

A burning jolt of pain pulsed through Abigail's cheek into her head. The cabin had gone cold and she could see her breath against the illumination from the flames in the fireplace and the bright light of the flames that poured in from outside.

In the corner of her eye, as Abigail inched backwards from Ivy whose face had changed and morphed into a hellish imitation of who she previously was, she saw Beverly heading for the door, and the shaking of the cabin had stopped, but then the door opened and shut viciously on its own, sending up splinters of wood in each direction.

"I've had enough of your games, Abigail. I've had enough of everybody. This is going to end here and now."

"Ivy there's still a good person in you. I know there is."

"The Ivy you knew is gone."

"No she's not. I know you're still in there. I know you can overcome this."

"The master only wanted the soul of the baby. Instead I'll take the souls of all of you."

Then Ivy went across the cabin, and Arnie stepped ahead of Hazel to block her off from Ivy.

"You're not gonna touch her."

Ivy grabbed Arnie's wrist and twisted it, then she tossed him on the ground effortlessly.

"You get to live, Arnie, but just for now. Just so you can see what I'm gonna do. If Hazel had done what I said then she wouldn't have to die."

"Ivana what are you doing?" Hazel said.

Abigail jumped to her feet despite the shaking cabin whose windows and doors were still opening and slamming of their own accord. After two steps she was knocked down again.

"No!" Arnie screamed, but there was nothing he could do.

Hazel's head was twisted fully around. Her lifeless body thudded to the ground.

37

Arnie cradled Hazel's body.

Between all the chaos there was something Arnie noticed: a flash of black that was circling around the cabin. It flashed in each of the windows as the creature made its trip around the cabin. Indistinct glimpses of a black goat.

Ivy neared Beverly who was screaming and backed into a corner with her baby.

Abigail reached into her back pocket and brought out a miniature Holy Bible with a green cover. She read from it: "For he said unto him, Come out of the man, thou unclean spirit."

The cabin stopped shaking and the doors and windows stopped opening and slamming on their own.

Ivy crumpled to the floor and Abigail held her Holy Bible over Ivy's chest. Beverly shielded her baby away. And that was when Arnie picked up Hazel's body and carried her outside.

Waiting for Arnie outside of the cabin was a robed black goat. Long horns protruding from his head. Sickeningly sharp teeth that he licked with his black tongue. The goat stood across from Arnie and smiled.

"Arnie," he said.

Arnie was mesmerized by the strange creature across from him that bathed in the glow of the massive flames.

"You two could be together forever."

"How?" Arnie said.

"The fire is your friend, Arnie. Walk her into my kingdom."

"I don't want to die."

"The fire is your friend, Arnie, isn't it?"

Arnie said nothing.

"You've known it was your friend your whole life. Ever since you were a little boy."

"Yes," Arnie said.

"Walk her into the flames."

Arnie's legs were moving despite his doubt, worry, and fears.

"You're doing good, Arnie."

Arnie descended the hill with Hazel's corpse. He felt the eyes of the black goat burrowing into him and watching him with every step he took. Down past the base of the hill, down into the trees, the fire had spread this way, and he stood in front of the wall of flames.

The heat that wrapped around his body was pleasant. He stared deep into the orange flames and thought about what would come next once he stepped inside. This was how it ended. Hazel in his arms. Him and Hazel forever.

He gave her a kiss.

Then they entered the fiery expanse.

He laid on the ground with Hazel's body. There was no feeling more pleasurable than burning, and watching everything around him become changed and destroyed and reformed into something different.

He smiled.

He waited for his soul to be taken away. He waited to be in the other life. He waited to meet Hazel again.

Together forever.

38

ABIGAIL HAD IVY PINNED down. Ivy was shaking and cursing, and her eyes were rolling back in her head.

"Ivy I'm going to help you," Abigail said, then she looked up at Beverly. "What worked last time?"

"Everything me and Cat tried failed and we had a dozen Bibles and—and don't you remember what you told me?"

"The wish."

"I wish this would all end."

Just then there was a loud rumble and thunder struck. A rainstorm was falling. Buckets of water fell through the open windows.

"Get out of here. Now."

"I can't leave you behind. We're in this together."

"Don't be stupid. You've got to get Ruth out of here."

Beverly stood in the doorway. "I know but... but..."

"Be safe," Abigail said. "I love you."

"I love you too."

And with that, Beverly and Ruth were out the front door.

Beverly went down the hill. The storm wasn't very strong now that she was out here under it. Rain was falling but it was hardly more than a drizzle. But it was doing the job. Behemoth flames still devoured and destroyed the land around her but the rain was helping to clear up a path.

She hurried down and buried Ruth in her shoulder, keeping her safe, trying to keep her dry. Ruth was sobbing dryly. Her poor baby—her poor baby needed to be home, needed water, needed food, needed to rest after the living hell she had been put through.

I love you, Ruth, Beverly thought, *and nothing is ever going to happen like this to you again.*

They were off through the section of woods where the fire had been put out...

...but Beverly had a feeling that this night was far, far from over.

"You tried this in your home, Abby. You know this won't work."

Abigail found the vile of Holy Water. One little drop left around the rim. Ivy was restrained by the Holy Bible on her chest and couldn't move out from under it. Abigail then kneeled next to Ivy again, and held the vile threateningly close to Ivy's face that was misshapen with the touch of the devil. Her bright eyes had dulled and her smile curved sickeningly. There was something grotesque lurking just under the surface of flesh, changing her from the nice girl she had once been. Now she was a monster that Abigail couldn't recognize.

Abigail touched her hand to Ivy's damnably cold face and pried her mouth open, then she poured in that last drop of Holy Water.

Ivy's face reverted back to her innocent, sweet self.

"Abigail this hurts. Please help me."

"You won't fool me," Abigail said. "I'll know when it's really over."

"You can't beat the devil." Ivy's face changed back into an abomination.

"Ivy, what happened to you? Why do you want this?"

"Because I'm in control of my life now. Is it that hard to understand?"

"You're a good girl. You shouldn't be mixed up in this."

"I'm not a good girl. You were completely wrong about me. And all of this morality coming from the girl who killed a priest, and who killed her friend, and from what my master tells me… you also killed Michelle."

Tears exploded in Abigail's eyes. "I… I…"

"What kind of person are you anyways, Abby?"

Abigail was silent.

"You're just like me. You've hurt as many people as I have. Is it excused because you didn't want to do it? Where's your punishment?"

"My punishment is the guilt I've had to live with."

"That's bullshit and you know it. You think guilt is punishment?"

"I—"

"Maybe you liked it. Maybe you liked getting away with murder."

"No I didn't—I don't—I—I'm sorry for everything I did."

Ivy laughed. "You're not sorry for a damn thing. In fact I think you're jealous of me. You're jealous because you didn't become the devil's bride."

Abigail cried. "I never said I was a good person. I only wanted to stop you from making the mistakes I made. I care about you, Ivy. You're the little sister I never had."

"Oh, spare me all this emotional bullshit."

Abigail wiped her tears away. "Earlier you said you were pregnant. Is that true?"

"I've never lied to you yet, Abby."

"Who's the father?"

"Doesn't matter, the only father the child needs is my master."

"I know you don't want my help, but I'm gonna get you out of this." Abigail flipped through the pages of The Bible that was on Ivy's chest still weighing her down.

As Abigail turned through pages finding what passage she was looking for, the cabin was shaken again and a loose wooden board in the wall flung across the room directly coming toward Abigail's face—she had a split second to think, and even less than that to act, and somehow her body decided to duck out of the way and avoid it. The piece of wood impaled one of the scattered couches that was on the other side of the cabin.

In her deflection she had landed over Ivy, knocking the Holy Bible off of her, and therefore breaking the little restrain she had had on her.

Abigail scrambled to grab her Bible but Ivy was already standing and kicked it away.

"I have plans for you, Abigail. You'll live perhaps a night more."

"What are you going to do?"

"I'm going to kill Beverly's baby. You'll see just what happens next."

Then Ivy left out the door and into the rainy night…

The rains stopped

Beverly rested against a tree in the tangle of forest.

"How are you doing, Mama?" Beverly said to Ruth, giving her a kiss on the cheek.

Ruth's snot was dried on her mouth. Her eyes were dry and she was tired. She had been through so much tonight… being taken from her crib, and being passed around by strangers.

"Just a little further now and I think we'll be out of here, okay?"

Her legs were sore and she felt stabs of pain with each step into the woods. She was moving without any certain direction in mind, only stepping where she could to avoid any burning patches of trees or vegetation. The rains had helped a great deal, and she hoped they would start up again.

Beverly stopped once more. "Sorry Ruthie, Mommy just needs to catch her breath."

A branch snapped in the forest.

Beverly looked over her shoulder. Since the flames had been mostly put out in the area through which she traveled, unsettling darkness had returned, and she couldn't tell if she really saw something moving far away or if her eyes were playing tricks on her or not.

Regardless of what may or may not have been lurking in that dreaded darkness, Beverly went forward through the woods, determined to find her way out.

Abigail picked up her Bible from where it had knocked into the wall. The corner was all bent up. She held it in both of her hands then she left the cabin. There was no sign of anybody else—no Ivy, no Beverly, nobody.

She had hardly noticed the rains had stopped, but as she went down the hill they started up again.

She had something she needed to get.

The pathway back toward the family cemetery had cleared up since the rains had diminished the flames, and Abigail followed it. Then she paused when she noticed the lump of remains on her right. Two carcasses. One on top of the other. Burned beyond recognition.

She wept for them then continued on to her original destination, the cemetery.

The first thing she noticed among all the charred remnants of what had once been the Engstrom Family Cemetery was Michelle's remains. That poor girl. Abigail shuddered. Why had any of this needed to happen?

Somewhere nearby, Abigail's cross necklace reflected a sparkle of faint moonlight. Abigail picked it up and put it back over her neck.

Beverly, I hope you're home. I hope you're safe.

The rains were heavier. Any flames that had once engulfed the forest were gone.

When Abigail came back to the Engstrom House she had expected it to be ruins. She had expected the fire to have overtaken it once and for all like it should have all those nights ago. But it still stood as tall and dreadfully evil as it ever had.

She opened the back door.

The house was chilly and quiet inside.

She passed through to the front room and needed to warm up. There was a box of matches on the table and Abigail struck and tossed it in with the half-burned logs that were already there. As the flames spread, Abigail noticed some drawings on the floor in front of the fireplace, and a paper that was left behind as well. Abigail held up the paper near the flames so she could read it.

Cat's missing person's poster.

Abigail sighed.

She sat as close to the fire as she could to take in its warmth, crumpled up the poster, then tossed it into the fire and Cat appeared. Abigail thought she had either lost her mind or was dreaming. She reached her hand to touch her old friend but she passed right through her.

"Cat. Oh my God."

"Abby, hey, long time no see."

"Cat how is this possible?"

"After all you've seen are you really gonna ask me that?"

"I—I just don't understand…"

"Look at you, still as beautiful as the day I met you."

"Cat I—I thought you hated me."

"I don't hate you."

"I haven't even told you sorry yet. I'm so sorry Cat. I deserve to be in your place."

"Don't be so silly."

"How can you be so calm?"

"I've had ten years to get over it. And besides, I'm not alone. Did Beverly ever tell you I had a baby girl? I've spent all this time with her. I wouldn't trade it for anything. I don't have much time before I have to go again, Abby. I just want you to know I forgive you. I forgave you a long time ago."

"Thank you Cat. But I'm still so sorry."

"Everything will be all right. Make sure you tell Beverly hello for me, kay?"

"I—I will." Abigail tried to give her a hug but passed right through her. "Goodbye Catherine."

"Goodbye Abigail."

Abigail left the house and went down the hill. Then she heard Beverly's screams.

39

BEVERLY EXITED THE WOODS to find herself at the neighboring farm.

She collapsed at the wishing well with Ruth in her arms. The off and on rain had halted for the time being.

"We're almost home," Beverly said. "I know you're so tired. You're so ready to get out of here. So am I, baby girl. So am I."

"Oh hi Beverly."

Beverly was disgusted hearing Ivy's voice.

She had remembered Ivy has a sweet little girl, but the Ivy that was standing ten feet down from her was somebody completely different.

"It's been a long night," Ivy said. "We've all been through a lot. Especially Ruth. Well, Hazel didn't have the heart to do it, but I do. I'd do anything for my master."

Beverly shielded Ruth then stood up, almost slipping face first from the slick mud that surrounded her. She attempted to keep her balance as she ran but she slipped and landed on her back. Her head pulsed with a fresh headache. Ivy laughed, coming forward and dragging one hand along the decrepit wishing well that Abigail and Beverly had thrown coins in so long ago.

Ivy ripped Ruth from Beverly's hands. Ruth let out dry cries and extended her arms back toward her mother, but before Beverly could move at all, Ivy's eyes shut and she strained against a sudden and new pain. Ruth dropped from Ivy's hands, and Beverly reacted in a split moment to save her daughter and grabbed her.

Abigail had found them and was holding her silver cross necklace straight ahead. When Abigail was close enough she slid the necklace over Ivy's neck no matter how badly Ivy fought against it, flailing her arms and kicking Abigail. Slowly Ivy dropped to her knees. Then she was shaking. She put both of her hands on her head and let out a scream that ripped through Beverly's ears as if tearing them up with sharp glass pieces.

Suddenly Abigail worked her arms around Ivy and lifted her up over the edge of the well. Ivy plummeted to the bottom.

Beverly reached one shaky hand into her back pocket and brought out a coin. "I'm gonna end this once and for all."

Abigail put her hand in front of Beverly's. "No, let me do it."

Beverly didn't say yes or no, but she didn't really care either way. Abigail took it from Beverly's hand and dropped it in.

"I wish this demon would leave us alone forever."

Abigail and Beverly peeked over the edge of the wishing well. They couldn't see anything in darkness. They exchanged a confused look, and each girl opened their mouth to speak but were cut off by the sudden explosion of violent winds that flared from the wishing well and ruptured with an explosion.

Abigail and Beverly staggered backwards then slipped against the pressure of the heavy winds. A dark spirit swirled with each blast, billowing toward the heavens. Strangely shaped skulls swirled with the continual whirlwind, and somewhere beyond the horizon lightning struck repeatedly and illuminated the hidden horrors in that thick dark smoke.

It all moved so dizzyingly fast, higher and higher, then it plunged back toward earth and Beverly realized she and Abigail were both screaming. The darkness sunk below the surface of the earth and all was suddenly still.

Her first instinct was to check Ruth. Ruth was alive. She was cold and wet and she needed to get her out of here quick.

She stumbled one step away then saw Abigail leaning over the side of the wishing well. She lowered the bucket down.

40

ALVIN BLOCH TAPED TOGETHER the torn Honus Wagner card.

When nighttime fell he crept through his new home.

The silent halls seemed full of eyes, as if there was always somebody with him. Nighttime chills slithered around his body. The horrors inside these walls were burned into his mind, and now here he was, the only person who might be able to put a stop to it. But how?

It all started with those dolls, and that's what he needed to get rid of.

Alvin sneaked up to the fifth floor and pulled open the dropdown stairs. Slowly he ascended them and peeked over the edge of the attic floor. Moonlight filtered in through the far end and spread across the room, granting him some visibility as he finished his climb off the final step and tiptoed closer to the dollhouse.

He opened it up. None of Jeanette's dolls were inside, so he shut it and left the attic, and went straight for Jeanette's bedroom, cracked her door open and tiptoed inside hoping not to wake her. She was asleep, and on the side of her bed that was pushed up against the wall, her four wooden dolls were scattered.

His hands clenched into tight fists. He wanted to rip them all apart and toss them into the fireplace.

He took a step and the floor creaked loudly and Jeanette's eyes opened. She gasped then moved back in her bed, realized it was her brother, then she rubbed her eyes and sighed because she knew she was safe and it wasn't an invader.

"Alvin, you scared me."

"Jeanette. I need to talk to you."

"Okay."

"Alone. Without your dolls."

"Miss Penelope told me you'd say something like that."

"You can't listen to Miss Penelope. You have to listen to me."

Jeanette reached backwards without having to look and picked up the doll that Alvin presumed was 'Miss Penelope.' Jeanette raised it to her ear and listened to it whisper, but its voice was too low for Alvin to even know any sound was coming out of it.

"Alvin, Miss Penelope says you'll be going away soon. She says that I'll become part of her family, we'll be together forever and ever."

"Jeanette you can't listen to her."

"Miss Penelope, I can't say that." Jeanette lowered the doll from her ear in shock. "No I can't, that's bad, I'll get in so much trouble."

"Tell me what she said, Jeanette."

Jeanette shook her head. "I can't."

Alvin moved slowly through the room until he was at her bedside. "Give me the dolls."

"Nuh-uh."

"Give me the dolls."

Alvin grabbed Miss Penelope from Jeanette's hands and tugged on it but his sister wouldn't let go. The siblings struggled with each other until the arms of the doll were popped off and came away with Alvin, and Jeanette held the doll's torso and feet. Alvin landed on his butt with a loud *THUD!* and Jeanette was crying.

"You broke Miss Penelope! Alvin how could you?"

Alvin slammed Miss Penelope's arms down and jumped to his feet then climbed over Jeanette's bed for the other dolls.

"These dolls killed my friend, they buried him in the walls with Abraham Lincoln! I think they killed Abraham too!"

"Stop saying that!"

Alvin grabbed the other three dolls. Abruptly they came to life with sudden animation and pried free of his grip and climbed over his arms and attacked him. They were digging their feet into his skin with more force than a living doll had any right to possess, and they were punching his head. One of the dolls reached into their thin cloth garments and removed a pin, but all the dolls paused when there was the stampede of footsteps in the hallway and Jeanette's door burst open.

It was Father.

"What is going on in here?"

"Father it was terrible," Jeanette said. She was going on a rant but Alvin cut her off.

"Jeanette's been practicing witchcraft with the dolls. They've come to life. They're the ones that killed Abraham Lincoln."

"What are you talking about, son?"

"The dolls are alive! Jeanette speaks to them! They told her that they're going to kill me!"

Alvin held up the dolls, who were now frozen stiff and pretending to be normal, but his dad dismissed them with the wave of his hand.

Jeanette laughed at him. Father gave her a kiss on the forehead and patted her back and told her to go back to sleep. Then Father grabbed the dolls away from Alvin, put them next to Jeanette, and left the room with him.

"What is the meaning of this?" Father said once they were in the hall and far enough from Jeanette's room that she might not overhear.

"I went into the walls yesterday. The dolls were alive and they were riding on rats. That's where my scar came from." Alvin touched his cheek where he had been cut. "They're alive and they're gonna kill us all. Jeanette told me that the dolls said so."

"Alvin you must have seen some scary motion pictures at the movie house. What have I told you about going to see those kinds of films?"

"But Dad trust me it wasn't a movie it was really the dolls they're alive they're—"

"Enough of this. I don't want to hear another word."

"But we're all in danger. I think Jeanette might be a witch. I think there's a curse on us, or maybe a curse on this house. There are things living in the walls, Dad."

"Things 'living in the walls?' Just look at you. Scared as if you've seen a ghost. Come on, off to bed. And when you wake up, you owe your sister an apology for these witchcraft accusations, boy."

"Father... please believe me. We're in danger."

"Goodnight, Alvin." Father had led him down to his bedroom during the conversation, and opened Alvin's door.

"Goodnight, Dad." Alvin gulped.

Father shut the door.

Alvin sat on his bed and wept.

What am I going to do? How am I going to stop Jeanette's dolls?

There was a creeping sound in his room; a scratching. Something that he hardly heard, and something that might have gone unnoticed if it weren't for the unending terror that he had been feeling since first setting foot inside the dreaded walls of this new house. It was an archaic terror, something that must have filled this house for the entirety of its creation.

Alvin's eyes followed the noise across the room but lost it somewhere in darkness. It was a brief crawling or scurry, like sharp talons against the wooden walls. But it had only been heard briefly then had vanished, if it had ever really been there at all. And now Alvin was not sure if he had really heard anything at all or if he were only frightened of what he had seen or heard in both the walls and in Jeanette's room.

He rubbed his eyes, stepped across the room, and turned on the light.

He thought about those that were lost in the walls. Billy. Samuel. Abraham Lincoln. None of which would ever come back.

Where had this hell all started? Why had any of this happened? Did evil have any reason for existing? How had Jeanette been corrupted so effortlessly?

Alvin sighed.

He laid in his bed but knew he wouldn't be getting any sleep. He laid with his back to his room and stared at the wall, anticipating hearing a noise within it. But his room remained silent; absolutely no noises aside from his own breathing.

Alvin's arm became numb from laying on it so he turned to his other side, and on his pillow was a monster. He was faced with a rat whose face was sickeningly misshapen, and riding on its back was its nightmarish master—Miss Penelope.

Jeanette hugged Miss Penelope and told her good morning, then she raised the doll to her ear to her what she had to say.

"There's really a hidden room?" Jeanette asked. "Can you show me where it is?"

Jeanette and Miss Penelope left her bedroom and went through the house, making a stop at Alvin's bedroom. She opened the door and the room was empty, and his covers and pillow had been flung from his bed as if he were in a struggle.

Jeanette picked them up and made Alvin's bed, although he wouldn't be needing it anymore. It was what Miss Penelope instructed her to do.

"Let's go."

They went to a hall that Jeanette didn't think she had been to yet—and with how big this house was, seemingly bigger on the inside than the outside, it might have been impossible to travel every hallway—and in the corner of the wall was a strange door that looked different from all the others. A green glow emanated from underneath it.

Inside the room was a blank stone interior suffused with that continually pulsing green light, and in the far corner of the room

Jeanette thought she saw two figures—a mother and a baby—but she didn't have time to fully take in the details because she moved from the doorway and shut it.

She raised Miss Penelope to her ear.

She knew what she had to do.

Jeanette went to Carrie's room and knocked on the door. There was no answer so Jeanette let herself in. Carrie sat up in bed when Jeanette's steps awoke her and she rubbed her eyes and said good morning.

"Do you want to see something cool?"

"What is it?"

"A secret room. Like we found in the dollhouse. But it's real."

"Are you joking?"

"No, I really found it. There's something inside waiting for you."

"What is it?"

"It's a surprise. Just come and see. Isn't that right, Miss Penelope?" Jeanette raised Miss Penelope to her ear. "Miss Penelope says you'll love it."

Carrie followed Jeanette to the mysterious door, and Jeanette opened it up for her.

"Are you coming in with me?"

"Yes," Jeanette said. "After you."

After Carried was inside, Jeanette slammed the door shut. There was no knob on the inside; no way for Carrier to get out of there. She was screaming at the top of her lungs, but her screams died away when the door disappeared.

"Now what?" Jeanette held up Miss Penelope to her ear. "What do you want me to do?"

Miss Penelope gave her the answer.

Her other brothers were Franklin and Daniel, they had neighboring bedrooms on the ground floor. She knocked on each door and sobbed until her brothers both awoke and met her in the hallway.

"What is it? Are you okay?"

"What's going on? Jeanette what's wrong?"

"Alvin's had a—had a…"

"Had a what?"

"Out with it, Jeanette."

"Alvin's had an accident."

"Where?"

"Take us."

"The basement. Come on."

Her brothers ran down ahead of her as if they knew where she needed them to go. They stood around the empty basement scanning their eyes across the open spaces in worry.

"Where is he?"

"That way." Jeanette pointed with one hand, while she clutched Miss Penelope tight with the other.

Her brothers entered the room where the Animal Control guy had tried to find Abraham Lincoln. Jeanette walked in behind him.

"Did he go inside that door?"

"Yes." Jeanette gave a fake cry.

Her brothers entered in, and she followed.

"Which way?"

Jeanette brought them down to the right side, going through the densely dark interior of the walls.

TAP! TAP! TAP!

Jeanette lifted Miss Penelope to her ear. Miss Penelope told her that everything was going as perfectly as they had planned.

The rats were coming with Miss Penelope's family on their backs.

Franklin and Daniel's screams never escaped the walls.

Jeanette went to her mom and dad's room and her mother and father were both asleep. She crept to her mother's side of the bed and tugged on Mother's arm until she woke up. Mother brushed hair out of Jeanette's eyes and gave her a kiss on the cheek.

"Good morning."

"Good morning Mother. Can you help me with something?"

"Sure, what is it?"

"Come and see."

Nathaniel Bloch was awoken by a scream. He turned to his wife and the bed was empty.

He ran out of his bedroom and heard the scream again—sharp and quick, it had died down as suddenly as it had begun. He went around the house barefoot, running up and down every hall and checking every room.

The house was completely quiet; his wife didn't answer any of his calls when he yelled out her name.

He was confused as he went up and down stairways, the house completely void of any signs of life.

He checked on his children. None of them were in their bedrooms.

Then there came that hideous scream again, and his heart thudded with terror... because when he heard it, he heard it coming from inside the walls.

41

HENRY CAME BACK HOME from the hospital. He sat with Ivy in her bedroom.

"How are you feeling?" She asked.

"So much better. The scar isn't even so bad."

"I'm still sorry for what I did, Henry."

"I forgive you." Henry gave her a hug then a kiss on her forehead. "You're my baby sister."

That night Abigail was making dinner and Ivy was helping her by washing the dishes while Abigail grabbed the seasonings she needed and opened and shut drawers looking for utensils. Then Abigail stopped for a minute and stood next to Ivy.

"Ivana, can I ask you something?"

"Yes?"

"Did you mean what you said, that you were…" Abigail hushed so Henry would not hear if he were nearby. "Pregnant?"

"Uh-huh." Ivy nodded.

"By who?"

"A stranger. Don't tell anyone, okay?"

"I promise I won't."

"Thank you. And thank you for everything you did for me." Ivy gave her a hug. "But how did you know the well would work?"

"I just had a feeling."

"You know, when I was down there, I thought I felt a vine wrap around my ankle. I thought something was pulling on me."

After dinner was ready, and Abigail and Ivy were setting the table, Henry came into the dining room and said, "Ivana, there's a couple guests arriving any second now who would like to see you."

"Uh, okay?"

Henry opened the front door two minutes later. It was their parents.

"Mom... Dad... hi."

They gave Ivy hugs and kisses. They were happy to see her.

Ivy didn't go back home with her parents despite their offer. She needed to stay here for just a little bit longer.

Ivy waited around her bedroom for nighttime to fall, and she waited to be sure that Abigail and Henry were both asleep. She tiptoed to their room and peeked in. Both in bed. Good. It would make things a lot easier.

She snuck out through the back door. Ashfall was quiet.

Ivy thought about everything that had happened, all the power she had felt, and all the things that had changed. Hazel, Michelle, Steve, Arnie. All dead. But she hardly cared about any of them anymore. All she really wanted was to be the devil's bride again. She wanted to be his. She wanted this baby to be the devil's baby.

Engstrom House seemed to be waiting for her. It was vibrant. It had escaped all touches of the flames that had devoured the forest behind it. Nothing could destroy this house, she thought. Nothing could ever get rid of it.

It was her favorite place on earth.

She entered the living room and struck a match from the box that was left on the table. She tossed it into the fireplace.

"I'm back," she said.

All was silent.

She waited...

And waited...

"Master?"

Quietness. Coldness. The empty house. Where had he gone?

His presence still lingered. He must have been around.

"I'm here," she said. "Come take your bride."

When there wasn't any answer, tears fell from her eyes.

"Come take me. Come take me. Come take me come take me come take me." Ivy screamed over and over. *"I am your bride. Come take me."*

CREEEEEEEEEAK!   *CREEEEEEEEEEEEEEEEEEAK!*
CREAAAAAAAAAAAAAAAAAAAAAAAAK!

That irritating noise constantly reverberating from the second floor. Ivy lit a candle and went to see what it was, and she arrived at the same room Warren had taken her into. She twisted the knob and pushed the door open. The black goat had taken on a new form so that his body was human in outline alone. Colleen—Mother Superior—was with him underneath the bloody sheets.

The black goat pulled away from Colleen and his body reverted back to its typical form. He met her in the middle of the room. She was moaning his name while Colleen laughed at her from the bed.

"Ivana. Is that you?"

"Yes—yes it's me. It's your bride." She petted him.

He licked her hand. "You don't look like your old self anymore."

"I'm ready to be yours again. I want to be yours again. All yours and yours only."

"It's too late for that, Ivana. I'm afraid I have found another."

She sobbed. *"What? What?"*

"You're damaged goods."

"I'm what?"

"You failed me when I needed you. I can't take you back now."

"Please. I need you. I am nothing without you."

"That may be true," he said, "but I am everything without you."

Ivy was screaming.

"There's one way out of this, darling."

"Yes? Yes I'll do anything. Tell me."

"Allow me to show you. Follow me."

"Don't take long," Colleen said behind them.

"Lead the way, my master."

"Did you bring the knife with you?"

Ivy removed it from her pocket.

"You know what you need to do now."

"Yes, my master."

He turned and walked away.

"Wait."

He halted.

"A kiss," she said, "before I go."

He nodded and returned to her. They shared one last kiss, then he was gone, returning to his new bride.

A face revealed itself on the wall under the touch of her candle-light. A big fat man.

"It isn't so bad."

"Who are you?"

"I don't see why it matters, but for the record my name is Howard. Who are you, young lady?"

"Ivana."

"Ivana. You'll have many friends here."

Spanning the hallway as far as Ivana's candle could illuminate, the faces of strangers popped through the walls. There were men and women, adults and children.

One woman said, "I know just the place. My old bedroom. Come now."

The hands of dozens of strangers protruded from the walls and floors and directed Ivy through the woman's bedroom to the neighboring bathroom. In a past life it had been grand and luxurious bathroom, but now the tub was rusted and filthy and the sides had chipped rapidly. Black gunk was collecting in the drain, and there was mold around all the edges.

Arms grew out of the porcelain and led her in. Faces grew from the ceiling and every square inch of wall; they all drooled. A warm mist emanated from their mouths. Their eyes glowed.

She laid down.

The house's collection of past lives excitedly watched her. They were ready for a new friend.

Ivy pressed the cold edge of the knife to her right wrist and pulled it across.

AUTHOR'S NOTES

If you read the author's notes for book two then you'd know that I struggled a lot when writing that book. I thought that that was the most I would ever struggle writing a book. And here I am finding out that it was, in fact, possible to struggle even worse.

I mentioned in that same afterward about not liking to bring back characters, preferring to write about a theme or location with different characters rather than using the same ones again. However, that just did not click for a third Engstrom book. I had done five drafts prior to this one, some of them finished and some unfinished, all of them awful, and all of them with new characters with a new scenario. But it wasn't working because it all felt dumb. Book one felt like it had a purpose, book two felt like it had a purpose, and just having some other kids around Ashfall stumble into the house, it just did not feel meaningful or right.

I tried messing around with some scenarios, like a girl whose grandmother or great grandmother knew one of the families that had lived there at the house, and perhaps this girl's family had some connection to the house, but it kept getting convoluted and kind of stupid. Like I had to figure out so many timelines for that situation, and since I don't like putting specific years on things it made it tough, because in book one it seemed like the Engstrom family and their timeline could have been 100 years before Abigail or 200 before Abigail and it didn't really matter, it just had to be long. But for somebody's grandmother to have known one of those families, and for there to be leftover clues and stuff, it made the timeline feel shorter, and I didn't know where to place it, and the story was not good anyways.

I tried another scenario, written after an early draft of book two, where the character Samantha brings something back home from her time at the Engstrom House and becomes possessed in her own home, committing suicide, leaving it up to her sister to piece together why her sister did it, but there was no mystery there to unravel. It was like trying to write a mystery without a mystery. And the character in that situation did not even live in Ashfall, so she had to—and this is so convoluted—have a reason to go on a road trip from her home to Ashfall to piece something together about this abandoned house and her sister, and there was just nothing there.

It's easy to make a house scary once. Twice, sure. But three times? Oh my goodness. I almost killed myself as I tried to write this book. Especially after I finalized book two, and published books one and two, and here I was with two great installments and no ending to the trilogy.

As much as I would have loved for this to be a scenario with new characters and for this series to be three one shot stories that could be read (pretty much) in any order, it did not work that way. You really have to read them 1 -> 2 -> 3, or 1 -> 3 -> 2 if you really want.

So where did this story come from? Well I kept thinking about Abigail and Beverly. I kept thinking how traumatic it would be to live with all of this. And after all Abigail did, could Beverly even be her friend anymore? I mean what were they up to now? After a month or after a year or even longer, how would everything have changed those girls? Well I couldn't get them off my mind. And one day I thought that Abigail had met somebody, she was dating somebody. And then one day I thought that it all went wrong and now Abigail has to tell him about her past and it could crumble their relationship. I thought that it could be her boyfriend or husband or whoever he is, whose sister gets overtaken by the house, and now Abigail kind of takes on Beverly's roll from book one.

It took me six months to work on this story coming at it fresh, from a blank page, throwing away FIVE previous drafts (again, some full drafts and some only partially completed), and writing fresh in this world again. I had to relearn who Abigail and Beverly were, but I also had to learn who the new characters were and how it all fit together.

And at the end of the story, it all brought me back to…. Why?

Why did any of this happen? Why was any of this necessary? What did anyone gain from any of these events happening? Why did the girls in book one, so effected by what happened, have to go through this again? What did everyone learn? What was the moral of the story?

And maybe there was no moral to it. Maybe sometimes in life you don't have the answers or a moral. Maybe sometimes you just have to do what you have to do, and in some instances it might be the right choice, but with a different set of circumstances it might be the wrong choice.

After completion of this novel I asked myself if I had a glar-ing problem with Abigail killing Michelle, and Beverly killing Steve. These two girls fought the whole novel to save Ivy, and what makes Ivy so special that they don't kill her right away—apart from Ivy being Abigail's future sister-in-law—and they try and save her?

Well I think I came to the conclusion that when your life is on the line and somebody is trying to kill you, you have to do what you have to do. It would have made no sense to harm Ivy if they were trying to save her. Michelle and Steve couldn't be reasoned with. They liked being possessed as much as Ivy did—in fact, I think it even broke their minds, since they were nonbelievers who became believers. I think it had a worse effect on them for that reason, since it broke their whole view of reality and unreality and what's real and what is not. So I think that while Ivy liked being possessed and did do a lot of horrible and wicked things, it's always the goal to try and save somebody rather than strike at them and kill them. And sometimes, you have to do what you have to do. If your life is on the line then you're gonna have to save yourself, no matter how much you wish you could also save that other person.

I think it might be a rather bleak outlook on life and events but that's just the way I felt when I came to the conclusion of this novel.

I hope it was a satisfying end to the trilogy.

I am always open to returning to the Engstrom House again, whether with these characters or others, if I get the idea for a fourth book.

You never know…